DUCK DUCK GOOSE
A ROSA GUZMAN THRILLER

JACKSON RIGGS

DUCK DUCK
GOOSE
A Rosa "Goose" Guzman Thriller
Book 1

By
Jackson Riggs

© 2020 Muonic Press Inc
www.muonic.com

* * *

www.JacksonRiggsAuthor.com
www.facebook.com/JacksonRiggsAuthor

No part of this book may be reproduced in any form, or by any electronic, mechanical or other means, without the permission in writing from the author.

CONTENTS

Want More Awesome Books?   v
Special Thanks   vii

Chapter 1   1
Chapter 2   11
Chapter 3   16
Chapter 4   22
Chapter 5   26
Chapter 6   33
Chapter 7   40
Chapter 8   44
Chapter 9   47
Chapter 10   51
Chapter 11   56
Chapter 12   61
Chapter 13   65
Chapter 14   67
Chapter 15   74
Chapter 16   82
Chapter 17   88
Chapter 18   92
Chapter 19   98
Chapter 20   104
Chapter 21   108
Chapter 22   111
Chapter 23   116
Chapter 24   119
Chapter 25   128
Chapter 26   131
Chapter 27   134
Chapter 28   141
Chapter 29   158
Chapter 30   159

Chapter 31	163
Chapter 32	169
Chapter 33	173
Chapter 34	175
Chapter 35	186
Chapter 36	191
Chapter 37	198
Chapter 38	204
Chapter 39	209
Chapter 40	214
Chapter 41	218
Chapter 42	225
Chapter 43	232
Chapter 44	235
Chapter 45	244
Chapter 46	251
Chapter 47	257
Chapter 48	261
Chapter 49	263
Chapter 50	273
Chapter 51	275
Chapter 52	281
Chapter 53	287
Chapter 54	290
Author Notes	297
About the Author	299

WANT MORE AWESOME BOOKS?

Join the Jackson Riggs Mailing List (books.to/riggsnewsletter) for free books and sneak previews!

If you're looking for great new thrillers to read, consider signing up for the Muonic Press Thriller Newsletter (books.to/muonicthrillers) to get gripping new titles!

SPECIAL THANKS

Special thanks to Tim Marquitz and Mark Posey who went above and beyond to make sure this was the best possible book it could be.

A huge thanks to all of my generous Kickstarter supporters without whom none of this would have been possible.

CHAPTER 1

The contoured rubber handle of the Ruger GP100 was as cold and rigid as Guzman's stare, her eyes glaring out from behind the tacky 1980s mirrored aviators.

For close to her entire life, Rosa had found solace in the firm and cool steel of a weapon, and although guns had taken so much from her, she continued to find comfort in them now. In this case, it was a .357 Magnum double action revolver with extended seven shot capacity and a six-inch barrel. Brushed metal gray with a darkened handle, formed to her grip, she cradled the weapon, turning it over, extending the rounded chamber and verifying it was loaded before clicking the cylinder back home. She leaned forward, sliding the weapon neatly back into a form-fitting leather holster, then resting it in her glove compartment. She pressed her narrow fingers against the smooth surface of the vinyl door and swung it shut with a muffled *click*.

Looking out through the windshield, she narrowed her alert gaze on the row of track housing in front of her, meandering along the side of the road, a parade of low budget constructs, continuing into the fog-soaked horizon. Through thinning layers of mist high in the sky, Rosa could barely make out the top stories of the sporadic, infrequent skyscrapers off to the east, such as they were in this small city. Springfield, Massachusetts wasn't considered a major metropolitan area by any stretch of the imagination, but it was home. One of the few places where she felt like she belonged. There were days when she wasn't sure why she felt so comfortable here. It had served as a perpetual prison, a place she continuously attempted to escape, but could never seem to break free of. She couldn't even find solace in Afghanistan, eventually ending up once again in her old backyard, dumped like a bag of wet leaves in the compost of this city. Everywhere she turned there was a different kind of traumatic memory, but in spite of these, it was still home. It still protected her.

The .357 helped do that, too, and her eyes darted towards the dashboard, but she held herself back. She didn't think she'd need it today and, frankly, she didn't want to take the chance. She avoided bringing weapons to these kinds of things if she could possibly help it, there was just too much that could go wrong. Still, it left her with some small measure of satisfaction to know it was there if she needed it.

"Goose, you awake?"

Rosa's head twitched upward.

"Yeah, Heath, I'm here. Sorry."

"They're on the way. Black Caddy, coming around the bend."

Rosa nodded, though her partner and fellow Army veteran Chuck Heath couldn't see her. He was in his own vehicle three blocks away, keeping watch over the only path to Alphonso Alman's house. They were both certain he would return here. He had no other place to go, and after skipping bail for the third time, he was quickly running out of friends to turn to.

While Chuck and Rosa both owned a chunk of the business, Chuck also split time doing some other things, supplementing his income as frequently as necessary to keep a roof over he and his brothers' heads. This particular job promised to be well-paying, and he was eager to play his role. Rosa often did the lion's share of the work, even though the business split was just slightly tilted her way, but the arrangement worked well for both of them.

This one could pay the electric bill for the next few months.

Up ahead, she saw the black Cadillac come around the corner and drift across the narrow street, then slip into its parking space next to the single floor home she had identified as Alman's. Even from a block away, she could see several heads inside the vehicle, the low budget window tinting already fading from time and a lack of professional application. This wasn't a surprise. The only thing more dependable than Alphonso skipping bail was the crew that rode around with him, guys who were big and tough, but not exactly the sharpest knives in the drawer.

"Eyes on them," Rosa reported into her wireless headset.

"Need backup?" Chuck asked in his narrow, tinny voice.

"Hell no."

Her eyes narrowed on the car ahead and the numerous shapes inside, shuffling around and maneuvering to exit. God damned clown car is what it was. Turning slightly, she focused her attention on the glove compartment, rethinking her previous hesitation.

Leaning over the passenger seat, Rosa unlatched the glove compartment and slipped out the clip-on leather holster wrapped tightly around her pistol. Opening her door and sliding out of the driver's side, Guzman fastened the slender holster onto her belt, over her right back pocket, close enough to her right side to have easy access if she needed it. Easing the car door shut, she stood in the street, her five foot-five inch frame looking downright demure in torn blue jeans and a white tank top. A red flannel shirt draped over her shoulders and covered her bare arms but was unbuttoned in the front. It hung just over the holster at the small of her back and fluttered slightly as she strode confidently forward, no hesitation in her step.

The doors of the Cadillac creaked open on ancient, unoiled hinges, and three mountains slowly emerged, pulling themselves from the car as if they'd filled up the entire inside with their massive bulk. A somewhat smaller man was enveloped by these three, a man who Rosa immediately recognized as their target. As Guzman slowly crossed the road, no rush in her movements, the large men walked across the brown and trampled lawn and disappeared into the side door of the house. There had been no sign they had noticed her, or if they had, no indication that they gave a crap. Rosa's eyes scanned the neighborhood, and she could clearly see each house sitting on their small lots, pressed up against a short ratty lawn with a tall, wooden fence at the rear. Just on the other side of the fence, Rosa knew there was a second access road, a barely paved, one-lane path running down the stretch of the subdivision back towards downtown.

"Moving in towards the front door," Rosa said into her earpiece.

"Here if you need me," replied Chuck.

Guzman's eyes snatched left and saw Heath's older model Ford approaching the corner, moving slowly, the narrow dark shape in the windshield a comfortable and familiar one.

The day was quiet in this part of the city, where most of the inhabitants were nocturnal, preferring to come out at night. Fog stretched low and wide throughout this row of houses, providing an ominous curtain of cotton ball light gray tucked against the surface of the low budget lodgings. Each step on the pavement sounded loud and abrupt against the nearly silent cloak of dim sky. Swinging her hand back, she pressed her palm to the comforting contour of the holster at her back, briefly touching the grip and testing how easily it might slide from its containment. Her heart slipped a few beats as it usually did in these moments, but she strode briskly forward, her eyes focused on the plastic staircase leading to the front door of the house.

Skipping two stairs, she drew up on the top platform, clenched her small fist, and smacked it three sharp times on the metal screen door. As loud as her footsteps had been, the sound of bone knuckle on metal was even louder. It was a flat *smack*, the sound of a frying pan being dropped onto a burner on the stove. Inside, she could hear the shuffling of footsteps and some murmured voices, calm, but rapid-fire, one voice to another, low and anxious. Things were quiet again for a moment, and she lifted her fist to knock again, but the inside door swung open and the screen door pushed out quickly, forcing her to take an uncertain step backwards, catching herself on the middle step.

A tall and wide man pushed himself out in front of a second man, his head round and smooth, a black shirt stretched tight around his massive chest. His teeth were bright white against his dark skin as he smiled, a look of true amusement crossing his broad face. Behind the two of them, Rosa caught a quick glimpse of a third man, every bit as huge as the other two.

"Hey there, little girl," The man in front snickered. "You selling cookies? Let me get some of them Thin Mints." Behind him, the second man snorted laughter.

"I'm here to see Alphonso," she replied, her eyes peering out from behind the oval sunglasses, perched underneath her favorite New England Patriots cap, faded blue and marred with small tears. It was turned backwards, the bill slanted flat against the long, dark ponytail that draped over her flannel shirt, down to between her shoulder blades. Rosa Guzman was a striking young woman, and the predatory glare of the man who answered the door gave her confirmation of this fact. Rosa didn't need confirmation, though, especially not from these dirt bags.

"He ain't here," the large man replied, the full girth of him threatening to burst free of his dark shirt. "And if you ain't a cop, you can get the hell off our stairs."

"I'm not a cop," Rosa replied, not missing a beat. "But I need to speak to Alphonso. Now."

"You got a warrant, bitch?"

"You got an escaped convict in there, asshole?"

The large man was no longer smiling, lips twisting over his white teeth into an angry sneer. Without warning, he slammed the door out, sending it crashing against the faux siding of the track home with an echoing *bang*. He lunged at her, moving fast for such a large man, but Rosa was well-prepared. She slipped and moved inside his range of motion, sending him sprawling down the staircase. His arms pin-wheeled as he tried to compensate, but he tumbled forward, his thick knees striking the plastic steps and sending his chest and face slamming into the dead grass and dirt. The second man charged, extending his arms as if he were trying to hug her, but she moved just as quickly, ducking under his closing grasp and driving a fist into his sternum. With a gasp, he lost his breath and stumbled slightly, allowing Guzman to push her way up the stairs and into the house, where she kicked the man in the knee, then elbowed him in the temple, one right after the other. He dropped to the cheap, stained linoleum floor and lay motionless.

Stepping over him into the kitchen, Rosa looked inside, scanning the rooms for any sign of motion. "Alphonso Alman! My name is Rosa Guzman! I'm a Fugitive Recovery Agent!"

Her identification was greeted with silence.

"Alphonso, I saw you come in here. Let's do this the quick and easy way, okay?"

Just to her left, a floorboard creaked, and her eyes darted behind the mirrored lenses of her sunglasses. Just at the edge of her vision, she caught the brief motion of another large, vague shape stumbling forward, a long object clasped between two clenched fists. The baseball bat was cocked tight to his right ear, his elbows locked, and as he burst into the small kitchen, he torqued his waist, swinging for the fences.

Guzman stepped backwards, the wooden bat arcing just in front of her and slamming into a ceramic lamp, exploding it into a hundred jagged shards and sending the cone-shaped lampshade tumbling awkwardly.

"Out of my house, bitch!" Alphonso screamed, pulling the bat close to himself again, preparing for a follow up swing.

"I don't want to hurt you," she said, remaining calm even as her target stepped forward again, preparing for another strike.

"Hurt me?" Alphonso asked, incredulous. "You got a baseball bat somewhere I don't know about?" With a grunt, he stepped forward and swung again, even harder, but also out of control. The bat wobbled in his grip as it soared just over Rosa's ducking head, and she struck out with a forearm, punching it into his intertwined limbs. His fingers burst apart, releasing the bat, sending it cartwheeling through the air, and she stepped forward, punching him in the ribs, sending him stumbling. With a *crash*, the bat shattered the living room window, and she moved forward again. But he was no slouch. Even as glass exploded onto his front lawn, he charged forward, barreling into her and sending her stumbling backwards, barely staying upright. As she tried to compensate, he turned and lumbered towards the rear of the house.

"God dammit!" Rosa shouted as he disappeared down a narrow hallway. "Chuck, he's heading for the back door!" she barked into the wireless headset.

"On it!" came the brief reply. As if to punctuate the response, she heard the telltale bang of American metal as his Ford door slammed shut. Drawing a breath, she threw herself down the hallway, running at a full tilt, then lunging right and bursting through the screen door at the rear of the house, out onto the lawn. Up ahead, she saw the gate slam back on tight hinges as Alphonso barreled through, Chuck drawing closer. Instead of veering towards them, Rosa ran straight forward, throwing herself in the air, wrapping her fingers around the top of the fence and pulling, torqueing her waist and bringing her legs over the top of the tall fence. Like a gymnast, she turned in the air, vaulted over the fence, and landed smoothly on the worn pavement of the access road on the other side. Alphonso was running at a full gallop a couple of hundred yards ahead of her as Chuck burst out onto the access road. Before he could even orient himself to where Alphonso was, Rosa dashed past him, legs pumping.

"Quit while you're ahead, Alphonso!" she shouted after him. He was already drawing larger as she ran forward, her swift pace quickly overcoming his clumsy lumbering. Up ahead, the thin, paved road intersected with a two-lane street, and she could see traffic buzzing back and forth.

"Scumbag," Rosa cursed to herself as she tried to pick up her pace. Just ahead, Alphonso navigated between hurtling cars, one blue Toyota screeching to a rocking halt, turning forty-five degrees in the middle of the road to avoid running into the large, lumbering convict.

Rosa pushed herself forward, easing past one slow moving car, then leaped into the air, sliding over the hood of a second, horns blasting in her ears from traffic that was suddenly all around her. Alphonso left the road and turned down a darkened alley, a narrow passage sandwiched between two small buildings, trash scattered throughout. Rosa was just behind him and ran towards the corner, just about to turn down when the swift, loud report of a pistol brought her to a stop.

It was a loud and sudden sound, a bark in the quiet darkness, rolling over the dull roar of the traffic just behind them. Rosa pushed herself backwards, slamming her spine against the brick wall of the building, the brief yellow flash illuminating the dim alley. It had come from a green dumpster sitting about halfway down the narrow path, pressed tight against the same building she was.

"Alphonso, think about what you're doing!" she shouted back at him. "Don't be stupid!"

"You shoulda just left me alone!" he shouted back. "This is my third gig! Third strike! I ain't going back in there!"

"Prison's gotta be better than a coffin!" Rosa shouted back.

"How the hell would you know?"

Rosa ducked slightly and brought herself around the corner of the wall, staying low and close. Up ahead, she saw the dumpster but saw no sign of Alphonso himself, though she could picture him huddled behind the green metal box, some low budget Glock clamped in his slick fist.

"You'd be surprised!" she shouted back.

"Come on, Alphonso!" came the high-pitched male voice from behind Rosa. She turned and saw Chuck coming up against the wall on the opposite side of the alley. He didn't have a gun in his hand, he didn't use them if he didn't have to. Being in the military had given him a begrudging respect for firearms, but he tried not to make it a habit to wade hip-deep into trouble, looking to shoot his way out. Clenching his fists, he slowly paced down the wall.

"Be careful," Rosa whispered, gesturing to him. He nodded back.

"Go to hell!" shouted Alphonso, swinging up around the dumpster, his automatic held in a lazy firing stance.

Before he could even fire, Rosa's own hands were up, her .357 in hand and firing, a swift series of two loud claps of thunder, slamming against the walls of the flanking buildings. Large, explosive sparks pounded off the metal surface of the dumpster, and Alphonso shrieked slightly, stumbling.

"Don't move!" Rosa shouted, her pistol leveled towards him. His own weapon was pointing towards the ground, held lightly in one hand while the other handheld him steady against the dumpster. "That was your warning shot, Alphonso. The next one will leave a mark."

His eyes darted between Rosa and Chuck as they both slowly approached, one on each wall, coming towards him. A look of resignation passed over his face, and the pistol trembled slightly in his grasp.

Rosa's heart thumped. She'd been here before, more often than she'd care to admit, and it didn't get easier. Life and death could be decided in a matter of seconds. One careless decision could change the lives of three people…. One minute, the world exists as it is, the next minute, everything is different. Rosa knew that feeling. She knew it well. She wished she didn't.

The scent of gunpowder clung in the air, mixed with the echoing rebounds of the gunshots. Her eyes stung, and her nose burned as if she was inside the barrel of the weapon, consumed by the smoke and sulfur. "Just drop the gun, Alphonso," she whispered as she drew in closer. "We can stop this right here."

Alphonso glared at her, and the gun barrel twitched. Rosa's muscles tensed, her finger dancing against the curved metal of the trigger, and a slick shine of sweat was suddenly on her forehead where it hadn't been before.

He didn't lift the weapon. It released from his grasp and clattered to the dirt-covered alley, falling amongst the rest of the discarded trash. Alphonso brought himself upright and lifted his hands, palms facing them, his eyes narrow and mouth a thin, set line.

"Fine," he muttered. "We do it your way."

Rosa nodded and glanced towards Chuck, seeing the same look of desperate, lifesaving relief that she felt. "You made the right choice," she said and moved in close, pulling some cuffs from her back pocket.

Just another day on the job.

CHAPTER 2

"What exactly the hell were you thinking, Goose?"

"Come on, Bruce," Rosa replied. "I didn't even wing him. I fired a couple of shots, he crapped his pants and gave up on the spot."

Bruce Kravitz pushed his hefty bulk up out of the ratty old wooden swivel chair and came around the desk gingerly, precariously balancing his three hundred-pound frame.

"Now I gotta fill out a police report. They need a copy of the bounty contract. Jesus Christ."

"Yeah, you're crying all the way to the bank, right? No broken bones, no damage. Bounty's intact, and you still get your cut, Brucie."

His eyes darted towards her, two narrow, milky ovals dug deep into his doughy face. "Lenny got away with that stuff, don't push your luck, Goose."

Rosa chuckled. "Yeah, Lenny got away with a lot of shit. Lenny wasn't a five foot nothing chica, so he had that going for him."

Bruce shook his head as he stomped across the office, heading towards a long, lateral filing cabinet. "I don't care if you're man, woman, or one of them trans-abled people. Get me my bounty money, I'm a happy guy. All I care about."

"You got it. So, where's that ole Kravitz smile?"

He looked back over his shoulder. "Ask your pal Bondalewski. She's the one who wants to see the bounty contract. Damn cops."

"She's just doing her job," Rosa replied, though part of her wasn't especially happy about Helen Bondalewski getting in the middle of this. Helen and Rosa worked together, off and on, and had a pretty decent relationship. Normally, she'd be going straight to her to get this stuff. Why did she go over her head this time?

"Yeah, fine, her job gives me an ulcer." Bruce flipped through the papers in the cabinet, all sorted by alphabetical order. Near the right-hand side, he dug up a folder labeled 'Alman' and pulled it out, then flipped it open. Looking at Bruce Kravitz, you would have thought he spent more time at the local donut shop than in his office, but his mind was a steel trap, and as a bail bondsman who'd been in this job for nearly two decades, he was mentally prepared for damn near anything. He had to be in order to make sense of the disaster that was his filing system contained within his small office.

Rosa turned from the filing cabinet and looked at the state of Kravitz's office, something she did often as she waited for a check or just for a ten-minute conversation with the man. As it generally was, its current state was a form of barely organized and contained chaos, filing cabinets strewn throughout, each set stuffed full of records until they could hold no more, at which time another one was brought in and shoehorned somewhere. In spite of doing this job for twenty years, Bruce didn't make a ton of money, and his office decor betrayed that fact. Cheap wood slat floors, bargain basement furniture and with nothing matching each other it was a haphazard jumble of conflicting styles, all crammed into the small two-room office, which sat in a squat, non-descript building just on the edge of civilization, almost tipping over into the inner-city projects, but barely grasping onto the ledge of actual reputable business. Even this far out of downtown, Rosa was certain the rent was ridiculous, and based on what she made for commission on jobs like this one, she had a hard time understanding how Bruce survived for two decades living from contract to contract. The fact was, he did, and because he did, she did.

Bruce had a long history with Lenny Goff, the previous owner of People Finders, the bounty organization that Rosa was now president and partial owner of herself. Lenny was a career cop until he wasn't any more, forced out at an early retirement when the city was having some particularly difficult financial issues. Lenny took retirement in stride, left the force and started up People Finders, using his many connections within law enforcement to land some especially lucrative bounties.

Rosa didn't have any of those connections, really, but still lived off Lenny's reputation, and it certainly didn't hurt that she seemed to have a knack for this work. Her and Chuck made a good team and had a decent success rate, good enough to cover the bills and keep operating.

Mostly.

"I've got us covered," Bruce said, lifting the folder grasped in his right hand. "Everything's on spec as usual."

"You're the man, Bruce," Rosa said with a smirk.

"Don't you forget it, sweetie."

"Call me sweetie again, would ya?" Rosa sneered, cracking her knuckles.

Bruce chuckled. "You don't scare me, half-pint. Get the hell outta here, Goose, let me handle the cops. I'll call you if I need you."

Rosa nodded. "Tell Bondalewski to come straight to me next time."

Bruce shrugged. "Whatever."

Rosa turned and walked towards the door, then glanced over her shoulder. "How much we pull in with that one?" she asked, acting as if she didn't already know.

"Five K," Bruce replied. "Minus my percentage."

"Don't want to forget your percentage," Rosa said, rolling her eyes. She settled her gaze on Bruce after a second. "Seriously, Kravitz. Thanks. This one will help."

Then it was Bruce's turn to roll his eyes. "Whatever. Hell outta here, okay?"

Rosa pushed out the door, moving past the high-pitched squeal of non-lubricated hinges, the narrow hallway beyond just as low budget and ramshackle as the office. A few feet down the hall, Chuck stood leaning against the wall. His clothes hung off him in wrinkled swaths, Heath's narrow frame barely filling the pants and shirt that he wore. Standing not more than five foot-five and likely weighing 140 pounds soaking wet, Chuck Heath was about the least imposing bounty hunter in the history of bounty hunters. A pair of sunglasses were perched high on his dark forehead, the black scrabble of recently shaved hair coating his brown scalp.

"How'd that go?" he asked, smirking.

"About like you'd think," Rosa replied, shaking her head. "But we're getting paid, so it's all good."

He pushed off the wall and joined her walking towards the front door.

"So, the cops going to make this a thing?" he asked.

"No idea. Bondalewski's already called Bruce, though."

"Helen?" Chuck asked, looking over at Rosa. "Doesn't she usually throw us a heads up?"

Rosa shrugged. "Usually, yeah. Not sure what's up this time."

"So, what's next?" Chuck asked.

Rosa stopped walking and glanced towards him. "Get home to your brothers. Make sure everything's good at home. We're caught up for now."

"You sure?"

"Yeah. I'll call you if I need anything."

Chuck nodded. As the sole caretaker of his small family, he spent a lot of time running home to check on his brothers, especially Travis. An impressionable fifteen-year-old, young Travis Heath was already getting mixed up in the wrong crowd, something all too easy to do as a kid living in Springfield's north end. Chuck had somehow managed to sidestep that crowd growing up, mostly because he was a devoted and unashamed nerd, but his youngest brother wasn't having the same luck.

Moving ahead of Rosa, he opened the door, then pressed his back against it, pushing it open so she could vacate.

"Thanks," she said quietly. He nodded, and the two separated, each to their own car to head back home to their respective lives.

CHAPTER 3

It didn't feel like she was at Kravitz's office for a few hours, but the sun had set and a low, gray sky watched over Rosa as she navigated her elderly vehicle around the final corner, heading towards the home stretch. A single lit eye glared out at her. Off to her right, a late train barreled along the tracks, it's light scorching the darkness ahead of it. Rosa's eyes were affixed on the train, and not for the first time, she wondered precisely what side of the tracks she was on these days.

Throughout most of her life, she had been decidedly on the *wrong side*, but as she'd worked hard over the past decade, give or take, she'd struggled to figure out if the work had made a difference. She wasn't convinced.

No matter how much time she spent in juvenile detention, how much time she'd spent with the United States Army, none of that could wash out those younger years, those childhood years that truly shaped the person she was destined to become. She had been destined to become something and had managed to become something else. Surrounded and raised by children throughout her life, Rosa had grown attached to that kind of life and had a strong nostalgia for reminders of her younger years. Those younger years, for better or worse, had shaped her and helped her become who she was. Was it fate, luck, or something else? Rosa Guzman had no explanation for how she had gotten where she was, and she was simultaneously relieved and petrified that one small misstep could take it all away.

Today had come close. She suspected it had come closer than she ever had before. You don't just fire a pistol within city limits without some repercussions, and the fact that Bondalewski had gone straight to Kravitz rather than come to her was proof of some narrow tightrope line she had managed to cross this time. She'd gotten the bounty. Alphonso Alman was unharmed, and she'd see the check in the next week or so, but what had it done to her reputation? There was a time that she couldn't have cared less, but that time had passed. It felt like something was at stake now, something beyond just her. Chuck. Lenny Goff. She had responsibilities.

Twisting the key, Rosa cut the engine, letting the car slowly settle into an even, background chatter before silencing completely. Sitting there in her quiet car, looking out at her office, which also happened to be her home, the silence felt overwhelming. A thick blanket, too warm and too heavy, lying on top of her, wrapping around her, unwieldy and too big, something she just couldn't seem to fight her way out of. All throughout her childhood, she'd been surrounded by noise. The coming and going of her mother's clients, the constant influx of neighborhood kids, boys and girls she'd adopted as brothers and sisters. Gunfire wasn't constant, but it happened often enough, and throughout every hour of her existence, there was just some kind of perpetual noise and activity, there was no such thing as quiet introspection.

These days, it seemed like all she had was quiet introspection. At least when she wasn't working.

Part of her liked it that way. Every year of her life had slowly separated her from her past, from the people she'd known in her youth and, at this point, she truly felt like she was forging her own path, regardless of how impossible it had become to leave her town. To push away this city that had given and taken so much. She'd tried time and time again to leave it, even traveling to the Middle East with the Army, but no matter how far she travelled, she found herself crashing back to the concrete of the north end, a prison of its own sort she just couldn't seem to escape. A constant endless reminder of times past, mistakes made, and lives changed.

Lives ended.

Rosa lowered her head, flexing and unflexing her fingers. The exhaustion of the day finally found her and settled on her shoulders, driving them down into a defeated slouch, the weight of the exchange with Alphonso Alman finally pressing down upon her. The swift, bright reports of pistol fire, the hurtling bullets that could have easily struck her down and ended her life. Returning fire, part of her actually hoping she might kill him.

How could she think that way? How could she still even consider taking another life after what had happened? Was she truly that bad of a person?

It was him or her. She chose him.

At the end of the day, they both survived the exchange, and she'd get the check in the mail and all would be forgiven, but the events would still linger. They'd still cling to her soul like used chewing gum, never fully pulled apart, always some thick, sticky residue left behind. It had been almost thirty years and there was plenty of used gum on her soul already. What was a little more?

Sitting there in the empty, silent car, Rosa looked out through the windshield at the small building, the lone yellow eye glaring out through the haze of evening fog, inviting her in. She was tired. It wasn't all that late, but she'd had a busy day, and a gunfight had a way of making her more tired than she probably should be. Finally feeling as if she'd sat there long enough, she pushed open the driver's side door, drew in a breath, and stepped into the night.

It was a quiet night tonight. Even so close to the north end, no stray noise caught her ears. It's not like this was the wild west with gunfights every night, but more often than not in her life there was this underlying racket, this sense of just something happening just outside her view, and the more silent the world was, the stranger she felt.

The silence tonight filled her with a moderate sense of unease, in spite of a job well done. Growing up amongst so much conflict, she had learned to understand and embrace the underlying noise of the lifeblood of a city, and a lack of that made her antsy, waiting for something to happen. It was an interesting aspect of survival instinct, something she had first developed on these very streets and further homed in the mountains of Afghanistan. If it was quiet, it didn't mean that nothing was happening, it just meant that you weren't aware of it yet, and it was looming around, ready to surprise you. She lived her life desperately hoping for the absence of surprise, and for her first thirty-five years, she'd been miserably unsuccessful.

There was still time.

Rosa stepped away from the car, easing her door shut. Fog was low and clinging to her vehicle and to the streetlights, enveloping everything in a light haze, taking the bright whiteness and reducing it to a dull gray. Enough to illuminate the world, but not truly brighten it. Rosa could see the pavement and buildings around her as she walked towards her office, but they were vague recollections, not a true view, a half-memory of the way things should be. Crossing the street, she approached the office and unlocked her front door, slipping inside and closing it behind her, quickly latching it. The one floor building was mostly made up of a main office with a pair of desks and computers, flanked by a scattering of filing cabinets. It resembled a real-life office, even having a coffee maker and water bubbler, but it all still felt unreal to Rosa. Lenny had been dead for two years at this point, and she still half-expected him to walk out of one of the doors and tell her to go home.

That wouldn't work these days. This *was* home. For better or worse, Rosa's work and Rosa's home were the same place, she couldn't afford separate ones. As she stepped into the threshold, her foot caught on something and slid swiftly, throwing her momentarily off balance. Looking down at the wooden floor, she saw an envelope firmly wedged underneath her foot.

An envelope? Who mails anything these days?

Slowly sliding her foot from the envelope, she bent at the waist, lowering herself down and spotted her own name neatly written on the surface of the paper which had been wedged underneath her sneakered foot. It had been sheer luck that she'd felt it there to begin with. Slipping her fingertips underneath it, she picked it up, lifting the corner of the paper from the wooden floor.

Standing, she held it in her hand, just looking at the flat surface of the envelope, her own name staring back at her as if accusing her of some mysterious crime.

She turned over the envelope in her hand, squinting at it, trying to decipher exactly what its purpose was, and she felt the folded piece of paper inside. A letter. Someone sent her a letter. Did she tumble back through time and not realize it?

Staring at the envelope, she took three strides towards the desk, just to her left, and dropped the envelope on the smooth, wooden surface, glaring down at it, unsure what she should do next. A letter could either be exceptionally important or completely unimportant and, at this point, she wasn't honestly sure which this was. Sitting down in the swivel chair tucked neatly under her desk, Rosa picked up the envelope and turned it over in her hand again. Tucking her index finger under the flap, she swiftly whipped it to her right, tearing the seal and opening the mysterious notation.

Inside the envelope was a single sheet of letter-sized paper, type written, about three paragraphs. Carefully unfolding the paper, Rosa looked down at what was written, but the words blurred together. Her vision naturally settled on the end of the letter and immediately focused on two words near the signature. Two very specific words. One word really. A name.

An all too familiar last name. One etched into the fabric of her memory, a name she had read in the newspaper all too many times in her young life, and to read it again, so many years later, drew her, kicking and screaming, back to those murky events.

Federov.

It was just a name. A name, that ultimately meant nothing, while at the same time meaning everything. Her eyes roamed to the top of the note and locked on a small wallet-sized photograph paperclipped there, a simple rectangular shape, the face looking as unfamiliar as the name was familiar. She knew the name intimately, she had burned it into her brain, repeated self-abuse carving it indelibly into every waking thought, and only recently had she even begun to absolve herself of those past sins.

And here it was. Again. After many years of failing to forget, someone went through the trouble of writing it down and sending it directly to her. Her vision faded and fogged, the paper shifting in front of her, the letters blurring together. Tears formed in her eyes, sudden and unexpected, and as she dropped the envelope back onto her desk, she couldn't help but wonder if this was all real or some elaborate trick.

She wasn't sure which outcome she'd prefer.

CHAPTER 4

The buildings felt so much taller back then, reaching towards the thickening clouds. Every memory Rosa had of that day, of the days surrounding it, were gray and cloudy, no hint of sunshine. She wasn't sure if that was because of the events themselves, or if the weather during those days was truly that bad. Did the sun ever shine during recollections of bad memories?

A fine mist spat down from the sky, not thick or steady enough to truly be considered rain, but enough so that a dull sheen coated the streets and sidewalks with dozens of rounded droplets clinging to the smooth surface of windows on the cars, beading on the metal surface surrounding them.

The weather mirrored her mood. It mirrored the mood of everyone she knew that day. It was a very bad day.

It was going to get worse.

"Doggie. They got Doggie."

"Son of a bitch. Doggie wouldn't hurt a fly. Why'd they have to do that?"

"He was wearin' the wrong colors. That's it. That's all it takes. Assholes."

"We gonna let that stand?"

Young Rosa Guzman stood among the older children, her foster family of sorts, boys and young men from her neighborhood, wrapped up in something they didn't truly understand.

Flanking Interstate 91, one of the main passageways running up the East Coast, Springfield, Massachusetts made for a convenient point of entry for undesirable elements. Less than sixty miles north of Hartford, Connecticut, and not too far away from New York City, gang activity in the largest city in western Massachusetts grew consistently for decades, with many children in the wrong neighborhoods getting caught up in the thrill of belonging to something larger than themselves. Overnight they went from roaming the streets of the north end with no direction and no ambition to working with older kids, being given responsibility and actual goals to work towards.

Rosa Guzman was one of those kids. She wasn't interested in drugs. She was too young and too obstinate to get pulled into a life of prostitution, yet she found a place among the older girls and was taken under their wing. Not just the girls, though. Her tomboy attitude and abrasive personality endeared her to the boys of the crew as well, and she grew close to many of them.

She was especially close to Doggie. His name was Douglas Menendez, but all the neighborhood kids knew him as Doggie. He was one of the younger and more naive members of their crew, riding the waves out of a sense of not knowing what else to do with his life. A devoted member of the Blades, he wore their colors, backed up his friends and for the first time in his young life felt like he belonged somewhere. But back then, you had to be careful. You had to watch where you wore those colors because the Blades weren't the only crew roaming Springfield, and even though the kids in this relatively small city all got along, the gangs in other parts of the northeast didn't. It didn't matter who you grew up with, someone wore the wrong colors in your backyard, they had to pay. Throughout the hidden corners of Springfield, the Russian Mafia had lodged a strong foothold through generations of migration. Slowly and methodically, they began consuming local business and turning parts of the city into their private strongholds. They didn't take kindly to the indoctrinated Blades, a low-level drug and weapon dealing gang trying to make their own move up the East Coast.

Doggie was heading to his cousin's birthday party, and nobody really knows why he didn't take off the bandana or why he didn't untie that yellow jacket from around his waist, but he didn't. He left them on and strolled down the street, proud as life until four quick gunshots took that pride from him and left him bleeding to death in the gutter, his dark blood mixing with runoff, twisting into the sewer system underneath the city. It had taken seconds. Mere seconds to change a kid without a worry in the world to a lifeless husk, blood-covered and limp.

"Are you sure it was the Russians?"

"Who else would it be?"

"Was he on their turf?"

"What does it matter? Yeah, he was on their turf, but it was Doggie, man. Doggie."

"I dunno, Switch. I mean, hell. He was wearin' our colors. Did they do anything we wouldn't have done?"

"The hell with you and the hell with them, man."

In her memories, Rosa couldn't always determine who was speaking, the voices just all bled together. One thing is certain, though, Carlos "Switch" Rodriguez was there. He was always there. Throughout every moment of her childhood, Switch was there, taking her under his wing, guiding her through her adolescence, protecting her from harm. Always at her side. The big brother she'd never had.

"So, what are we gonna do about it?"

"What we always do. Get our pound of flesh."

"Against the Russians? You're crazy, yo."

At this point, Rosa had some clarity. She saw Switch turn and look over his shoulder, the wide, straight brim of his old school Hartford Whalers baseball cap sitting slightly cockeyed as if sneering at the other kid. Rosa couldn't remember the other kid's name, just another nameless face lost to the fog of history, but she still remembered Switch's narrow eyes, his furrowed brow, two shining gold teeth visible against his rows of white. Thick rough of dark hair stretched out on his face, an untamed lawn that was never quite mowed short enough.

"I don't care if it's the Russians, the Spanish, or the goddamned Chinese. They take from us, we take from them. That's the way this stuff works."

The silent response told Rosa all she needed to know back then. There would be no more discussion, no more arguments, no more defense. Doggie was dead, and for damn sure, someone would pay for that.

CHAPTER 5

It was the best time of the day, in Mitchell Capozza's unbiased opinion. Darkness had settled over his city, a deep cloak blocking out the light, allowing him to move more freely and less encumbered. A few blocks outside of downtown, where the rent was just a little too expensive and the clientele just a little too upper class, the small Chinese restaurant sat nestled among a throng of larger buildings. Just to one side there was a pair of office buildings, not the upper echelon twenty floor models, mind you, but the four or five floor middle class offices where the mom and pop insurance companies set up shop. The smaller law firms in town, all those places that couldn't quite afford the penthouse view provided by the glass and steel superstructures closer to the center of the action.

The Emerald Lotus was a fixture here, a restaurant that had been family owned and operated for nearly fifty years before Mitchell Capozza made the owners an offer they couldn't refuse and added yet another real estate transaction to his already long laundry list of them.

Like every other transaction, the Emerald Lotus was a good restaurant, but not the best. It had acceptable decor but would never be considered fancy. It was a place where families came on Friday night, though, if you were hosting a business guest from out of town, it was the last place you'd think to take them. The food was good, the inspector had never shut it down, though he had regular complaints about the kitchen.

In short, it existed much like Capozza himself, as a recognizable fixture in the city, an icon that everyone knew and accepted as a part of everyday life, but not necessarily a desirable destination or respected venue.

Capital Industries was built upon a stockpile of disrespected venues. Restaurants, buildings, riverfront property, all manner of investment opportunities that did okay, but never quite put Capozza over the edge. Never quite thrust him into that upper class he so desired to be. If his parents had still been alive, they would have been immeasurably proud of the third generation Italian, but they weren't still alive, and the only person he could please was himself.

He was not pleased.

The Emerald Lotus sat mostly dark, the front door locked and the parking lot lights dimmed. It rarely had guests this late at night as it was but, tonight, Capozza wanted a nice peaceful meal, so tonight they closed early to give him what he asked for.

Gleaming under the low-slung stars, the freshly cleaned black sedan eased into one of the front parking spots. Washed and detailed like it was the finest in German engineering, the Cadillac cut its engine and a well-dressed driver stepped out of the front seat, sweeping around to the rear opposite door and easing it open.

Capozza stepped out, draped in a neatly pressed dark suit, nothing made by Armani, but nice enough, and smoothed his pants as he pulled himself upright slowly. Capozza wasn't what anyone would call fat, but he had the typical paunch of a fifty-year-old man who didn't work out regularly. A narrow face, thinly covered in a neatly groomed gray beard, his alert eyes brushed across the empty parking lot as he adjusted the rectangular glasses perched on top of his bent nose. His hair matched his beard, though it was in full retreat from his forehead, revealing more of his bare scalp than he cared to admit. All of his gophers and toadies went out of their way to tell him how dignified he looked, and mostly he let himself believe it. However, he longed for the day when someone he didn't pay a full salary to give him a similar compliment. As the years grew longer, he became more doubtful that day would ever come.

The driver stepped ahead and beat him to the front door, swinging it open and holding it so Capozza could enter. He halted for a moment, regarding the empty restaurant with a mixture of disappointment and satisfaction. There was a brief moment of pleasure at the fact that he could enjoy his meal in peace, but this brief moment was quickly scattered by the realization that there were almost a dozen employees he was paying by the hour with not a single paying customer to offset the expense.

Considered one of the wealthiest men in Western Massachusetts, Mitchell Capozza held the secret of his lack of wealth very close to the vest. The truth was, if you looked at his books, and looked at the value of his property, one could easily surmise that he was worth millions. Several millions. But Mitchell was not a simple man and did not live by simple means. He desired and lived a life of extravagance, the kind of extravagance that came dangerously close to outstripping his means.

But he had a reputation to uphold. It had taken him decades to wedge his way into this position of power in this city, and he only held that power based on the misguided belief that he was almost immeasurably wealthy. Shuffling money around to the right people at the right times greased the wheels for many of his transactions, and with each purchase and each allocation, he told himself this would be the one that paid off. That the improvements he made to this property would net him that ten-million-dollar windfall that would finally get him out from under this mountain.

It never seemed to happen, but he lived as if it already had.

The corner booth sat waiting, the deep red vinyl seats neatly wiped down, though a few stray rips caught his eyes.

"What would you like, Mr. Capozza?" asked an engaging young host, stepping up from behind a podium to the left of the front door. "Your normal seat, sir?"

Capozza nodded. "Please." His voice was a quiet confidence, never wavering.

Following the escort as if he didn't know exactly where he was going, as if he hadn't sat at this seat seventy times before, he wove between the thickly packed tables, which never seemed more than half-full, and deftly stepped between two waiters cleaning up. They both nodded respectfully and obediently as he passed.

With a gesture, the host guided Capozza towards the rounded booth, and he dropped down, then slid all the way to the back, laying his arms on the wooden table in front of him. Looking out over the empty restaurant, for a brief second, he felt a sense of pride. This was his. He owned this. It belonged to him.

"What can I get you, sir?" a waiter asked, stepping in as the host stepped away.

"Sweet and Sour Soup," Mitchell replied quietly. "Egg Fu Yung. A side of dumplings."

The waiter nodded. "And to drink?"

"Bring a bottle of Riesling, please. Italian Riesling."

"As you wish," the waiter nodded and stepped backwards gracefully. He turned and was gone.

Mitchell pressed his palms against the table and drew in a deep breath, looking out at the restaurant. Glasses clinked and waiters lifted chairs, turning them upside down and setting them on the tables. The front door eased open and the glow of the starry night outside shone through before two large silhouettes appeared to merge together into a single, thick, formless organism, which pressed into the restaurant. In the low light of the Emerald Lotus, the shape separated again and became two tall, broad-shouldered individuals, each one dressed in a dark suit and weaving gracefully between the scattered tables.

"Pietro. Jerome. Come, come." Capozza gestured towards them, signaling the chairs opposite him. Pietro nodded and eased one of the chairs out, settling his bulk into it. Jerome repeated the motion. The two men could have been brothers if not for their different ethnicity, both tall and wide, more muscle than fat. Pietro's head was shorn clear, a bare scalp gleaming under the artificial light of the restaurant, without even the scant covering of hair fuzz. A thin goatee surrounded his thin lips just over a squared chin. Next to him Jerome placed his hands on his lap, a thin coat of dark hair on his head and a full beard, also well-manicured, stretching across his wide face.

"Any word yet?" Capozza asked, looking at Pietro specifically.

"Not yet," Pietro replied. "We've checked his home, we've checked in with his parents and known associates. Nothing so far."

"When was the last time he missed work?" Capozza asked.

"His attendance has been exemplary up until last week," Jerome replied. "Rarely missed work, and when he did, it was usually something for his son."

"I assume we've checked his son's school?"

"Of course," Pietro interjected. "His last day was the same last day at work as his father. Since last Monday, both of them have essentially been off the grid."

Capozza grimaced, leaning back slightly. The cheap, red vinyl squeaked amusingly underneath him, and one of the smaller tears stretched, threatening to vomit a small handful of foam filling.

"Have you heard back from the security team?" Pietro asked.

Capozza nodded. "The infosec team detected a large download of data to his laptop the evening before his departure. Network permissions were edited to provide access to certain previously restricted files."

Jerome shook his head. "Not good."

Capozza's eyes snapped tight and flashed towards him as if attempting to wound. "That is an understatement, Jerome. A massive understatement."

"How was he able to gain access? We have protocols for this type of thing, don't we?" Pietro clasped his fingers together nervously.

"Of course, we do," Capozza replied. "He was in charge of the department. We expect better from our leadership."

Pietro nodded.

"Since this happened, we have instituted a new set of checks and balances, but too little too late in this case. Now, we just have to pick up the pieces."

Jerome looked down at the table, not wanting to risk the sharp edge of Capozza's glare again. "The letter was delivered earlier today," he said. "I believe she has it."

Capozza nodded. "Good."

This time, Jerome did lift his head. "Is she the right choice?" he asked.

Capozza seemed to work this question out in his head for a moment. Footsteps *thumped* along the carpeted floor, and the three men turned as the waiter approached. He elegantly arranged the Egg Fu Yung, sweet and sour soup, and a full bottle of Italian Riesling on the table. Reaching back onto the plastic platter, he retrieved three upside-down wine glasses and spread them around the table, one by one.

"I don't think we have any other choice," Capozza replied as the cork from the wine bottle popped as if to emphasize his point. A slow slurp followed as each of the glasses were filled to near the top with the lightly amber beverage.

"She's good. And she's affordable."

Jerome nodded and didn't press, still slightly recovering from the previous eye knives.

Pietro had no such compunctions. "Are you concerned with her connections to the subject?"

Capozza actually smirked. "I'm banking on those connections, Pietro. I think it gives us some leverage."

Pietro nodded. "Understood. But what about Federov? Will he suspect anything?"

"No. Those records are sealed." Capozza smiled thinly. "Sealed to most."

Jerome and Pietro both grinned, supporting their boss's self-inflated sense of importance.

"So what next?" Jerome asked.

Capozza pulled the Egg Fu Yung in front of him, picking up a fork and knife to start digging in. He steadily scraped the silverware against the ceramic plate, carving the egg dish into smaller pieces methodically and patiently. Stabbing a fork into the egg, he pushed it into his mouth and chewed, relishing the anticipation of his two lackeys. Picking up the nearest wine glass, he took a long, deep swig to wash down the egg, then set the glass back down and dabbed his chin with a napkin.

"More of the same, gentlemen," he finally replied. "Keep looking for Federov and his son. Talk to security, see if we know exactly what files he accessed. If I don't hear from Guzman by tomorrow morning, I'll be in touch."

Pietro and Jerome both nodded.

Capozza scraped his fork, piling up more dinner and lifted it to his mouth. He glanced over his nose, looking at the two men. Setting his fork down, he gestured with his fingers, waving them away towards the front door.

"You can go," he said quietly in between chewing. The two men nodded and pressed their palms on the table, pushing themselves to their feet, then turned away and walked towards the door. Watching their retreating forms, Mitchell Capozza drained the remainder of his glass of wine and slid it aside, then shifted and retrieved one of the other filled glasses on the table. He tipped that to his lips and drank.

Setting down the glass, he leaned back and placed his hands on his lap, letting the food settle and the wine buzz low in the back of his head. Good food and solitude brought him some small measure of happiness, but his nagging sense of betrayal was thick and sharp and sat in his gut like a volleyball of nails. It prevented even the simplest of pleasures from truly being pleasures, and for that crime, he would never forgive Stepan Federov. Capozza was a calm man. An intense man, but ultimately an understanding and forgiving one. But he did not tolerate betrayal. He could not tolerate disloyalty. Make a mistake or an error in judgment, and that was okay. Deliberately defy him or shrug off your loyalty like an old wet ski parka?

That had to be punished.

CHAPTER 6

"Come on, Nichole, I know you better than this. That shit that went down last week...you gotta give me something, girlfriend."

"I tol' you, Officer, out here on the streets, you gotta call me Silent H. Don't call me Nichole, streets got ears, right? They got lots of ears. I can't be on no first name basis with no cop!" Her eyes darted out from under the thick lock of blonde hair. One hand wrapped around officer Bondalewski's forearm and squeezed gently.

"Yeah, yeah, Silent H, I get it. All I know is we had the wild, wild west down here with Alphonso Alman, and I know you know his crew. What did you hear about that? Did you see anything?"

Nichole Janell shook her head. "I ain't seen jack. I ain't heard jack. I don't know jack."

"Then what am I paying you for? You're my CI, you forget that or something?"

Nichole twisted around, glancing down the street to make sure no other eyes were upon her. "I didn't forget. Just cut me some slack, okay? Honest, I don't know nothin' about this Alman thing."

Helen held up her hands. "All right. Fair enough. I'll let you off the hook on this one, H, but don't make me regret it."

Nichole nodded furiously and turned away from the female officer, making her way back down the sidewalk.

Helen Bondalewski often relished her role as a female cop, one of few in Springfield proper, especially when it came to the cops walking the streets. She was relatively young but had already experienced an entire life's worth of on the job moments, not the least of which came ten years ago on a day much like today. An early morning, fall day, cool to the touch, but not yet cold, just a lingering threat of worse still to come.

Clouds covered the sky, reaching towards each other and linking hands, blocking out any semblance of sun. Like that day ten years ago, a light drizzle fell, spattering against her blue hat and dark blue windbreaker, pulled tight over her light blue button up shirt underneath. The days of the typical beat cop attitude were swiftly fading in the rearview mirror, but she went out of her way to make sure she walked her streets as much as she could, not just for some face time with the locals, but because it helped keep her in shape. For as active an occupation as being a police officer felt like it should be, she felt like she spent a hell of a lot of time on her ass either in a car or at her desk. She needed to get some fresh air.

As she walked down the sidewalk, eyes scanning, the familiar and comfortable weight of her service pistol at her hip, she didn't hear the low rattle of the engine as it approached back and to her left.

"Hey, Helen!" the voice was low and shrill, a woman's voice. She halted and turned, shielding her eyes from the light falling rain.

"Rosa?" she asked, glaring at the car, which sat idling in the road, the passenger window rolled down.

"Yeah. Can you talk?"

Bondalewski's face hardened slightly, her smile faltering. "Look, I know what this is about."

"So, come talk to me."

Helen glanced to her right, then to her left. No other traffic approached, on the sidewalks or on the road. She sighed and stepped off the walkway, then opened the passenger door and slipped inside.

"Thanks," Rosa said. "The rain was ruining the upholstery."

Helen glanced down at the worn and faded fabric she sat upon, some of it nearly threadbare. She couldn't help but smile. The car lurched forward, navigated a left turn, and proceeded down a one-way street.

"Rosa, let me explain about Alman."

"This isn't about Alman," Rosa replied. "Although that was pretty messed up."

Helen looked over at her. "What's this about then?"

"Well, now that you mention it..., why the hell did you go over my head? I thought we were on better terms than that?"

"Come on, don't be like that. I have to do my job. Gunfire was exchanged, Rosa, I can't take convenient shortcuts when that stuff happens."

"Nobody got hurt."

"And you're damn lucky they didn't."

"All right, all right," Rosa said, lifting a hand and showing her palm, a sign of willing acceptance of events. "Open the glove box, will you?"

Officer Bondalewski looked over at her, then her eyes darted back to the glove compartment. "Okay?" She leaned forward and unlatched the clasp, bringing down the curved handle. It was stuffed full, as she figured it would be, and most of the stuff in there was stuff that Rosa probably hadn't even looked at in a handful of years but perched on top was a pearly white envelope with the words "Rosa Guzman" written in fancy writing.

"What the hell is this?"

Rosa shrugged as she drove, making another series of swift turns, trying to stay on empty streets as much as possible.

"Open it," she said.

The police officer did. She withdrew a piece of folded paper and carefully unfolded it, her eyes scanning the typewritten note that had been contained within. Evenly spaced type, neatly composed, tightly organized, like some kind of old school cover letter that a kid wrote a little too meticulously for his entry level job application.

Rosa glanced at Bondalewski's face, saw her scan through the whole letter, then return to the top, squint a little tighter, and read through again. She lifted her head, a look of utter confusion on her face as she folded the paper back up and held it in her lap.

"Where did you get this?" she asked, looking over at the driver.

"It was in my office," Rosa replied. "Hand delivered."

"And it really came from Capozza?"

Rosa shrugged. "How should I know? I don't even know the guy. I can't imagine someone would have faked that."

Helen opened the paper again and read back through.

"Federov?"

"Federov."

"And you think it's the same Federov?"

"How many can there be? He would have been in the papers back then right?"

Helen nodded. "And you think Capozza...you think he knows about your connection to people named Federov?"

"Kind of seems that way. I can't think of any other reason why he'd choose me out of anyone to look for this guy."

"When did you get this?"

"Last night."

"Have you done any looking yet?"

"Not a bit. Came straight to you first. It feels squirrelly."

"It looks squirrelly."

"Anyone reported him missing yet?" Rosa angled the car to the right and began coming back around to where she had picked Helen up.

"Not that I know of, but I'm not in the loop on all of that."

"What should I do about it?"

Helen folded the paper back up and stuffed it inside the envelope. "The guy is loaded. Owns half the city. I'd accept the offer and see what he wants. Nothing illegal here that I can see."

"You don't think it's strange that he's looking for..." Rosa's voice trailed off slightly. "That he's looking for *him?*"

"Maybe a little. There's probably some connection. I can start looking into it if you want."

Rosa shook her head. "No, not yet. Let me dig first. I don't want you getting wrapped up in anything."

"Okay."

"I'm just a little freaked out. It could be a coincidence, or it could be something else."

Glancing out the window at the steadily increasing patter of rain, Officer Bondalewski snorted slightly. "You believe in coincidence as much as I do, Guzman."

Rosa rolled her eyes. "Yeah, no kidding." Surprisingly, she felt a sharp pinch of tears in her eyes. A sudden and aggressive melancholy flooded her chest, feeling like a fist closing around her insides and squeezing slowly. After all these years, just seeing that name…that damned name.

Helen seemed to notice the shift in emotion. "Hey, you okay?" she asked.

"I'll be fine," Rosa replied a little too quickly.

"Bull, Goose," Helen replied. She didn't use Rosa's nickname often, but when she did, it was her motherly way of telling the young girl to stop being so damned stubborn.

"Really, I'm all right. Just seeing that name again. It stirred some stuff back up."

"I know. Let's try to get to the bottom of it."

"What do you know about this Mitchell Capozza dude, anyway? I mean, besides what's in the papers?"

Helen shrugged. "Not sure. I know he's a good friend of the police. Often one of the biggest sponsors of our fundraising efforts. I've seen him in the precinct from time to time, nobody seems to have a bad word to say about him."

"Can you ask around a little?"

"Sure."

"Thanks."

The car eased to a stop on the same block where Officer Bondalewski had been walking. Rosa left the motor running as she nudged up next to the sidewalk, the streets still empty before her.

"You sure you're okay?" Helen asked.

Rosa nodded. "I'll be fine."

"What's your next step?"

"Figure out why Capozza's looking for Stepan Federov, and what his relationship is to..."

"To?" Helen asked, pinning her eyes on Rosa's.

"You know who," Rosa replied, her voice low.

Helen did know who. She knew the name Federov as well as Rosa did, but Capozza's connection to him? That was still unclear.

"Okay. I'll talk to some of my folks and see if I can dig anything up on Capozza. See if I get an insight as to why he'd be hiring a bounty hunter rather than just going to the police."

Rosa looked over at her. "Aren't the implications pretty clear?"

"The world isn't black and white, Rosa."

"Tell me about it."

Helen shrugged, opened her door, and stepped out. "Take care of yourself, okay. Give me a call if you need to talk."

Rosa looked out of the opened door at her and nodded but didn't reply. Helen stood, easing the door shut, then watched as the car pulled away and drove off underneath the sheer curtain of light rain.

Ten years. In many ways, Rosa Guzman had grown up quite a lot since then. In other ways, she was still that scared sixteen-year-old hyperventilating in the rain, eyes wide as if she had looked into the soul of Satan himself and somehow came out alive.

Helen didn't believe in coincidence…, but the records had been sealed, and Capozza couldn't have known about Rosa's connection to the last name Federov.

Could he?

Something was rotten in Denmark, Helen decided as she crossed the street to resume walking her beat. She'd passed up more than one promotion since that day ten years ago, and here she was, walking the streets the same way she had been back then. She wasn't old, that much was certain but, suddenly, she felt exhausted and weary under the potential implications of what Rosa Guzman had just showed her.

CHAPTER 7

The junky old sedan barely got him where he needed to go, but it was better than the alternative, which was mass transportation. It's not like he made enough working with Goose to afford anything better, and even if the beat-up Ford was a hand-me-down from one of their clients in an effort to pay off their bill, it ran well, got him where he needed to go, and helped get his brothers where they need to go as well

That was the most important part.

Prentiss and Travis were Chuck Heath's brothers, but it was more complicated than that. He was also their sole caretaker, their protector, and their surrogate parent. It was a lot of responsibility for him, but he was handling it a lot better now than he had when he was forced to give up his military career to move back home in order to care for them. Back then, he hardly paid attention to his own difficulties, he was too busy burying his mother.

His two younger brothers took it much harder than he did. He had been off in a foreign country by then, learning to be an intelligence officer and, already, Springfield, Massachusetts had faded into a vague memory, a place he never envisioned going back to. A part of his past.

Everything changed with the car accident. T-boned by a delivery truck, his mother was pronounced dead at the scene, leaving two orphaned brothers alone at home, and forcing Chuck to take an early and unexpected retirement from what had, at that point, been his dream job. Officer Candidates' School with a straight line to intelligence, using his brains as well as his well-conditioned body to defend his country and see the world.

Springfield was a part of the world, at least.

Stepping out of the sedan, he slammed the door shut, pulling out his shirt and pulling it down over his narrow arms. The shirt hung loose on his thin frame, as every article of clothing seemed to. For over ten years, Chuck had worked religiously in various weight rooms to build his body, but no matter what he did, he remained that skinny kid from the block that he'd been since school. No matter how much he lifted, how often he went, how much protein he forced down his throat, he still looked like he weighed ninety pounds soaking wet.

Moving around the car, he trotted up the stairs to the apartment building, his legs aching slightly. After getting done with Alphonso Alman, he'd made one of his usual stops to the local YMCA and pounded out an hour's worth of lower body work, which always left him a little sore and slow moving. Going up the stairs to the second-floor apartment was an exercise in focus, trying to look past the dull ache in his thighs and the bark in his calves. Moments later, he pushed open the door to his apartment, squeezing in and stepping over some discarded trash piled on the floor. Shaking his head, he bent over and scooped up an empty pizza box.

"Travis, who ordered the pizza? We don't have the extra money for this!" he shouted into the empty stillness of the apartment.

"Prentiss did it!" a faded voice shouted back.

A lanky twenty-year-old with a loose fitting T-shirt and thick, baggy pants emerged from one of the rooms to Chuck's right. "Yeah, I bought the pizza," he said in his deep, gruff voice. "I got a good tip at the restaurant last night. A pizza ain't gonna break us, bro."

Chuck nodded and walked over towards the kitchen, depositing the box on the counter. "At least take care of your own trash next time."

"Sorry, man."

"Travis, what's your homework look like tonight?" Chuck asked, walking around the counter and heading down the hall towards his youngest brother's bedroom.

"The hell with that, man," Travis replied.

"Watch your mouth," muttered Chuck. He reached the bedroom and leaned in, looking at his youngest brother, who was sprawled out on the bed, shirtless with basketball shorts. He clutched an X-Box controller in his curled fingers and looked at a small screen where some random soldiers were moving in squad formation, firing weapons. A white headset was pressed tight on his curled mop of dark hair, his eyes narrowly focused on the screen ahead.

"Travis, come on, man. Homework first, then *Call of Duty*."

"Almost to the checkpoint, yo," Travis replied, not even looking towards him.

"Ten minutes. Then homework. I don't care about the checkpoint." Chuck tapped the wall and stepped away, shaking his head. All things considered, having Travis at home playing X-Box was a heck of a lot better than the alternative, which had become an increasing problem in recent months. He'd been spending more time outside of home, hanging out with the wrong crowd, and Chuck could see him getting drawn towards the gangs.

Towards the Blades. He wasn't going to let that happen.

"Prentiss, you gotta watch out for him, man, okay?" Chuck said as he emerged back into the living room where his twenty year-old brother was rooting through the refrigerator.

"I'm trying, Chuck," Prentiss replied. "I got my life to live, too, though, right?"

Chuck just stood there looking at the skinny kid in front of him, bent at the waist, half-buried in the appliance.

We all have our lives to live, he thought. Well, most of us anyway.

Normally, a happy go lucky kid, Chuck had grown up fast when his mother died and had learned to live with the added responsibility, even if he didn't like it a heck of a lot. It didn't help that his two younger brothers were typical teenage boys, having a hard time seeing life outside of their little circle. In a way, they resented Chuck more than appreciated him, a feeling that did not go unnoticed.

So, Chuck typically withdrew into himself. Focused on his training. Harnessed his anger and frustration into an extra rep on the weight bench or an extra round at the local kickboxing gym. Every moment of the day, it seemed, was spent either conditioning his mind or conditioning his body, but at the end of the day, what would it get him? Would his brothers ever outgrow their need for him? Would he ever feel less responsibility again?

Walking over to his backpack, which leaned against the living room wall, he bent over and yanked the slim, black laptop out of it, tucked it under his arm, and withdrew to his corner of the universe, trying to figure out the quickest and easiest legal way to forget his troubles.

CHAPTER 8

"Captain Hunger?" Helen Bondalewski asked as she propped open the door, rapping her knuckles on the frosted glass. "Can I come in for a minute?"

"Yeah, come on in, Bondo," Hunger replied. He sat at his ancient wooden desk, which likely gleamed when it was new but, at this point, it was scuffed and worn and covered with months', if not years', worth of past due paperwork in thickening piles. Among the scattered sheets and leaning stacks, his flat panel computer screen sat like a blank, black billboard with nothing on it, blocking any view of his face as his fingers slapped at the keyboard. From around the black slab of a monitor, Helen could see his rounded shoulders covered in rumpled white cotton, a black tie half unknotted, streaked across his chest.

She stood there for a moment.

"Bondo? What do you need? Speak up, I can't read your mind."

"What do you know about Mitchell Capozza?" she asked. It just kind of spewed from her mouth, a series of barely connected words tumbling forth.

His fingers immediately halted their thumping, ungainly dance across the keys. Leaning to the side slightly, he narrowed his eyes at officer Bondalewski around the monitor screen.

"What did you say?" he asked, but his expression betrayed the fact that he knew exactly what she had said.

"Mitchell Capozza," she repeated. "He's a friend of the police, I know. Just wondering what we know about him."

The captain gestured towards the door for a second, then waved Helen over towards him. "Shut the door and come in."

She did as he asked, walking around the desk and sitting at a small wooden chair pushed flush against the wall. Leaning forward, she rested her elbows on her knees and looked at him, waiting for some sort of amazing enlightenment.

"What are you asking about him for?" Captain Hunger asked, his lips twisting underneath his thick, caterpillar mustache, a dull gunmetal gray, streaked with white.

Helen drew up slightly. "I'm just asking, Cap. Apparently, someone who works for him is missing. Instead of coming to the cops, it looks like he's paying a bounty hunter to find him. Just seems weird is all."

"Bounty hunter?"

"Yeah. Rosa Guzman."

"That's Lenny's old place, right? People Finders or whatever?"

"Yeah, I guess. I don't know the history like you do, Captain."

The Captain smiled, his mustache twisting up. "Man. Lenny Goff was real police," he said. "Vice cop. You knew that, right? Twenty years before he got forced out. I could tell you some of the collars he made, holy crap."

Officer Bondalewski nodded slightly. She didn't know many of the specifics, but she'd certainly heard her share of the legends surrounding Detective Lenny Goff, and they always seemed to be mixed with outrage at how he was forced out, then undoubtedly punctuated with remorse at his untimely death.

None of these fond memories seem to extend to Rosa Guzman, however. To many of the police within these walls, the success of People Finders began and ended with Lenny Goff.

"So why her?" Captain Hunger asked.

Helen shrugged. "I was hoping maybe someone in here might be able to shed some light on that."

Hunger shook his head. "Don't bother. You ain't gonna dig up any dirt on Capozza in here. Like you said, he's a friend of the police. A good friend."

"What exactly does that mean?"

"So, what did you tell Guzman to do? She going to help him?"

"I really don't know. I just thought it was strange that this guy is missing and instead of filing a missing person's report, he's hiring a recovery agent. I don't get it."

"Who's the guy?"

"Stepan Federov," Bondalewski replied.

Captain Hunger paused for a moment, stroking his chin. "I know that name?"

"I'm sure you do," Helen replied. "At least the last name. In connection with Rosa Guzman?"

Realization seemed to settle within Captain Hunger's eyes, though he didn't speak his memory out loud.

"Let me run him through. We'll see if anything comes up. Check hospitals, morgues, all that stuff."

Helen nodded. "Sounds good. No APB, though, okay? I want to find out why this is so hush hush."

"Sounds fair. Like I said, though, don't push the Capozza issue, okay? He's got a lot of friends on the force and elsewhere. Nothing good will come of it."

Standing from the chair and nodding softly, Helen straightened her hat and tipped it briefly to Captain Hunger.

"Thanks, Cap. Let me know what you hear, okay? I'll go touch base with Guzman."

He nodded and waved her towards the door. She followed his lead, wondering what exactly she was going to do with this next.

CHAPTER 9

As the day drew closer to afternoon, Helen Bondalewski stood at the long, lateral filing cabinet, pulling out folders and leafing through individual documents. She'd spent a few hours of her day cross referencing case files on the Department's intranet, but with no luck there, decided it was time to go physical.

After leafing through folders and pulling out paper for an hour, Helen lowered her head and slid the drawer slowly shut. Not a single speeding ticket, moving violation, domestic disturbance...none of it. At least not in the past ten years. Before then, Helen knew what she would find, but that felt like ancient history.

She walked back over to her desk and slid into a chair, tapping her keyboard and bringing up what little information existed about Stepan Federov.

Married to Dalia Federov. An eleven-year-old son. Currently works as the Director of Information Technology for Capital Industries, one of the largest companies in Western Massachusetts. According to Rosa Guzman, he stopped reporting for work a week ago, and both he and his son simply vanished, but no missing person's report had been filed.

"Okay, now how about your kid?" Helen asked nobody in particular as she keyed in on Stepan Federov's son. Glancing at the clock on her desk, she gauged she had just enough time and scooped up the handset, punching in a few numbers.

"Springfield Public School System," said the monotone voice on the other end of the phone.

"Good afternoon, this is Officer Bondalewski from the Springfield Police, how are you?" Helen said in a voice as calm and kind as she could muster.

As usual, when a police officer calls, the person on the other end took a moment to respond again. "What can I do for you, Officer?"

"I have a question about a student. I'm not sure which school he goes to."

"Name and age?"

"Jorge Federov is his name, age eleven. We're trying to solve a little dilemma here."

"I'm very sorry officer, but as a minor, I can't authorize the release of Jorge's information without some kind of legal authority."

Helen placed her forehead in her hand. "Can you confirm any kind of attendance? Give me some idea when he was last in school?"

"I'm not sure that would be appropriate, Officer Bondalewski. Not without his parent or guardian's permission."

"I understand. Please understand me when I say this may be a matter of life and death, ma'am. I empathize with protecting minors, believe me, but this is a potentially dire situation. I'm happy to get something written up providing us access to this information, but with these kinds of cases, I'm sure you can appreciate how time sensitive it is."

On the other end, Helen heard keys tapping on a keyboard. "All I can tell you," the voice said, thin and firm, "is that Jorge was called out of school by his father last week. A family emergency. He said he could be out indefinitely."

"His father made that call? Are you certain?"

"That is my understanding, yes."

Helen sat, phone in hand, staring at her computer screen. "Okay.

This has been very helpful. Thank you. I know you didn't have to share that."

"Good day, Officer Bondalewski."

Helen hung up and rested back on her swivel chair, interlocking her fingers behind her head. As she leaned back, she caught movement out of the corner of her eye. Crossing the precinct, she saw Detective Ryan Sargent, a familiar face in the department. A thick bush of curly blond hair spiraled off his head, cascading down across his jaw in sheets of blond beard. He wore a pink button-up short sleeve shirt, holster strapped across his chest, with faded blue jeans. Ryan truly was the prototypical undercover vice cop, and that was exactly the kind of person Helen needed.

"Ryan!" she shouted and waved. "Got a minute?"

Ryan stopped and turned, flashing his charming 'aw shucks' smile. "Anything for you, beautiful," he said in a way that actually didn't sound sleazy, amazingly enough.

Helen took a few steps towards him, gesturing to an interrogation room on a wall to her right. He fell in behind her, and they retreated to the relative solace of the ten by ten room, a table and three chairs in the center.

"What's up?" he asked.

"Hoping maybe you've heard something on the streets. Something about a missing guy and his son."

Ryan shook his head, looking somewhat confused. "Nah, nothing specific. Who we talking about?"

"A former executive for Capital Industries, guy named Stepan Federov. His son's name is Jorge. They've been gone for about a week, though nobody has been around to file missing persons. Supposedly, his boss is paying a bounty hunter to try and track him down."

"Definitely sounds fishy," Ryan replied. "But I've got nothing for you."

"Damn."

"Sorry, gorgeous."

Helen rolled her eyes. Ryan had been after her for several years, ever since she was a fresh-faced recruit. She was no longer so fresh in the face, but he hadn't let up. She'd seen him on the arm of too many women to count since she first met him and had no desire to be another addition to the roster.

"It's all right," she replied. "Just keep your ears open, okay?"

"Sure thing."

Helen walked towards the door and reached for the knob.

"Hey, wait a minute."

She paused and looked back at him.

"Federov you say?"

"Yeah. Federov."

"Russian?"

Helen thought for a moment, then shrugged. "Not sure. I guess he could be?" She grew pensive, thinking back to that day ten years ago, then nodded softly. "Actually, yeah. You're right. He's definitely Russian."

"Okay. Well, this may mean nothing, I don't know, but I did talk to a contact last night who said the Russian mob is unusually active. They seem to be shuffling people around. A typical shell game when they're trying to hide something."

Officer Bondalewski cocked her head, looking at Ryan. "Or someone?"

This time it was Ryan's turn to shrug. "Can't say for sure. But if the Russian mob's involved..."

"Dammit," Helen said, closing her eyes. That was an angle she hadn't considered and, frankly, didn't want to consider, especially with Rosa Guzman involved.

"Sorry if I'm the bearer of bad news," Ryan said, then stood up from where he was leaning on the table, walking towards the door.

"It's all right. Thanks, Ryan. That helps. I think."

He smirked his bashful little boy smirk, offered a wink, and stepped out.

Helen crossed her arms over her chest, watching him leave. She had to call Rosa. She had to call Rosa right now.

CHAPTER 10

"Rosa? Rosa Guzman?"

"Hey, Cristina. Yeah, it's me. Long time no talk, right?"

Cristina Kovacs leaned back in her wooden swivel chair and pushed her narrow glasses up into the untamed wild of light-colored hair. Scattered around her was an assortment of other desks and chairs remarkably similar to hers, some occupied and some not. A constant blur of activity swirled around her, with people walking back and forth, lifting hands in signal, and even shouting.

"Yeah, right. Listen, it's almost deadline here, what can I do for you?"

Deadline was always a little crazed at the *Springfield Examiner*, the small homegrown newspaper that evolved out of Mitch Crabtree's backyard and turned into a one-time juggernaut of independent journalism. Along with many other newspapers over the past several decades, years of slowing subscriptions and a shift to online content more or less decimated the paper, but through it all, the *Examiner* maintained its stringent adherence to quality and unbiased reporting, in many cases burning contacts to ensure the truth was told. As a result, the small, but aggressive, newspaper created its firm niche, establishing a reputation as an impartial source of truth and integrity

Cristina Kovacs jumped on board straight out of journalism school and never looked back, truly finding her place in a paper she believed in. And as so many reporters do, built plenty of relationships along the way.

Her introduction to Rosa Guzman hadn't been an especially positive one, but they'd been introduced, and they'd communicated from time to time over the years, though when her phone rang that afternoon, Rosa's was among the last people she expected to hear from.

"Sorry to interrupt," Rosa replied. She fought hard to keep the stammer out of her voice. "Just wanted to run a few things by you. I can call at a different time if that would work better."

"No, no," Cristina replied. "My stories are submitted already, it's just noisy and chaotic here. Everything okay?"

"Yeah, I'm good," Rosa replied, though Cristina could sense some hesitation in her voice "Listen, you guys get any stories across your desk recently about Capital Industries? Anything that doesn't pass the sniff test?"

Cristina placed her bent elbow on the table, holding the phone close to her face, clamping pure white teeth against the eraser in her mouth. She knew of Capital Industries......of course she did. Everyone in Springfield knew about them.

"Nothing's coming to mind," she replied.

"What about Mitchell Capozza? Anything on him outside of his business?"

Kovacs clamped the phone in the crook of her neck and scattered her fingers across the keyboard in a swift dance of tapping. Reading the screen, she navigated with the mouse, hopping to other screens and repeating the motion, deciphering her centralized index of recent news stories.

"Hmmm...no. Nothing that I can see."

Rosa sat in her driver's seat, cell phone to her hear, her fingers tapping on the steering wheel impatiently. "How about Stepan Federov. Anything on him?"

"Federov... F, e, d, e, r, o, v?" Cristina asked, spelling out the name.

"Yeah," Rosa replied, bracing herself for the question she assumed would come next.

Cristina whacked away on the keyboard, then guided her mouse through a few different search screens.

"I got nothing, Rosa," she replied.

"All right. Thanks for checking," Rosa said and started to lower her phone.

"Hold up!" Cristina said. "Rosa, what is this about?"

"Nothing special, Cristina. Just a job. Trying to find someone."

"A job for Capozza?"

"I haven't signed any papers yet, but I probably shouldn't talk too far out of school," Rosa said. Not every bounty came with confidentiality agreements, but sometimes they did, and she suspected that any work she did for Capozza likely would.

"Just be careful, okay?"

"Why do you say that?"

Cristina straightened her chair and glanced around the office quickly, alert eyes scanning her surroundings. Leaning forward, she placed her elbow on the desk and pulled the phone in more tightly towards her face.

"Working in this job, you hear things," she said. "He's got his hands in a lot of cookie jars."

"What do you mean?"

"Well, we don't know anything concrete, but you hear rumors. Stories of some of the wheels he's greased. He's got connections, but they're not all legitimate."

"He's a Massachusetts businessman, Cristina, that's not exactly a surprise."

Kovacs smiled slightly. "Fair point. Let's just say we hear more about him than others. He stands out in the crowd."

This didn't necessarily surprise Rosa. After all, a completely legitimate businessman typically wouldn't hire a bounty hunter to find someone before they even were reported missing, would they? Something about this case smelled funny from the get-go, but she couldn't seem to separate herself from it. *The reason for that is pretty obvious,* she thought, but it didn't change the fact that there was something else going on here, something that Mitchell Capozza hadn't told her in that stupid letter. Something she would have to talk to him face to face about.

She wasn't sure if she was looking forward to that particular conversation or not.

"Understood, Cristina. I really appreciate your help on this."

"Yeah, of course, Rosa. But hey, now that we're talking about this, have you thought to check with Devereaux Detective Agency at all?"

"Devereaux?" Rose asked, holding the phone more closely. The name grew a hard pit in Rosa's stomach. Davis Devereaux meant well, of that she knew. She'd run into him once, not too long ago, and he'd inadvertently blown up her entire operation and almost cost Rosa her life. She told herself she held no ill will for the man, but even she wasn't convinced.

"Yeah. New guy in town, I think he came up from the south somewhere. Cajun country. Guy's name is Devereaux Davis, he's a PI, set up shop about a month ago."

Rosa narrowed her eyes. "I know him, Cristina," she said, solemnly. "We've, uh… had a run in."

"Ah," Cristina replied, sensing the hesitation in Rosa's voice. "Sounds like the first impression wasn't a positive one."

"Not especially. But do you think he might help with this? What's his connection?"

"From what I've heard, he's normally Capozza's go-to guy for stuff like this. The dude he leans on with these things that skirt the outside of the law."

Rosa shook her head. Another reason not to like this guy a whole lot. Anyone who was on Capozza's speed dial didn't feel like the kind of person she wanted to be around.

"So why didn't he use him this time?"

"I think that's the million-dollar question, right?"

It wasn't. At least not for Rosa. She'd spoken with Capozza and she knew his motivations. Knew he was twisting the knife in her gut to encourage her to help. But Cristina didn't know that and she didn't need to know that. But if Devereaux did spend some time with Capozza, maybe it was worth talking to him anyway.

"You've been a big help, Cristina," Rosa said, actually meaning it for a change.

"Any time, Rosa, you know that. We should grab a coffee one of these days."

Rosa's mouth turned up slightly, forming an even, straight line. Coffee. Right. Isn't that what normal people did? Rosa didn't consider herself a normal person by any stretch. She wasn't even sure what 'grabbing a coffee' might entail. Would she actually have to talk? Have some kind of normal conversation?

Yeah, not her gig.

"That sounds good. We should set something up. I think that would be fun."

About as fun as a full day root canal. In general, Rosa Guzman didn't really get along with…well…people in general. She tolerated Chuck Heath, but the one person she may have actually cared for at one point along the way wasn't around anymore. Because of her. Because of what she did.

"Great! I look forward to it." Cristina's cheerful demeanor sent goosebumps racing up Rosa's arms, and she closed her eyes.

"Thanks again, Cristina. I'll talk to you soon."

They both hung up, and as the sun worked its methodical progression towards the horizon, leaving pink clouds and gray skies in its wake, she made up her mind that the only next step was talking to Capozza himself. The sooner the better.

CHAPTER 11

Bad memories are only sometimes in color. More often, they're in varying shades of gray.

The rain wasn't a curtain now, it was a diagonal sheet of pelting bullets, a constant roar of pounding water, shrouding a gray day even grayer.

In front of the building, a vaguely rectangular collection of crumbling brick, the collection of young men, boys really, gathered, talking in low, hurried voices and handing out weapons as if giving out treats for Halloween.

"A'ight, Switch, who we looking for?" one of the boys asked, tying the yellow bandana around his clean shaven head.

"East side, right around two o'clock. Next shift turns over, a bunch of those commie sons of bitches leave and most of them are in the gangs."

"So we're just gonna open fire?"

"Don't be stupid. According to Joel and Frankie, Doggie was put down by a dude named Andrei. He works first shift, he'll be jettin' around that time."

"What's the brother look like?"

"White dude. Bald, big bushy beard. Always wears a Yankees

jacket just to mess with everyone." Switch stuffed his hand in his pocket and pulled out a crumpled photograph, barely viewable, but clear enough. He handed it off to the kid, who nodded at it.

"This asshole? He killed Doggie?"

Switch shrugged. "That's what Frankie tells me. Look, scumbag is part of their crew, whether or not he pulled the trigger on Dog. Like for like, that's how we do it."

Heads nodded around the semi-circle.

Rosa Guzman stood several feet away, watching the boys. Part of her wanted to be in the circle with them, a bigger part of her wanted to be as far away as she possibly could. She was a kid, and these boys were her protectors. Her family. What was she supposed to tell them? At a hair under sixteen years old, she hardly held any weight with this crew of young tough guys, and even if she was older, she was still just a girl. In the world of Springfield gangs, there was no equal opportunity.

As she watched the group talk, pistols appeared and began making the rounds, passing from hand to hand, chambers sliding open, magazines being checked. It was a strange and deadly choreography, an intricate hand-dance with tools of death as the props. Her eyes narrowed on those small black rectangles as they jogged back and forth between skilled fingers. Fingers that knew the feel and the heft of these weapons far more expertly than they should at the ages these boys were. Aged far beyond their years, these kids who should be in school or in camp, or on their way to higher education were, instead, planning the ambush and execution of other living humans.

Rosa wasn't sure why these thoughts occurred to her. She was just as much a part of this twisted culture as they were. She was raised by the streets just as much as any of them. All of them. They were a part of her, too, but for whatever reason, her mind just worked differently. She saw things very black and white, where nearly every one of her peers just looked at the world in shades of gray, each tint darker and more obscure than the next.

The group talked amongst themselves for a brief moment, then began to separate, Switch directing some of his brothers to side roads and streets. Apparently, the mission was a go.

As the crowd dispersed, Rosa walked towards Switch, her eyes darting around the surrounding crowd slowly dispersing.

"I don't like this, Switch," she said quietly, trying not to let the others hear. Out of everyone in her crew, she was closest with Carlos Rodriguez, the boy who had truly taken her under his wing when her mother wandered off and just never bothered coming home.

"Don't have to like it, Goose," he replied. "It's the way the street works. We don't take care of this, they just come back harder."

"So what next? We kill some of them, they turn around and kill some more of us? When does it stop?"

"Ain't no stopping it, *chica*. It's the way of the world, whether you're on the streets here or in the mountains of camel country. Whoever carries the bigger stick wins."

"This is wrong."

"Wrong or right don't mean jack," Switch replied. "There is no wrong or right here, kid. Life or death, that's all we got. Someone dealt Doggie a hand, it's our job to deal it right back at them."

Rosa shook her head.

"You gotta learn sometime, little girl. I ain't gonna be around forever."

She looked up at him. He stood almost a foot taller than she did, a beanstalk of a boy with olive skin, close-cropped brown hair, and a baseball hat turned backwards on his head. He had a low fuzz of facial hair just above a series of chains draped down over his narrow chest. A large, puffy red jacket swamped him, working hard to conceal his skinny frame. Pulling the jacket to the side, he reached his hand in.

"What are you doing?" Rosa asked.

Carlos pulled out a pistol. It was a smaller one, but still an automatic, a compact Sig Sauer, .380 caliber, the perfect sized weapon to slide into a teenage girl's grasp.

Rosa shook her head and took a step backwards. "No, Switch. I don't want it."

"Just take it, dammit." He growled. "You're coming with us, you're learning the streets. It's past time you did."

Rosa looked at the taller boy, working hard to conceal her lip quiver, trying to keep her emotions in check. In her young life, she hadn't run across many people she looked up to and wanted to please, but Carlos "Switch" Rodriguez was one of them.

"Don't cry, kid," he said, his voice low so the boys around couldn't hear. "Just take the pistol. You don't have to fire it, but if you get in trouble, I want you to have it."

Rosa nodded, reached out, and wrapped her small fingers around the contoured grip that felt way too large, even on such a small weapon. Switch wrapped his hands around hers and showed her how to take the safety off, how to check the magazine, and how to load a round in the chamber.

"You got all that?" he asked. "Tell me you got it, Goose."

Rosa nodded softly. "Yeah. I got it, Switch."

"All right. You're with me, cuz. Let's roll."

The rain continued to fall, slapping the pavement and the buildings all around them as they walked. Slowly drifting apart and separating into groups, the small collection of local boys seemed to transform into highly-trained warriors, stealthily taking cover around corners, behind parked cars, and moving in even, well-planned, calculated movements. They all acted nonchalant, hands in their pockets, acting as if they belonged exactly where they were going, even as they slowly ventured into Russian territory. Even as every step brought them deeper into a strange enemy land that was not delineated by borders or watch towers, instead, by an invisible divide of low rent neighborhoods. There was no local embassy here, there was no refuge, and no place to run. Once they made their move, it would be a frantic rush back to their side of town and a hope that they all made it back alive.

Rosa kept pace with Switch, just off his right foot, her own eyes staring straight ahead, her own small hands pushed tight into her jacket pockets. She could see the street stretching up ahead, the street she had heard the boys talking about, and she knew they were getting close.

Close to what?

For as tight as she was with the Blades, she had never been too mixed up in any actual gang activity. She had been one of their little sisters, joining them in grief when one of their own fell, helping the boys mend their wounds, once in a while transporting some sort of contraband from one place to another. But as far as violence went, as far as firing an actual weapon in an attack on other living being, she had never stepped close to that line, and here she was, tempting fate and encouraging retaliation.

"Stay cool, Goose," Switch said, glancing over towards her. "Just a few more minutes and it will all be over."

Switch was right about one thing. It would be just a few minutes.

But nothing would be over. The trouble was just beginning.

CHAPTER 12

Outside the windows of the precinct, the sky had settled past dusk into darkness, the dim glow of streetlights and downtown scattering across the pale glass. Helen Bondalewski pulled her jacket on over her blue button-up shirt and ran the zipper up, checking to make sure she had situated her desk for the next morning.

"Good night, Bondo," Captain Hunger said, nodding to her as he passed, crossing the floor towards the exit.

"Night, Cap," Helen replied. "Hey, any luck on what we talked about earlier?"

He glanced back and shook his head a few times, though it wasn't a very enthusiastic motion. Helen narrowed her eyes at the back of her Captain's head as he pushed open the door and vanished into the night.

Capozza has a lot of friends, and some friends in this building. Who'd said that? Had Captain Hunger said that? Whoever had said it, she wasn't feeling all that comfortable all of a sudden.

Her phone chirped enthusiastically, and Helen rolled her eyes. Every damned night, right as she was about to leave.

"She said it was important!" shouted the dispatcher from behind the large desk, getting a clear view of the officer's frustration with the last-minute phone call.

"Better be!" Helen dropped her bag on the floor and stepped back over to her desk, snaking the phone from its cradle and pressing it to her ear. "Officer Bondalewski."

"Helen, it's Rosa."

"Hey, Rosa. It's about time, I've been trying to get a hold of you." Helen settled herself back into the chair, letting out a quiet sigh so as not to let on to Rosa how soon she had been to going home.

"Just checking in. Any luck?"

"Well, matter of fact, nothing concrete, but I did get some word off the street."

"I'm listening."

"According to one of our vice contacts, there's been some rumbling in circles of the Russian mob. Some talk about trying to move someone...or hide someone."

Rosa didn't reply. In fact, Helen thought she heard a sharp, wet intake of breath.

"We're not entirely sure what Federov's connections are to the Russian mob, but he does have the lineage, so we think it might be worth checking out."

"Okay, great. Thanks. What else?"

Helen's eyes darted, looking at the wide precinct room around her. Desks and chairs were haphazardly filled by the arriving night staff, but nobody was nearby.

"Rosa, you have to understand, to a degree, this is police business. I shouldn't be just spreading this around."

"Last I heard, nobody had reported anything. No complaint filed. Nothing to indicate foul play. Anything you have is because of what I told you, right?"

Helen leaned back, pushing her hat back on her dirty blonde hair. "All right, fine. I just had to make that clear."

"It's clear."

"I talked with the Springfield school system and, apparently,

Federov's son was pulled out of school a week ago by his father. So, wherever dad is, the kid is there, too."

"So, it sounds like they're hiding from something...but what?" Rosa asked, her voice quiet.

"Well, sounds like they're hiding from Capozza. I mean, he's the only one looking for them, right?"

"The only one I know."

"So, what's next?"

Rosa thought for a brief moment. "What's next is I need to talk to him. I haven't officially agreed to the contract yet."

"Should you?"

"What do you mean?"

"Isn't this a little close to home?"

"Springfield's a small city, Helen. Everything's a little close to home." Rosa leaned back in the driver's seat of her car, parked out on the side of the road outside her squat little office. She'd arrived twenty minutes ago but had no desire to go inside. "If I don't do this, he'll find someone else who will, but they won't do it as well as I will."

"Probably true."

"Plus, he chose me for a reason. I want to know what that reason is."

"So are you going to talk to him?"

"That's the plan," Rosa said, her voice growing more and more firm with every word.

"Well, don't tell anyone I told you this, but you know that Chinese place over by the North End? The Emerald Lotus?"

Rosa could picture it in her mind. A slightly rundown place. Nice enough, but far from the nicest Chinese place in the town limits.

"Yeah, I think I know the place."

"Word is, he has dinner there a few nights a week. Usually gets there around eight or nine."

Rosa smiled. "So, you think I oughta take him by surprise maybe?"

"Lot of times people like him want to have these conversations on their own terms. Keeping them off balance may help you out."

Rosa nodded and smiled softly. She liked the sound of this.

"But be careful. It may also set off his radar. He may put up his defenses. That's not always a good thing."

"Fair enough," Rosa replied.

"Anything else you need?" Helen asked, leaning forward in her chair again, mentally preparing to head home for the second time.

"I don't think so," Rosa replied. "You're a big help, Bondalewski. Thanks."

"Protect and Serve, right?" The memory flashed in Helen's mind. The gray, rainy sky. Water running down the side of the street, tinted red with spilled blood. The shocked eyes of the teenage girl looking off into space, knowing that life as she knew it had likely just changed irrevocably. She hadn't been able to protect then. Would she be able to make up for that now? Would anything she did from here on out make up for that one afternoon almost twelve years ago? Somehow, she doubted it. That die was cast and it wasn't coming back.

"I'll talk to you later," Rosa said and thumbed her phone off.

Helen nodded, surprised to feel the slight prick of tears in her eyes. Time to get out of here.

CHAPTER 13

It had taken a lot for her to build up the courage, but as she pressed her foot to the accelerator, her old beat up car navigating the back streets of Springfield, she could feel the steel coming to her spine. She felt brave. She felt tough. She wasn't going to let this asshole Capozza push her around, that was for sure. Too much had happened in her life already and she'd survived it all so far. Was she going to live through two tours in Afghanistan just to be pushed around by some jerk hole slumlord in Springfield?

Guiding the car around a loose right turn, she could see the lights of the Chinese restaurant up ahead. He was there tonight, as he always was. She'd decided then and there she was going to take a stand.

Take a stand against what, though? Against a big paycheck? Take a stand against a millionaire businessman whose motives she didn't know? She needed the cash and she needed the work. Not only could Capozza pay well, but he could recommend her to others, working for him could literally change her whole career.

But at what cost? What cost to herself and what cost to this man? This man she knew, or at least thought she knew.

As the parking lot opened up in front of her, the steel bar in her spine felt narrower and weaker, a flimsy support that wasn't nearly as rigid as it had been only minutes before. Her heart fluttered as she pulled in and she let her eyes close, wondering what she should do next.

CHAPTER 14

It was a name she hadn't seen for a long time, a name she'd hoped she'd never see again. But more and more, Rosa Guzman was becoming convinced that hope was a thing of legend, a myth. Something meant for other people. A vague reflection in the water, it appeared close, but twisted and rippled away the moment you reached it.

Gripping the paper in tightly clenched fingers, she closed her eyes, pulling it together into a twisted, crumpled ball, her anger the smallest bit satiated by the crunching of tree pulp. Even through the crinkled ball, she thought she saw that name glaring at her, accusing her.

She couldn't remember how long she'd been sitting in the parking lot, and she looked out through the windshield, narrowing her alert gaze on the flat front of Emerald Lotus, the small Chinese restaurant resting alone in the rare empty plot of land this close to downtown. It was a squat, square building with a sloped oriental roof, flanked by small artificial palm trees. Neatly manicured shrubs stretched along its base on top of a gravel lot, with the parking lot paved over it in a U, surrounding the small eatery.

That name? Why that name? Of all the people. Was it a coincidence?

"Goose, you awake?"

Rosa's head jerked a bit, pulled harshly out of her uncharacteristic daydream.

"Yeah, Heath, I'm here. Sorry."

"He's here. Corner booth. Just him and a few goons. He's alone in the booth eating, the goons are milling around."

Rosa nodded. Helen had said he might be here, though part of her didn't want to believe it might be this easy.

The Emerald Lotus wasn't the only local business that Mitchell Capozza owned a piece of and, in fact, he was quietly one of the wealthiest members of Springfield's elite. He was one of those quiet millionaires, a man who preferred to slide under the radar, using their partially ill-gotten gains to leverage more ill-gotten gains, all the while trying to bury the traces of those illicit funds underneath well-structured, established businesses. However, as wealthy as he might appear to the more normal clientele of this fair city, he was constantly moving his money, shuffling his funds. In truth, many of his peers suspected he was not quite as flush with cash as things might look.

While the Emerald Lotus was probably the business he was most known for in town, the truth was he held majority stakes in at least two dozen others, and was the all-out owner of Capstone Development, a land management conglomerate that had made a business out of buying low and selling high in the real estate world. There was some debate as to how Capozza managed to stay even with the competition in this highly competitive industry, but the fact remained that he was merely a plump cat among a community of fat cats.

Rosa Guzman hadn't been surprised when she received the letter from him. As well as being a Massachusetts licensed Fugitive Recovery Agent, she also contracted out services as a more under the radar bounty hunter. Her past ties to criminals did her a disservice throughout most of her life, but in this one aspect, it was quite valuable to her.

Federov was a name woven within the fabric of those things. One of many life changing events for Rosa Guzman, an event she had no desire to relive. Capozza had taken that option away from her, he'd forced her to remember.

Standing next to her car, Rosa glowered towards the glass covered entrance to Emerald Lotus. She could feel the churn of her gut roll over, then tighten into a crystalline core. Her muscles clenched, and she steeled herself. Yes, the name had been a surprise, and an emotional one, but she wouldn't let it hurt her. She'd harvest it and use it for motivation. Stepping forward, she slammed the car door closed, her left fist clutched around the crumpled paper with the name on it. With *that* name on it.

Rosa drew in a breath as she pushed through the glass door, standing straight, her eyes focused on the rear corner where Capozza was eating. A host stepped from around the podium, false smirk on his face.

"My apologies, ma'am, we are closed for the night,"

Rosa continued her stride, her shoulder striking his, and knocking him aside, his eyes drawing wide, and breath sucking in through pursed lips.

"Well, I never—" he grumbled as she passed through.

It was a large and ornate restaurant with extravagant decorations on the post of each booth and the scattered circular tables surrounded by hand-carved wooden chairs, each one filled with a red vinyl cushion. The appearance of lush elegance with none of the actual quality. There was just enough room through the tables for Rosa to walk, her body pointed straight towards Capozza who sat in that right, rear booth, alone except for the rounded white plate overflowing with Lo Mein and glistening pork. At the table to his right, a well-dressed waiter was tipping a chair upside down and resting it on the round surface, while two other men in suit jackets were repeating the motion at the table to his left. As he twisted a pair of wooden chopsticks in his hand, Capozza's eyes raised from the plate, meeting hers but showing no sign of surprise.

His face was broad, but not fat, his jaw an angular line, leading up to a thinning hood of graying hair. He wasn't bald, but was heading that way, choosing to beat nature to the punch with a short trim. The short hair led down into a well-manicured graying beard, which did a decent job concealing whatever expression might have been hidden underneath. Even in a seated posture, hunched over his plate of food, he looked as if he could have been a football player, and not a wide receiver or quarterback, but one of those 350-pound linebackers. His black clad frame nearly filled the corner booth, but if his face was any indication, he didn't have much fat on him, just thick layers of rounded muscle, covered by hand-woven Italian linen.

As Rosa walked near, he gently set his chopsticks down and pulled the cloth napkin from his lap, dabbing his lips.

"Mr. Capozza, we need to talk," she said in a low hiss.

"Ms. Guzman?" he asked, folding his hands together. She paused.

"You know who I am?"

"Of course. I make it my business to know anyone I might choose to work with." His steel blue eyes drifted to the crumpled paper in her hand, then flicked quickly back to her own.

"How did you know about this?" she asked, squeezing her left fist just a bit tighter, the crumpled paper rustling in the silent restaurant.

Capozza's mouth tilted into a crooked grimace. "You don't get to where I am without being able to dig up dirt, Ms. Guzman."

Rosa didn't reply.

"I need someone found, and your name came up. That is what you do, right? Find people?"

"Not all people."

Mitchell Capozza leaned back against the vinyl cushion of the corner booth, creaking noisily under his wide bulk.

"I pay very well, Ms. Guzman."

"You think this is about the money?" she asked, lifting her fist, twisted paper spewing out from between closed fingers.

"Isn't everything?"

"No." Rosa snapped her hand open and tossed the crumpled paper, sending the ball smacking into Capozza's chest. It struck him, then tumbled down his arm and disappeared under the table. He didn't react.

"Chew that up and choke on it," Rosa snarled.

It was a calculated risk. Rosa wanted the job. She wanted to be fully in the loop on this man's quest for Stepan Federov, but she also wanted to keep him at arm's length and make sure he knew she wasn't happy about the arrangement. In truth, she hadn't known what she was going to say or do when she walked in here. As usual, she was flying by the seat of her pants and hoping for the best.

Among the ornate decorations and the thick red furniture, Rosa hadn't noticed that the floors of the restaurant were wooden, but she heard a slight *squeak* to her left, like a plank trying to withstand a large weight. The looming presence cast a brief shadow in the corner of her eye, and she barely stepped right before one of the oversized well-dressed men came upon her, arms outstretched. Sidestepping and rolling backwards, she slid away as his momentum carried him forward. Pressing her palm to the back of his head and thrusting forward, she drove his face into the wooden surface of the table. The resounding impact clattered the plate of Lo Mein and rattled the chopsticks on the smooth table, as the large, bald-headed man grunted, then rolled left, off the table and onto the floor.

Capozza grinned like a cat watching two mice play, as if deciding which one would be dinner.

They stood there silently, the very air in the restaurant still, a thin cloud of steam lifting from the plate of Lo Mein. Capozza leaned over, reaching his long arm under the table and retrieved the crumpled piece of paper.

Methodically, he unfolded the paper and pressed his palms into it, straightening it out on the table, pushing the surface smooth. It took a few moments, the unfolding loud and isolated against the silence. Rosa could smell the lingering simmered meat coming from the kitchen, the strange silence in a usually busy restaurant accentuating all of her other senses.

Capozza smoothed out the paper and slid it across the polished surface of the table to Rosa, who remained standing, glaring at him defiantly.

"Ms. Guzman, I'm willing to give you a second chance."

Rosa started to reply, but he held up a hand.

"I need you to find this man and bring him to me. I don't care what happened in the past, but this man is very important to me."

She stared down at the paper and could once again see the name written there, a blue-stained gouge on the surface of her memory.

"You can trust me, I will make this very much worth your while," Capozza continued, giving her a look that emphasized what he said. "And you won't get a second chance to say no."

Rosa rested her fingertips on the table, leaving them inches from where the paper lay, creased and worn with the crumpling and smoothing. Carefully, bit by bit, she walked her fingers towards the paper, her eyes never leaving Capozza's smile, a false crescent of white teeth.

"If you find this man, I can guarantee your money troubles will be over. You can pay off your debts. Grow your business. Get out of your old neighborhood. That's what you've been wanting, isn't it? To finally outrun your past?"

It had been. Maybe what Rosa was seeing was her way out? Things often came full circle, and maybe by closing this door, she could finally move on. Move on in ways she'd wanted to do in the Army but had been unable to accomplish.

Her fingers walked towards the damaged paper again, finally resting on it.

"At least think about it," Capozza said, his smile still carved into his smooth skin.

Rosa didn't reply, she merely swept the paper from the table, drawing it closer, then spinning around and walking back towards the exit. She could feel the hot glare of Capozza's eyes on her back as she walked away, and the heat there matched the flush of her cheeks. The flush of shame? She wasn't sure.

Chuck Heath took a long stride towards the front door, nervous that Rosa had been in there so long, when that same door swung swiftly open, ejecting his female partner in a swift, no nonsense stride. Chuck took an uncertain step back as he watched her cross the parking lot and approach her car.

"We're done here," she said simply, easing open her car door. Chuck glanced back in the restaurant, his eyes narrowing on that back corner booth, just barely visible through the windows. He turned back to face Rosa again, but she was inside her old car, the engine rolling over, her face an emotionless mask.

As she pulled away, her tires grabbed pavement in a swift squeal, and he walked to his car, looking at the taillights fading in the distance and getting the distinct impression that whatever path had opened up for them could potentially change things forever.

The real question was, would it be a change for the better or for the worse?

Too soon to tell.

CHAPTER 15

Rosa couldn't sit still. Back pressed flush against the brick corner of the building, her heart raced, and she kept leaning out to glance down the street. From where she stood, she could make out the general shape and form of the factory, a huge concrete and brick fortress built a century ago, now staffed with dozens of members of Russia's northeast Mafia. The bell rang loud and long, signaling the end of the shift, and she almost jumped in her shoes, knowing that each moment marked the slow passage of time leading towards someone's inevitable death.

Would it be a Russian death? Would it be one of her crew? Would it be her?

Down the road, the doors to the factory opened and people spilled into the paved parking lot next to the large, thick, square structure. Human forms dispersed and moved towards vehicles, but a tightly-grouped clutch of younger men drifted together and separated from the throng as one organism, meandering out onto the sidewalk. Rosa glared at the group, squinting, trying to tell if she could see the boy in the middle of all the other bodies. The boy who killed Doggie. She'd laid eyes on the crumpled photograph, but it revealed dreadfully little, especially considering the Blades were preparing to lay down corporal punishment on any poor soul who might slightly resemble the boy in the picture.

"Be ready, Goose," Switch said from her left. He was hunched down behind a parked car, his pistol already out. The factory was the center of this little section of neighborhood, with ripples of broken down buildings circling out from the center. Streets were not typically busy this time of day, and no cars appeared to be rolling by. Scattered throughout her field of vision, she could see mostly her friends, her family, all in a defensive posture, all holding weapons. All preparing to kill or be killed.

How had she never seen this side of them before? Had they kept it from her on purpose? Had Switch been so protective as to shield her from something so much a part of who they all were?

A hundred or so yards away, a young man in a backwards black baseball cap stuck his head out and made a motion with his hand. Rosa had no idea what it meant, but everything started happening at once. Bodies started moving, shuffling forward, staying low to the ground. Where weapons had been casually clutched in one hand, a second hand came up to support the first, lifting guns slightly as figures lurched forward, bent at the waist.

"What's happening?" she asked as Switch took a step back and started to walk around the car.

He glanced back at her and gestured, palm sweeping downward. "Stay back, *chica*. Shit's about to get real."

Rosa froze, looking down at her hands, the small pistol resting in her relaxed fingers, still not sure what she was going to do with it if she had to.

The main road stretched out next to the factory, running west to east, a large parking lot perched just next to the huge building and attached to the street, protected by a chain link fence and unlocked gate. Parallel parking spaces were methodically placed down the left side of the road, just next to large and crumbling brick structures that were at one point storage warehouses in this part of town.

Just to the west of the largest abandoned building was a vacant lot, a square of pounded dirt and not much else. Behind that lot sat a small parking lot with a handful of cars, which was where Switch was moving, slowly but with intent. Rosa remained behind the largest building, eyes fixated on the vacant lot and the factory workers moving along the street just on the other side. More cars were parked at the edge of the main road, with another building on the far west side of the lot, as well. They were flanked and surrounded.

Rosa had little experience with anything of this sort, but even she remained nervous about the way this looked to be unfolding. The vacant lot was just that, vacant, and was surrounded by cars and buildings. While the main group of targets the Blades were moving in on was small, supposedly the factory was staffed with Russian immigrants, and any one of them could be a member of their crew. If bullets started popping, how many factory workers would come flooding out to back them up and where would the Blades run? Where would they take cover?

"Switch!" she yelled in an elevated whisper. "I don't like this, Carlos! This is not good."

"Street justice, Goose! Shut up and grab cover. It's goin' down whether you like it or not!"

"There's no cover! No place to hide!"

Switch looked back at her and grinned his lopsided grin. It was a grin Rosa would remember every day for the next twelve years.

Up ahead, she could see the familiar forms of her friends begin lifting up from their previous low crouches. Almost immediately, shouts echoed across the empty lot, accusatory bellows and indignant anger.

"This is for Doggie, you commie sons of bitches!"

Rosa wasn't sure who said it, but right after the words emerged, a staccato *pop, pop, pop, pop* rebounded from the lot, the sharp, snapping noise repeating off into the emptiness. Quick bursts of words followed, a jumble of consonants, strung together like no words Rosa had ever heard before. She glanced around and saw the small group of factory workers scattering like cockroaches under a quick flash of light.

One of them spun and fell, more pops exploding in the lot and another one flew backwards, shouting random, nonsensical gibberish. Other members of the group spread and ran in different directions, and a few of them reached into shirts and pants and produced their own weapons as if from nowhere.

More swift popping answered the first few volleys, echoing fireworks, this corner of Springfield sounding much like the Fourth of July. Everything was chaos. Another series of pops and shouts sent the Blades pulling backwards and spreading out, running towards cars, taking cover. Rosa turned her head and saw a blue truck flying down the road, then slamming on the brakes, coming around into a screeching halt, with a small group of men tumbling out, pistols in hand. Shouting rang out, interspersed with the rapid snaps of gunfire, and somewhere in the distance, a shrill scream erupted.

"Cover, Blades, cover!" shouted Switch as he lifted his pistol and squeezed off three shots, the weapon thrashing in his tight grasp. Tough gangsters throwing bullets around, no skill, no trigger discipline, just random fire to see how many bodies dropped.

He backpedaled as a pair of bright sparks pinged off the roof of a car to his left, then a third shattered the side window, sending him scrambling to his right. As he moved towards another car, more shots echoed and another window exploded, with Switch backpedaling and swinging his arm around randomly, squeezing off gunfire. Rosa's head whipped around left and right, then back again, trying to follow the action. This wasn't anything like the movies or TV shows she'd seen with tightly choreographed action sequences moving from one place to the next. Everything was moving at once, everything was happening at once, and nothing made sense.

In the near distance, Rosa could hear the faint warble of sirens.

"Scatter, Blades, scatter!" Switch shouted, and they pulled back further, then turned and started to run. More pops echoed and, suddenly, the Russians were everywhere. Switch stayed behind, clutching his gun with two hands, directing fire towards the approaching group, dangerously close to the oncoming crowd.

"Switch, move back!" shouted Rosa, leaning out from the building.

His head spun around. "Goose! Get the hell outta here! Go!"

It only lasted for a moment. Switch turned to face her for the shortest period of time, just that one brief moment, but that's all it took. Another volley of shots rolled over the air, echoing from the hardened surface of the surrounding buildings, and Switch stumbled, shouting.

"No!" Rosa shouted. "No, no, no!" Without even thinking, she charged from her corner, pistol in hand, running straight for her adopted brother as he sprawled towards the ground. The sirens were louder. They seemed to be everywhere, and even as some Russians continued to approach, others separated and moved away.

Rosa heard frantic shouting and glanced over towards the street, briefly noticing a huddled mass by a streetlight on the side of the road, an oddly draped collection of clothing next to some strangely shaped shopping cart, some poor bystander caught in the crossfire, just trying to protect himself.

A bullet slammed off the back of a pickup truck, sending Rosa scrambling down and forward, ducking her head and lifting the pistol, this strange block of metal in her hand that felt so alien to her, even as it felt so natural to everyone she knew.

"I'm coming, Switch!" she shouted.

"Don't!" he screamed, reaching towards her as he pulled himself upright. She could see blood staining the leg of his pants, but other than that, he seemed active and very much alive.

Completely ignoring him, she charged forward, staying down, trying to ignore the occasional whine of bullets overhead, and then, finally, she reached the last parked vehicle, the last inch of cover before several yards of open ground between her and the young man...the boy really who had carried her through the past several years. The closest thing she had to family lying on the ground, the dirt beneath him darkly stained with his blood. The men who shot him drew closer, weapons raised and trained. She was the only thing that stood between him and them, and the only thing that could save him. In the distance, the huddled mass looked around from behind the streetlight, calculating whether or not it was safe to move. Whether the bundled groceries in the cart were worth risking their lives for.

Rosa charged forward. Bullets pounded into the dirt at her feet, and she glanced to her right, seeing just one man approaching. The rest of the Russians had peeled away and ran as the sirens bellowed from all corners of the world, nearly screaming now as the police must have been less than a block away. The man leveled his weapon, the black bar of metal wavering slightly as it directed towards them both. Rosa didn't know what else to do.

She threw herself forward, towards Switch, closing her eyes and whipping her arm around, hauling back on the trigger of her small Sig Sauer, her hand tightening and straining, her arm muscles tensing as the weapon kicked as if trying to loosen itself from her grip. So close, the pops were far more than pops. Even with the low caliber .380, they sounded like sonic booms rolling through the heavens. Her finger pulled and pulled and pulled again, repeatedly jacking back on the trigger until there were no more sonic booms, there were no more ragged thrashing of metal on flesh, there was just the unenthusiastic, empty clacking of spent ammunition.

Sirens wailed, but the gunfire had stopped. Rosa was hunched over Switch, draped across his body, the boy squirming underneath her.

"The cops!" Switch yelled. "We gotta move!"

Rosa lifted her head and turned, her vision clouding. The man was on the ground on his back, his arms askew, his pistol tossed several feet away, sitting in shallow grass. His body was still and lifeless. She couldn't tell if his chest rose or fell, but they were moving, and he was not.

Switch pushed himself upright, gently shoving Rosa from on top of him. "Come on, Goose, pull it together!"

Car doors slammed all around them. Feet slapped on pavement, and the sirens kept screaming.

Rosa looked at the body and felt a mixture of dread and satisfaction. A strange lack of guilt and feeling of victory settled over her, and she almost smiled, even as the thundering feet of approaching police officers emerged from the alleys around them. Then her smile faltered.

Her eyes settled on a second shape, one behind the gunman, several yards past, on the sidewalk. Previously a huddled mass behind a streetlight. A formless shape who had apparently decided their groceries were worth risking life for. This shape was also down on the ground, lifeless and not moving.

And as Rosa's eyes fixated on the prone form, the vague shape of nothing that used to be something, she realized that the cart was not a cart at all...it wasn't groceries. It wasn't some homeless person wandering the streets, pushing their entire life's worth in a wire frame basket on wheels. The cart was a stroller, and the shrill cry of a baby inside was the loudest noise she had ever heard in her life.

"Too late!" Switch screamed. "It's too late. They're here."

Rosa continued looking at the covered shape, the barely human contoured form draped in a long cloth coat. She couldn't pull her eyes away.

"Rosa!" Switch screamed. "Give me that!" he reached forward and wrapped his hand around her pistol, yanking it from her. Rosa whirled her head around, glaring at him.

"That's mine!"

"The hell it is!" Switch shouted. He rubbed his hands all over it, grasping the handle, pulling the trigger on the empty chamber. He stroked the barrel and took the pistol in both hands, making sure he touched nearly every single inch of metal and contoured rubber. "This is all mine. You never touched it you hear me. I was shot, I returned fire with my pistol. That's what happened. That's all that happened. That's all that will ever happen, you get it?"

Rosa shook her head, tears brimming in her eyes. "I don't... what... I can't..."

"Bottle it up, Rosa. This is on me."

All around them, feet slammed and voices barked. Loud voices bellowed telling Switch to drop the weapon, telling him to get on his stomach. All around her, blue uniforms blurred together, weapons jolted up, arms spun, hips pivoted. Bodies moved, but she sat still, her eyes looking back across the lot at the two fallen bodies and that endless scream coming from the discarded stroller.

The rain had stopped.

The world of gray would go on forever.

CHAPTER 16

The popping of sporadic gunfire echoed in Rosa's ears as the memory faded. Eyes fluttering, she could feel her lashes slapping rapidly against her cheeks as she struggled to fight her way back into the waking world, the rattling tapping clarifying, slowly shifting from gunfire to a thick, sharp rapping.

Rosa opened her eyes, momentarily disoriented, but realizing quickly she was still sitting in the driver's seat of her car, the vehicle parked outside her office, not running, just parked silently. Night had fallen, surrounding her, the bare illumination of sporadic streetlights telling her where she was. Rubbing a hand through her dark hair, Rosa sat upright trying to clear the fog from her eyes and the unpleasant memories from her mind.

Wrapping her fingers around the steering wheel, she pulled herself closer to it, shaking her head.

"Dammit," she whispered to herself. Was she really burning the candle at both ends this much? She pressed her forehead against the steering wheel and closed her eyes, then the swift and sudden rapping slammed her eyes back open and whipped her head around. That sound hadn't been remnants of her memories, it had been someone at her window.

Glaring out the passenger side, she could barely make out a man standing outside her car, slightly bent at the waist, tapping something on her window. Something hard and metal. Something that looked suspiciously like a weapon. As her eyes adjusted to the dim light of the surrounding streetlights, she could see that it was indeed a man, a bald-headed guy with a dark jacket and a thin beard, and he was indeed tapping the barrel of a pistol against the safety glass of her passenger window.

"Rosa Guzman?" he asked, his voice thickly accented.

She leaned back slightly but made no motion to leave the car. "The hell do you want?" she asked.

"Just to talk. That's all."

"Funny way of showing it," she replied, nodding towards the pistol. "Real funny."

"Come on out. We don't want to hurt you."

We?

The driver's side door suddenly cranked open with a screech of unoiled hinges, and she jerked, spinning towards it, but not before a thick arm reached in, fingers wrapping around the loose fabric of her coat. She felt the tug as the jacket tightened and the arm clenched, then hauled back, pulling her from the driver's seat. She lurched, then toppled, falling from the seat and landing in a painful crumple on the asphalt sidewalk, her shoulder slamming first, then her back, though she managed to tuck her chin and protect her head.

As she rolled and tried to correct her momentum, the first man came around the front of the car, his gun still in hand, but pointed towards the ground.

"What the hell?" Rosa asked, pushing herself up with one arm.

"Chill the hell out, Pietro!" the other man yelled, coming up on the second man and shoving him with the hand that didn't hold the weapon. "We were told not to rough her up."

Rosa reached up towards her car, planted her hand and got slowly to her feet, rubbing her shoulder with her free hand.

"Who told you not to rough me up. What the hell is this even about?"

"My apologies," the first man said, extending a hand, wrapping his fingers around her arm and helping her up. "My name is Gregor."

She squinted at him as she finished getting to her feet. "Russian?" she asked.

He returned a glare that she couldn't quite translate. "Does that matter?"

"Maybe."

Under the pale streetlights the three of them stood. Gregor continued to hold his weapon, the barrel pointing towards the ground, though Pietro wasn't holding his weapon. Rosa felt sure it was buried in a holster somewhere under his dark jacket. She stood near her car, still rubbing her sore shoulder, and still working to clear her head from the rude awakening.

"What do you want?" she asked.

Gregor's eyes darted towards Pietro's and he looked away.

"We hear that you are looking around for a friend of ours," he finally replied.

"Who? Stepan Federov?" Rosa asked.

Gregor didn't answer her question directly. "The man you are looking for is safe. Do not worry."

"I'd like to be the judge of that," Rosa replied.

"That is not your right," Pietro replied. Gregor flashed him another look.

"The man who has hired you," Gregor said, "he wants harm to come to Mr. Federov. We cannot allow that."

"I'd like to hear that story from Mr. Federov," Rosa replied. "You'll have to excuse me if I don't take the word of men who sneak up on sleeping women with guns in their hands."

Gregor's eyes flashed to the pistol he held, then flashed back to her. "You'll have to forgive me, Ms. Guzman." He slid his weapon back in its holster. "I did not mean to intimidate."

Rosa shook her head. "Not intimidated, believe me."

"Good," Gregor replied.

"So we can count on your cooperation?" Pietro asked, taking a step towards her. "You will help us with this simple request?"

"Hell no," Rosa replied. "I've got a contract. I'm being paid to find Mr. Federov, I intend to do that, whether you assholes want me to or not."

Gregor's face hardened. "I'm not sure you understand the gravity of this situation," he said.

"I'm not sure you understand how little I care."

Pietro actually smiled at this, then looked towards Gregor. "I like this girl!"

"I'm flattered," Rosa replied. "Now why don't the both of you get the hell out of here and tell whoever sent you they can go screw themselves."

"I don't think you want us to do that," said Gregor. "That would not end well. For anyone."

Rosa shrugged. "Fair enough."

The three of them stood in silence, standing in a triangle, each one looking at each other.

"Point's been made," Rosa finally said. "If you don't mind, I'm going to head to bed. It's much more comfortable in there than in my car." She started to move towards the building, but Pietro moved first, taking two long strides and getting between her and the sidewalk.

"Not so fast, little lady," he replied. "We must insist on these points we are making. They are not optional."

Rosa looked up at the man, her eyes narrowing. "I heard you. I understand. Please get the hell out of my way. I'm tired and cranky and not in the mood to deal with you."

Gregor stepped up behind her, placing a firm hand on her shoulder, squeezing slightly. "We can understand your frustration, Ms. Guzman. We hope you also see our point of view."

Rosa stood there, muscles tensed. She drew in a deep breath and closed her eyes. "Please, release me," she said calmly.

"Ms. Guzman, we must insist, as Pietro said."

"You can insist all you want," Rosa replied. "Just let me go so I can go to bed."

Pietro didn't move. Gregor's hand flexed slightly but made no motion to release her shoulder. Rosa dropped her chin to her chest.

"I've had a rough day, okay?"

"I think we all have," Gregor replied, an edge to his voice. The calm, kindly demeanor had evaporated from his voice. "We don't want this to end badly for you."

Rosa glanced back towards him and shook her head. "It won't end badly for *me*, trust me on that."

Gregor squeezed for just a moment, some non-subtle reminder of who he perceived was in charge. Rosa drew in another breath, each one tensing her muscles, making her body more rigid, the tendons in her shoulder tightening up.

"Don't make this difficult," he started to say.

Rosa relaxed her shoulder and his grasp loosened. Just enough. She spun and slapped aside his hand, then placed her opposite hand against the side of his head and shoved, driving his forehead into the metal side of her vehicle. His right temple collided with the door frame, just to the right of the window, with a thick *bang*. He clenched his eyes shut and pressed his lips tight together. As his head rebounded off the door, she released him, letting him fall as Pietro moved in, reaching into his jacket for his pistol.

Rosa was already moving towards him. She lifted her knee tight to her chest and thrust out, slamming her foot into Pietro's stomach, knocking the wind from his lungs and sending him stumbling backwards. Moving forward, she drew close to his clumsy form, pressing her body into his and slipping her hand around the handle of his pistol. As she withdrew it, she stepped backwards, pivoted on her heel, and drove her other foot high up into his chest. The piston motion of her kick caught him on the left pectoral and drove him backwards with such momentum that his feet left the pavement and he struck the ground, the base of his skull smacking dully on the sidewalk. Rosa stood there, looking over the two fallen men. Already, Gregor started to stir, pushing up onto one hand, the other hand moving to his head, slowly rubbing it.

"Go back to your boss," Rosa said. "I want Stepan Federov. I want to at least see him. Talk to him. Figure out what the hell is going on."

Gregor scowled at her. "This was a mistake, Ms. Guzman. This was the worst move you could have made."

"We might be on the same side," she replied. "But if he sends goons to my house with guns again, we won't be. Got it, Gregor?"

Gregor glared at her as he moved to a sitting position, his back resting against her car, the side of his face red and already starting to swell slightly. Somewhat reluctantly, he nodded his head.

"I'm not a pushover. I'm not some little woman you can intimidate. Understood?"

Gregor nodded again.

"Get the hell out of here. Tell your boss I'll be coming to talk to him."

Rosa turned and stepped up onto the sidewalk, wanting to get far away from the two Russians before they could see just how uncertain she was. She stepped into her home office, turned, locked the doors, and drew an uncertain, lingering breath, desperation for sleep slowly overcoming her.

CHAPTER 17

Even with the events of the previous night so fresh in her mind as she woke, Rosa opened her eyes upon the new day with a renewed sense of drive and purpose. The Russians had made their presence known, but she thought they'd overstepped their bounds, and only gone to prove to her that she was poking the right nest. Federov and his son were no longer vague objects, strange, mythical goals for Mitchell Capozza, they were starting to form into physical beings, people that needed help. People that Rosa could help and to hell with Capozza's dirty money.

There was plenty of good news about their visit last night, most notably was that Federov was apparently still alive, and in the hands of the Russians, who seemed very eager to keep him that way.

That was good, wasn't it?

Rosa wasn't entirely sure. While the Russians were adamant that Capozza wanted him dead, Rosa didn't yet know that for sure, and with a big money contract riding on the location of Federov, she had a certain motivation to not just let this ride.

Not only that, but a part of her suddenly had a distinct interest in the outcome of this case, as well. Federov was a name engraved into her memories, a permanent piece of her existence, and she felt strangely connected to him. She needed to do what she could to find him and to make sure whatever happened, he and his son were safe. Part of her believed the Russians were the best place for him and that they would keep him protected, but without knowing exactly what Capozza wanted from him, she had to play this by the book.

Swinging her legs out of bed, she took three long strides across the makeshift bedroom. Her office was small, a square room with a desk and front door, a tiny bathroom off the north wall, and her bed was shoehorned into a secondary room, most likely originally designed as a kitchen. Instead, the kitchen was built into the main office area, more or less a counter with a dorm-sized fridge underneath it and a microwave on top of it. One of these days she had to get a real place to live, an actual apartment or home that she could consider a permanent living area, but that felt like very far away at this point. If she could land Stepan Federov, she would be distinctly closer to having an actual residence and some semblance of a life rather than sleeping in a spare room in her office.

She was determined she wouldn't let money drive her whole existence and wouldn't sacrifice the safety and security of her clients simply for a paycheck, but the longer she lived in this relative squalor, the easier it was to overlook some of those core beliefs.

At least there was a coffee machine.

Setting the low budget bubbler burbling, she moved on towards the phone and made a quick call to the police precinct.

"Officer Bondalewski please," she asked.

"She's out on patrol," came the reply.

"Can I get her voice mail?"

"Hold please."

The line rang and Helen's voice sounded. Rosa waited a moment, then left a message. "Hey, Helen, this is Rosa. Just wanted to let you know I got a visit from a couple of Russian gentlemen last night. I think we settled our differences, but just in case anything happens, I wanted you to know. Let me know if you get any more details on Federov. Thanks."

She hung up and glanced out the front window. The street

outside was clear, no cars, no sign of people wandering around. Good.

For whatever reason, she didn't feel threatened by her visit from the Russians last night. It meant to her that she was asking the wrong questions, already starting to turn over the wrong stones. Certain people wanted to put a stop to that, which was a sure sign to her that she was on the right track. Even for an unofficial investigation, some contract work she was doing on the side, things had seemed to escalate already.

The police. This thought stuck in the back of Rosa's mind, clinging there, wormed in the way of her other thoughts.

So Mitchell Capozza was involved. The Russian mob was involved. And here she was, caught right smack dab in the middle. This wasn't going to end well. Rosa glanced at her watch, already knowing she had woken up far later than any other normal people in this part of the world, and she needn't worry about what time she was calling.

Punching the familiar number, she waited for a few distinct rings, then the high-pitched voice picked up.

"Hey, Goose, what's up?"

"Hey, Chuck. Everything okay your way?"

"Good as can be expected," Chuck replied, though Rosa knew full well it was doubtful that things in his life would ever really truly be *fine*.

"I got a visit from some Russians last night."

"What?"

"Yeah. Pure goon squad. Nothing to worry about, I sent them packing."

"They'll be back."

"No doubt."

"So, what do you need?"

"Well, they were telling me to stay away from Federov, so obviously, they've got some fingers in this pie. You got anyone you know on the inside there?"

Chuck Heath thought for a moment. "Yeah, you know, there's a dude down at the gym who I know pretty well. Talks with a pretty thick accent, though I'll be honest, I have no idea if it's Russian or not. He usually hits the heavy bag around lunch. Besides that, I got nothing."

"All right, that works. I'm going to do some checking, see if I can find any links at all between Capozza and the Russians. This doesn't smell right, I'm not sure if they're connected, but it's worth a shot."

"So, if we know the Russians have him, why are we poking the hornet's nest? Can we just tell Capozza what we know?"

Rosa sat in her office chair, narrowing her eyes and running a hand through her tangled mass of brown hair. "I don't know. Something smells funny about this. All of this. I don't trust Capozza for a second, but the Russians aren't exactly generous. They wouldn't be protecting him unless something was in it for them. The pieces aren't quite fitting together here, Heath."

"I get it. I hear you. Let me see what I can dig up, okay?"

"Thanks, Chuck. Call me around noon?"

"That's in twenty minutes."

Rosa rolled her eyes and cursed herself for her terrible sleep discipline. "Dammit. Sorry. Call me at three. Okay?"

"Will do."

Rosa hung up and sat in her chair for a moment, trying to sort out the last twenty-four hours in her head. She wasn't having much luck. The conversation with Chuck had been a positive one, that much was certain, but there were still many things that were uncertain, and the more she thought about it, the more she came back to the Russians. In this part of the world, the Russian mob was nefarious and infamous, and it was well known in Rosa's circles that you didn't cross them. So, as it currently stood, she was square between one slime ball, Mitchell Capozza, and a whole group of slime balls, the Russian mafia. If things didn't start turning her way soon, this little adventure would be over before it could even truly begin.

CHAPTER 18

Chuck never needed arm twisting to go to the gym, so the minute he hung up the phone with Rosa, he grabbed his bags and headed out of his apartment, walking briskly down the narrow sidewalk towards the small building only a few blocks away.

The place was called Ernesto's, and it was a fixture in this part of town. The current guy running it, a round, but surprisingly fit man by the name of Joe Michaels was Ernie's cousin, and inherited the family business when Ernie passed away a few years back. Michaels wasn't a fitness fanatic, he had actually been in the music video business when it all happened, but family pressure had led him into taking over the business. The relatively low upkeep costs and decent monthly revenue certainly didn't hurt.

Slinging his bag over his shoulder, Chuck turned up the stairs and pushed through the door, eyes scanning the sparse crowd inside. The midday crew was already there, and while Chuck didn't yet see the guy he told Rosa about, Joe Michaels himself looked over, smiled, and gave him a wave, gesturing him to come over.

"`Sup, Joe?" Chuck asked as he crossed the wooden floor towards his old friend.

"Chuck, my boy! How are those brothers of yours, huh?" Joe

asked. A tent sized blue T-shirt draped over his shoulders and swung as he walked, partially covering the black basketball shorts he wore underneath. His voice was thick with an Italian accent, which Chuck couldn't ascertain the validity of, but he'd known him for years, and the guy treated him well.

"They're all right," Chuck replied. "As all right as punk ass boys can be, anyway, right?"

Joe threw his head back and laughed. "Your mom always had a heck of a time with them, God rest her soul."

Chuck forced a smile. Talking about his late mother wasn't high on his list of things he liked to do, but a free monthly gym rate with access to heavy bags, weights, and treadmills made any kind of momentary suffering worthwhile.

"I've been trying to get them down here. I keep hoping they'll take some of that negative energy and turn it into something positive," Chuck said, bending down and setting his duffel on the floor.

"Like you did, huh?"

Chuck looked up at Joe who stood over him, smiling.

"Eh, I wouldn't go that far," Chuck replied. Reaching into his bag, he pulled out a pair of thickly padded gloves with individual fingers, the tips cut off. Michaels looked at him, and Chuck knew what he saw. All skin and bones, narrow body swimming in a gray tank top and blue shorts. Chuck knew what his legs looked like, intertwined narrow branches of clenched muscle, each ligament clearly visible. He knew he was short and skinny, but he also knew he was strong and fast. These are things he knew, but Joe didn't.

"You're not usually here around lunch," Joe said, grabbing the heavy bag and maneuvering it between him and Chuck as he bounced on the balls of his feet gracefully.

"I was actually hoping to run into someone," Chuck said, dipping left, lashing out with his left fist, striking the bag, then following up with two more rapid-fire bursts. The vinyl surface of the thick, cylindrical bag thumped loudly as it jerked in Joe's tight grasp.

"Oh, who's that?" he asked.

"Actually, don't know his name," Chuck said, then launched

another brief volley of punches. "I think he's a Russian guy. Usually in here at lunch pummeling the heavy bag."

Michaels narrowed his eyes at him, his mouth turning slightly. "Ben? Ben Magnússon? What do you want him for?"

"Magnússon? That doesn't sound like a Russian name."

Joe shrugged again. "You think I know his life story? I just know his name that's all."

Chuck punched again, then followed up one more, then with a swift third. "It's for a job. Just looking to talk to him for a few minutes."

Michaels pressed his shoulder in the bag to hold it firm and nodded softly, signaling for Chuck to turn up the heat. Chuck did. Lunging in and out, he slapped at the bag with three quick strikes, then lurched left and repeated the motion before back pedaling slightly and pounding the bag four more times. Ten strikes in a matter of seconds. Joe couldn't help but smirk and shake his head softly.

"Haven't seen him yet," Joe replied. "But he should be here. Doesn't miss too many lunch breaks."

"Sounds good. I'll keep an eye out."

Joe's expression didn't soften. "Just watch yourself, okay? That boy doesn't hang out with the best crowd."

Chuck laughed. "In this neighborhood, who does?"

Michaels stepped back, holding the bag still and smiled. "Good point." He walked away, letting the thick bag sway slightly as Chuck continued to dance around it, shuffling back and forth, eyeing it, stepping back, and launching with a burst of punches.

For twenty minutes, he battled against the heavy bag, alternating with punches and the occasional roundhouse kick, pushing the bag one way, then countering, stopping, and striking again. Around the gym, eyes glanced over, fixated on the scrawny kid prancing around and landing deep, explosive thuds on the massive bag. Walking down the street, any one of these guys would have passed him right on by, thinking he was some gaunt kid who might benefit from a few hours in the gym. Here, in his shorts and tank top, his wiry frame pulled tight around fully packed muscle, he was admired. Strong and fast, smart, and swift, no matter what gym Chuck used, he generally drew a crowd.

He stopped for a moment, bending over and placing his palms on his thighs. His breath was harsh, but even, his tank top dipping off his skinny shoulders. From near the front of the large, open room, he heard the front door push open, and he glanced up.

There he was.

Chuck didn't know the guy well, he'd only seen him and heard him in passing throughout his many trips to Ernesto's, but he was easily recognizable, both by sight and by sound, his thick, Eastern European accent catching anyone's ear who was nearby. Unlike Chuck, the guy was thick and broad-shouldered, a nearly square-sized man, not very tall, but built like a snub-nosed tractor trailer. He wore a red tank top stretched tightly across his barrel chest. His massive, vein-covered arms at a permanent state of flex. As he looked around the gym, searching for a place to settle, his eyes caught Chuck's. The two men stared at each other. Their eyes lingered a little long than either man was comfortable with, but the other guy eventually broke off and strode towards the free weights, tossing his ragged duffel by the nearest bench.

Chuck watched his back as he moved towards the nearest rack of dumbbells, his arms swaying out to the side because they couldn't quite tuck tightly to him. Before he could get into his first set, Chuck walked over to him and gestured, just catching the corner of his eye.

The Russian turned and scowled slightly, acknowledging Chuck's signal, but going out of his way to not look happy about it.

"Do I know you?" he asked in the familiar accent.

"No, not really," Chuck replied, putting on a friendly smile. "I mean, I've seen you here, but we've never really met." Chuck extended his hand towards the man, who glanced down at it like he was clutching a fist full of dog crap.

Chuck pulled his hand back and started to rethink this strategy. He'd been working out nearly side by side with this guy for a year or more, he was anticipating a little more camaraderie.

"Sorry to bother you," he said. "Just had a question. A kind of personal one, if you don't mind."

The large man crossed his large arms across his even larger chest. He became a vaguely human-shaped stone wall in shape, thickness, and expression.

"Correct me if I'm wrong," Chuck continued, "but you're Russian, right?"

The man narrowed his eyes. "Technically, my parents were Scandinavian. But I was born and raised in Russia, yes."

"Okay, good. See, I have this friend of mine. Guy I know really well. We hang out all the time."

"Good for you," Ben said stiffly.

"Well, it was good. He's a good friend. He has a son, and they both vanished a week or so ago."

The Russian's expression shifted, his head drawing back and eyes narrowing. For the briefest moment, a flush blossomed at his cheeks and forehead. An actual human emotion.

"I know this is a shot in the dark, and I know it's stupid to think that one Russian guy knows another just because they're both Russian, but I don't know what else to do."

"I am sorry," the large man replied, showing some genuine concern. "What is his name?"

"Federov," Chuck replied. "Stepan Federov. His son's name is Jorge."

If the weightlifter recognized the name, he showed no sign. "When did he disappear?"

Chuck glanced around the gym, making sure there was nobody within earshot. "We're not quite sure, but it was sometime last week. That was the last day his son was in school."

"Very well," Magnússon replied, seeming to choose his words very carefully. "What do the police say?"

"They've got nothing. Can't find a trace of either of them, which is why I decided to hit the streets. I remember you, I was always impressed by your sets." Chuck gestured to his own skinny frame. "I'm jealous, man."

At this, Ben smiled warmly. He slapped Chuck's chest with his palm a few times lightly. "You have good muscle," he said. "Nothing to be embarrassed by. Good speed, too."

"Thanks, man."

The large man followed Chuck's eyes, scanning the floor near them to make sure nobody could hear them speaking. "I am sorry I cannot help more."

Chuck shrugged. "Hey, it was worth a try, right?"

The other man held up a finger. "But there is something else you maybe should try. Another place."

"Is that so?"

"It is so. There is Russian bar in Hartford. It is, how you say, infamous."

"Infamous? For what?"

The large man leaned slowly in, his eyes still shifting. "Connections to Russian mafia. They have their fingers everywhere."

Chuck nodded softly.

"If something bad happened to your friend, they may know about it there."

"Thank you," Chuck replied honestly. "That's very helpful."

"Maybe not too helpful," the Russian replied. "You don't want to mess with the Russian mob. Nothing good comes of it. Best to let police handle it."

"You're probably right."

The larger man stood back upright, pulling away from Chuck, looking down at him. "You want to run through a few sets, my new friend? Maybe we put some more beef on you? My name is Benedikt, I can help you get bigger. Big like me."

Chuck smirked and looked at the clock on the wall. It was just after one, and Rosa didn't want to talk until three. Plenty of time.

"Stack 'em up," Chuck said. All around them, metal plates clanged and slammed.

CHAPTER 19

Rosa stepped out of her car, easing the door shut, her eyes narrowing over the sloped roof towards the small structure ahead. It was a squat brick building with white shutters, a narrow driveway just to the right of the paved asphalt walkway leading to a single step entrance. A fairly new two-door coup sat in the driveway, some fancy looking blue car that Rosa's eyes landed on. She couldn't help but make a mental comparison between her own beat up sedan and this nice-looking pseudo sports car and wonder just what Devereaux Davis was doing right that she was doing so wrong.

She walked up the asphalt walkway towards the metal entrance door, a brass plaque bolted to the brick wall saying *Devereaux Detective Agency, est 2015*. She'd heard her share of tales about Devereaux Davis, and she'd seen what he could do firsthand, but she'd come away unimpressed. He seemed smart, capable, and well put together, seemed like he had a great head on his shoulders, but with their last interaction, pretty much every step he'd taken had been in the wrong direction.

But he'd been used, she told herself. Someone else was pulling the strings, it was tough to blame him for that.

She rapped her knuckles on the door and waited for a few moments, hearing the scuffed footfalls of someone on the other side.

The door swung open and the man appeared just as she remembered him, youngish, probably in his late thirties, the close fuzz of an unshaven face twisted into a grimace.

His face brightened momentarily when he saw her, a glimpse of recognition, and pleasant recognition, but slowly, the look shifted to a recollection of past interactions and times gone wrong. It was like watching a statue collapse into a barely formed clump of clay.

"Rosa?" he asked simply. "Rosa Guzman?'"

"Mr. Davis," Rosa said.

"I have to admit, I didn't expect you to stop by this soon. Or, well… ever again. Not after the way I screwed the pooch last time around."

Rosa couldn't help but smile. Yes, he had screwed the pooch, but he'd recognized that and was apparently taking full responsibility for it. One point in the Devereaux Davis column.

"I just have a few questions," she continued. "About Mitchell Capozza."

Davis scowled at her, then pulled back and unhooked the chain behind the door, peeling it open. He was wearing a black t-shirt and blue jeans, but no socks or shoes. As she got a better look at him, she saw brown hair pulled into a tight, wet ponytail behind his head, and vibrant green eyes glowering out at her. About the response she expected for mentioning Capozza's name.

"What is this about?" he asked, ushering her in, suddenly appearing far less friendly.

"You know my name, but I'm not sure you know what I really do. I'm a licensed Fugitive Recovery Agent. A…bounty hunter if you will."

"I'm aware," Davis replied. "What's this have to do with Mitch? With Mr. Capozza?"

"Mitch? So you're on a first name basis?"

Dev seemed uncomfortable with the direct question. "We have a mutually beneficial relationship," he said.

Rosa glanced out at the sports car parked outside the office, then nodded back towards Dev. "So I see."

"It's not like that."

Rosa held up a palm. "Listen. What arrangements you and Capozza have are your business. But now, he's made it my business, and that's why I'm here."

"Did he hire you for something?" Dev asked curiously.

Goose nodded. "Yeah. I can't really go into the details, but word on the street is you're normally his guy, so I'm just trying to get some perspective."

Dev crossed his arms. "I haven't done a whole lot with him lately," he said. "The guy's obsessed with that new office building downtown. Pouring a lot of cash and attention into it."

"I think I've seen it. The one down by the bridge? Tall building, right?"

Dev nodded. "Yeah, that's the one. Ever since they started clearing the lot for that, I haven't heard much from him."

"What kind of work do you typically do?"

Dev shrugged. "All sorts. Background checks for employees, reconnaissance on competitors. Mostly just rinky dink things that he pays me to do because I can do them quickly."

"And quietly? Without a paper trail?"

Dev looked at her suspiciously.

"No judgements," Rosa said. "Like I said, just trying to figure out what I'm dealing with."

"No judgements," Dev replied. "Hey, you want a cup of coffee or something?"

"Hell yes."

Dev nodded and broke away, walking across the lobby of his office, which was really a glorified living room of sorts. It was a long, narrow, carpeted room with a couch against the far wall and a desk perched just ahead of a door. A small kitchenette was shoehorned into the opposite corner of the couch and he made his way there, snagging the coffee pot. Rosa navigated to a cushioned chair that sat nearby, dropping herself down into it.

"So. Mitchell Capozza called you?" he asked, not turning around.

"Yep. Who knows maybe next week I'll be driving the sports car..."

Dev twitched almost imperceptibly, but covered it up with a soft, manufactured chuckle.

"Do you know the name Stepan Federov?" Rosa asked.

"Think so," Dev replied. "Used to work for Capozza."

"Used to being the operative word."

"Okay. So he skipped out?"

"Yeah. And Capozza wants me to find him. Way I understand it, he usually asks you to handle that stuff."

Dev turned towards her, a coffee cup in each hand. He approached her and handed her one of the mugs, thin wisps of steam rising from the dark liquid. As she drew the mug to her lips, he leaned on the desk, taking a chug of his own.

"Thanks," Rosa said.

"You're right," Dev said. "He usually asks me to do that stuff."

"Any idea why he didn't this time?"

Dev shook his head. "Nope."

"How friendly are you with Capozza?"

"Friendly? I wouldn't say we're friendly. I mean… yeah, I call him Mitch, he calls me Dev. But, it's just that he's got me on a decent retainer, and I do what he asks when he asks. That's about the extent of our relationship."

"How did you get connected with him?"

"Couple years ago, I think? When I first came up North."

Rosa took another sip of coffee. "I can tell from your accent you're not from the area."

Dev chuckled. "New Orleans. Born, raised and became a cop. Both the best thing and worst thing to ever happen to me." He said it in an off-hand way, but Rosa could sense some genuine pain contained underneath the words.

She nodded. "I can relate. Had a few of those in my life. I keep trying to get away, and just end up right back where I started."

"Oh I don't think I'll be going back home any time soon."

"Why's that?"

Dev shrugged. "It's a bit of a long story. Maybe we can talk about it sometime."

"Okay?" Rosa asked, a little confused.

"Over coffee or something? Dinner?"

Rosa flushed and set the coffee down on the desk, then rose from her seat.

"Maybe," she replied simply.

"Sorry," Dev replied, flashing a tooth-filled grin. "Maybe I should wait until I've known you for twenty minutes before I ask you out, huh? I've been accused of being a fast mover."

"It's all good. But I'm just here on business, all right?"

"Fair enough."

"So, what can you tell me about Capozza?"

"Not much, I'm afraid. We've got a purely business relationship. He asks me to do things, and I do them. So far there's been nothing illegal. Nothing that even ventured close to the police. After what happened down south, I'm steering far clear of that up here."

"What did happen down south, if you don't mind me asking?"

"Oh, so you want the life story without the dinner, huh? Story of my life."

Rosa chuckled. "Sorry."

"It's all right." Dev's face grew suddenly serious, and once again Rosa sensed the hurt. The vulnerability. He had an outgoing and friendly presence, but inside there was a windstorm…he reminded her of herself.

"There was a case. A few cases really, but most of my issues hinged on one. I was a really good detective, so good that I solved a case that a lot of people actually didn't want me to solve. Certain people made it very clear to me and my family that I had overstepped my bounds."

"This does sound like an interesting story."

"If you want the good parts, it'll take some beers and red meat. Sorry, I'm holding fast."

"Fair enough," Rosa replied, grinning in spite of herself. There was something about Dev Davis that she liked. Something that she identified with. He had secrets, maybe as many secrets as she did.

"Thanks for the coffee," she said quietly, turning towards the door.

"Hey, keep me posted on what you're doing for Mitch, okay?"

"Sure," Rosa replied. "Good to meet you. Maybe I'll be in touch, all right?"

Dev nodded and she stepped out the door, out onto the walkway. Her thoughts raced as she walked towards her car, parked near the sidewalk, trying to figure out Dev's place in all of this, and whether or not he could be trusted. He and Capozza were obviously close. Just how close remained to be seen, and how that would impact her own investigation was still to be determined. Without even knowing it, though. Dev had given her something. Given her something valuable, something that had been right under her nose the whole time.

CHAPTER 20

"This is ridiculous." Mitchell Capozza sat in his long back, ornately decorated swivel chair, perched behind the mahogany desk, a long and curved wood surface highly polished and smoothed to a nearly reflective finish. His hands were folded into tightly curled fingers in front of him, squeezing so tightly the pink of his flesh was receding into pale white.

"I don't have time to waste on this. We need to find him now."

Pietro stood on the other side of the desk, arms crossed behind his back, his face a mask of poorly feigned uncertainty. "We have not yet heard from Ms. Guzman today. We're hoping she has some idea of next steps."

"Then what am I paying you for?" Capozza asked, glancing up. His face was set and stoic, with little emotion creasing his skin or forming his expression.

"Mr. Capozza, we are trying to help."

Capozza's eyes narrowed, and he placed his palms on the desk. The door to his office creaked open and a middle-aged woman thrust herself past it, catching Capozza's eye.

"Mr. Capozza, you have a visitor," she said quietly.

"Who is it?"

"It's Selectman Gregg, sir."

Capozza eased his eyes closed and drew in a deep breath. "Tell him I'll be right with him," he said. She nodded and pulled herself back out of his office, shutting the door.

"This shit, Pietro. This shit is why we have to find him."

"We are working on it, sir," Pietro replied.

"Have you checked with the Russians?" Capozza asked. "Are they protecting him for some reason?"

"We've tried a few contacts but are having no luck."

"Try a few more contacts. I need to talk to the selectman, but I trust you'll have something for me later this afternoon."

"Of course," Pietro replied, nodding, and turning to walk away.

Capozza pressed a button on a phone sitting on the table to his right. "Go ahead and send in the Selectman, Ruby."

Pietro opened the door to leave, sliding to one side so Selectman Gregg could pass by into the office. Gregg was dressed well in a neatly pressed suit and tie. His hair was slicked to his scalp, a narrow, graying helmet, and his slate eyes peered out from behind circular glasses. He glanced back as Pietro removed himself and shut the door behind him.

"Selectman?" Capozza asked, easing himself to his feet.

"Mitchell," the man replied. The two shook hands briefly. "Tell me you have some news?"

Capozza gestured towards a chair, and the politician took a few steps towards it and sat down, crossing his legs. He wrapped his hands around his narrow knees and cocked his head at the business owner as if to say, "well?"

"We are still looking for him," Capozza replied, "but we have some leads."

"For Christ's sake, Mitchell." The Selectman hissed. "That man knows far too much. For three years we've been working together. Your business has exploded thanks to us."

"You've been very helpful with my zoning requests, Ralph. I owe you all more than I can repay."

"Oh, you will be repaying," Gregg said, nodding crisply.

"Of course, of course."

"Do you know yet what he left the building with?"

Capozza drew in a breath and glanced around the office. "I don't like talking about this here. Can we go somewhere else?"

"No, we cannot. You have beaten around the bush enough. I'm not the only one who is worried about this, Mitchell. You're going to get cut out."

"You can't do that," Capozza said, his voice a low, haggard whisper.

"Oh, we can. We cleared the path for you, Mitchell, and all you've managed to do is shuffle some businesses around and conveniently lose gigabytes of incriminating data! If Federov releases any of that information, we could all end up in prison!"

"And he'd lose all leverage. He'd be dead less than an hour after it got out there and he knows that. That's not his game."

"What is his game?"

"I wish I could tell you. Once we find him, I'll let you ask him yourself."

"I look forward to that."

Capozza struggled to keep his voice low and steady. "I appreciate your concern, Ralph, but I still maintain that the person here with the most to lose is me. Trust me when I say I have the appropriate motivation."

Selectman Gregg scowled but did not deny that what Capozza said was true. He pressed his hands on his thighs and pushed himself upright, standing.

"I'm glad to hear you're appropriately motivated," he said. "You're dangling by a narrow thread, my friend. You are an eyelash away from this whole thing falling apart," he gestured to the office around him as a form of emphasis. "And if this falls apart, you fall apart with it. Not us. You."

Capozza joined the man in standing. "Then what are you so afraid of, Ralph?"

The two men glared at each other, a noiseless heat broiling the air around them.

"I'll be hearing from you soon," Gregg said. Capozza didn't reply. The well-dressed politician spun on a neatly polished heel and thrust himself out of the office in five swift strides, slamming the door behind him.

Capozza stood alone in his office wondering where it had all gone wrong.

CHAPTER 21

Rosa stood up from her cluttered desk, the phone chirping loudly not too far away. She'd just returned from her visit to Devereaux and hadn't taken two steps into the house before her phone started going off.

"Guzman," she replied, pressing the receiver to her ear.

"Hey, Goose, it's Chuck."

"What do you have for me, Chuck? Tell me you've got something." She could almost picture him in his apartment, sitting tight to the kitchen counter, probably trying to find a place to rest his elbow between cereal crumbs, discarded trash, and empty bowls.

"I talked to the guy at the gym."

"And?"

"And…he has no idea."

"Damn it."

"But he did make mention of a night club in Hartford."

Rosa sat back in her chair and leaned forward slightly. "There are a lot of night clubs in Hartford," she replied.

"But supposedly only one of them is owned by the Russian mob."

"What the hell, Chuck. What am I supposed to do with that?"

"Well, according to my new lifting buddy, that's our best bet to try and find Federov. He'd never heard of him himself but said almost anything that goes on in the Russian community around here passes through that club at some point."

"Snooping around at a night club owned by the Russian mob doesn't strike me as being the best career move, you know?"

"You wanna live forever?"

Rosa chuckled. "Well, you know, another fifty years might be nice." Might be. Though she wasn't sure she could take fifty more years of living contract to contract, barely surviving in a ten by ten room attached to her office. She wasn't sure she could take two more years of that.

"Where's your sense of adventure?"

"Jesus," Rosa said, "you mix it up with some Russian musclehead for the afternoon and suddenly you're John Rambo. Dial it back, Heath."

"Oh calm down, Goose. We're on the same side here."

Rosa touched her chin to her chest. "I know we are. Sorry, Chuck. Didn't mean to be a bitch. I'm just feeling a little over my skis."

"No judgments," Chuck replied.

Rosa sat back, closing her eyes. Federov. Did he have some connections to the Russians beyond his lineage. Is that why she had been there that day? And did she really want to open this can of worms?

"You got any nice clothes, Chucky?"

"I'm sure I can scare something up."

"All right. We're going dancing tonight. Pick me up at seven?"

"I'll be there."

Rosa hung up the phone, immediately regretting her chipper demeanor. Dance clubs were not her thing. By and large, she hated people in general, and the more people who were at any given place, the less she wanted to be there. But a job was a job.

She'd have to make sure to pack the Ruger tonight, though. She wasn't crazy about feeling this way, but she needed this contract. If she was going to get out of this bad situation and start an actual life, she needed this to happen.

So why did she feel so terrible about it?

Truth was, the Federov family was an indelible part of her life already and for all the wrong reasons. Did she really have it in her to further wreck whatever life they had left? Or could she turn this job into some kind of redemption story?

She wasn't big on the concept of redemption. She didn't buy it.

Some things just couldn't be redeemed.

But this wasn't a time to live in the past. This was a time to look forward, to follow the word of the contract, take a big pay day, and put her life on a better track.

At least that's what she kept telling herself.

CHAPTER 22

"Is this thing going to get us all the way to Hartford?" Rosa just got a glance of Chuck's sedan as it sat under the faded glow of the streetlights. It was a good thirty years old, a faded dark blue with a scattering of barely painted Bondo holding it together.

"And yours is so much better?"

Rosa glanced back, looking at her own ancient hatchback and found it tough to argue the point.

"Point taken, kid," she replied. She glanced back over at Chuck and smiled thinly. He was wearing a bright blue button-up shirt, which hung comically on his narrow shoulders, nicely tailored pants cinched tight around his waist, bunched up and wrinkled. As she watched, Chuck jingled a small key in his hand, then knelt on the sidewalk, slipping it into his sneaker. She glared at him.

"Never hurts to have a spare," he said with a wink. Rosa shook her head.

She was wearing a nice pair of black jeans and a satin blue shirt, pretty much the only clothes she owned that could pass for night club apparel. They were a couple of rock stars out for a night on the town.

"All right, let's hit it," she said, sliding into the passenger seat. As she lowered herself to the seat, she reached behind herself and lightly touched the holster at the small of her back, her breath easing at the heft and contour of the pistol wrapped tight within. Her security blanket.

"You brought the gun?" Chuck asked, glancing over at her.

"Felt like the right thing to do," Rosa replied, obviously a little embarrassed about it.

Chuck started the car, gunning the engine. "Some of these places have metal detectors."

"We'll deal with that when the time comes, smart guy."

The drive was quiet and unremarkable, a straight shot down the highway from Springfield to Hartford, Connecticut. Chuck guided the sedan off the highway and through a myriad of confusing turns until he turned left onto a gravel parking lot, the small rocks crunching under the steadily rolling tires. Turning and applying the brakes, he placed his car in line with several others, the night club a couple hundred yards away, flanked against the dim light of late evening, and bracketed by the light show of downtown Hartford a few blocks away.

By the looks of the building, it was an industrial complex of some kind at one point, as so many of these buildings were. A large gravel lot surrounded the massive concrete building, a series of crammed together rectangles with visible fire escapes zig-zagging up the dark concrete walls. Windows littered the outside wall, many of them casting pale yellow light out onto the dirt, reflecting small, bright squares in even patterns on the rocky ground. Cars were parked evenly throughout this huge area, and there were lots of them, stacked up in even rows. A large, cylindrical smokestack perched on the rear corner of the building, but nothing came out, it was dark and silent, converted from essential part of daily life to just so much useless ornamentation.

Facing Rosa and Chuck was the flat front of the looming building, four large windows looking out towards them and a single rectangular door down near the ground. Even from this distance, they could see the door was flanked by at least three men. Three *large* men.

Chuck looked over at his partner. "I'm thinking the Ruger may not be our best play."

Rosa didn't look away from the trio of bouncers perched at the front of the building. "You might be right." She eased open the door to Chuck's sedan, and leaned in, popping the glove compartment. With the other hand, she skillfully unhooked the holster from the small of her back, slipped it from her pants, and slid it inside, then latched the door again.

"Feel better?" she asked as she tugged her shirt back down, straightening herself.

"Not especially."

"I feel you."

They walked forward, shoes crunching on gravel, human-shaped shadows drifting around them, all heading towards the same destination. At the door, they could see the three men taking steps towards anyone who approached, asking them questions, checking the clipboard in their hand, and ultimately letting them walk past and into the club.

Rosa's sense of unease was only increasing by the moment, and the more she thought about the approach they were taking, the more uncertain she was about where it might lead. Still, she stuck shoulder to shoulder with Chuck as they continued their steady progression forward, the building growing larger and larger ahead of them. They could hear the music inside now as well, the rapid-fire slam of techno music chased by a low screeching of complimentary electronica echoed in the air around the building, to the point where Chuck could almost feel the impact of the bass.

"You bring your dancing shoes?" he asked Rosa, leaning in towards her.

She smiled lightly but, inside, her heart was slamming in tune to the raucous music. She could feel the cool sheen of sweat on her flesh as she pictured the building filled wall to wall with writhing bodies with no space to move, no space to turn, and no space to breathe. Not her idea of a fun evening activity. Since her upbringing as an only child, Rosa had grown accustomed to being alone, or at least one of very few people in any given place at one time. Her experiences growing up had generally led her to believe that the more people who were someplace, the more likely there was to be trouble.

As if her experience with the Blades wasn't enough to reinforce that, her last field operation in Afghanistan certainly put a nail in it. The less people around, the better, especially in a confined space like this one.

"Name?"

Rosa jerked her head up, pulled out of the fog of her angst.

One of the three bouncers cocked his head at her. "Name, please."

"Oh, right, sorry," she muttered. "Rosa. Rosa Guzman."

"And I'm Charles Heath," Chuck interjected.

The man lifted his clipboard and scanned down through the paper, his eyes narrowed and finger darting across the page.

"I do not see you here," the bouncer replied. "You are not on the list."

Rosa tried to look wounded. "Look, we just need to ask some questions. We're not going to be staying long. Is there a manager or someone we can talk to?" she found her voice elevating slightly, trying to get the edge over the background music, which seemed as if it was almost rattling the windows.

"A manager?" the man asked. "What you think this is some fast food restaurant?"

"Look, we need to talk with someone if we could," Chuck said. "We don't even need to go inside."

"Get the hell out of here," the bouncer replied, gesturing past them with his clipboard. "Go back home."

"This could be a matter of life or death," Rosa said.

A second Russian bouncer stepped towards them. "Yes, it could, especially if you don't leave. This place is not for you."

The two men flanked each other, creating a flesh barricade coated in tight jackets. Shoulder to shoulder, there seemed to be no way to squeeze through. Rosa glared into the eyes of the one on the left, then shifted to the one on the right, then back again. The third man hung slightly behind them, his hands stuffed in his pockets and looking threatening.

"Stepan Federov sent us," she said. She wasn't even sure why she said it, it just came out.

Both men narrowed their eyes. "What the hell did you just say?" the man on the left asked in his thick accent.

Rosa stood firm, not stepping back. "Stepan Federov. Do you know him?"

The two men glanced at each other, then back at Chuck and Rosa.

"You stay here," the man on the right said, then broke away, leaving his partner standing there alone, watching them. They all stood there in silence, Rosa and Chuck not even looking at each other. A few moments passed, and the first man emerged again, striding towards them, his face hard and narrow.

"Spread your arms and legs," he barked. They both did. The men frisked them both, checking them carefully for weapons, looking under jackets, at their backs, their sleeves. After a few seconds, they appeared satisfied that neither of them were armed.

"Come with us," the man said, his voice a low, accented hiss. "I'm not sure where you heard the name Stepan Federov, little girl." He growled, glancing over his shoulder at them as he led them towards the club, "but you might not be glad that you did."

CHAPTER 23

In her memories, Rosa couldn't tell if the rain was still falling, her eyes were in a permanent state of fog, her flesh moist and clammy, and the pungent odor of spent smoke lingered in the air, masking any indication of wet pavement. Above, the sky was still a vacant shade of gray like deep, dark pencil scratches barely erased.

Red flashes danced off the buildings around her, streaking through the smoke-filled air, the damp coolness of the sidewalk starting to seep through her blue jeans. A few feet away, Switch was being tended to by EMTs, with police officers standing close by making sure he didn't try a sudden cut and run.

He wouldn't have made it far.

The wound on his leg was nasty, a ragged tear through cloth and a deep gouge through skin and muscle, red staining denim, leaking through and running into the rainwater gutter. They'd stopped the bleeding and wrapped him up in bandages, but he was still looking a little pale, his round eyes glaring off towards nothing.

"Hey, you all right?"

Rosa's head turned slowly, drifted really, and her eyes tried to focus on the woman standing next to her. She was a cop, like everyone else, but her long blonde hair spilled down out of her blue cap, touching her shoulders. She was young and pretty, but her voice was hard and sharp, even when she was trying to be kind. Dropping down into a low squat, she touched Rosa's shoulder with a gentle palm.

"I'm officer Bondalewski," she said quietly. "You can call me Helen. Are you hurt?"

Rosa shook her head.

"Did you see what happened?"

Rosa looked towards her, fixated on her eyes, then everything grew foggy, and she glanced away again. Helen looked down at the sidewalk, then pulled herself upright, stretching slightly. She turned and looked towards the vacant lot where two lumps of lifeless flesh were covered in emotionless, dark plastic bags, their final statements to the world at large a dramatic lack of identity. Two more motionless piles with no names and no lives, lost in the shuffle of life around them. Everyone focused on the living while they simply faded into the background, blurred and soon to be forgotten.

On her right, a male cop approached, peeling off his unnecessary sunglasses and glancing down at the small notepad he held in his hand.

"Male vic was a member of the Russian mob from what we can tell. Two priors, nothing serious, but on all sorts of known associate's lists."

Helen kept looking, her gaze now moving and focused on the second pile, the one over on the sidewalk. The one that had been pushing a baby stroller not an hour before.

"What about the woman?"

The male cop joined Helen in looking out towards the sidewalk. "She has some family ties with the Russians, pretty far up the food chain," he started, then looked down at his pad. "But it looks like she was just an innocent bystander here. Caught in the crossfire."

Rosa sat on the sidewalk, listening to them speak, barely hearing the words but understanding them clearly. Understanding the meaning behind them. The impact. The immediate effect on life and death.

"Who was she?" she heard Helen ask.

A few pieces of paper flipped and the guy cop adjusted his stance. "Name was Federov. Dalia Federov."

CHAPTER 24

"Yo, you coming or what?" the accented voice barked over the rumbling din of the dance floor. Rosa snapped to attention, her head springing up and eyes slamming open. Her momentary shift into the past was completely evaporated, the gray pencil-lead skies blown apart by streaking pink and yellow neon lights, searing through fog machines, clasped between the shattering bass of the dance music. All around them, bodies writhed and moved, dancing both in and out of time to the background noise. Far to the left, beyond the throng on the dance floor, a polished bar stretched from end to end, with two attractive bartenders sliding up and down it, artfully tilting bottles, filling glasses, and handing out drinks, conversing with the clientele.

Rosa could barely focus. Ever since she had first received the letter from Mitchell Capozza referencing Stepan Federov, she had known it was the same man. The man whose wife she had killed. The man whose son she had taken the mother away from. Yes, Switch took the blame. He wasn't about to let her rot in jail for something he dragged her into, so he did what a man would do in his twisted little mind and took the hit.

He took the hit in more ways than one.

Tears stung Rosa's eyes as she walked. She tried to blame them on the thick smoke in the club and the throbbing music, but she couldn't even fool herself at this point, and all she could do was try and blink them away.

She recovered and glanced towards the Russian bouncer talking to her.

"I'm with you, sorry," she said and picked up her pace. They were walking the perimeter of the club, around the dance floor and towards a narrow door pressed against the right wall. The door was unmarked with no windows, just a simple handle on a plain rectangle of wood, flanked by two large, well-dressed men. Chuck glanced at the two men as he approached, just behind the lead Russian.

"You guys have a weight limit?" he asked.

One of the men looked at him and shook his head. "Obviously, you do not."

The man on the right shifted, hooked his fingers in the door handle, and opened the door, allowing the three others to slide through. A long staircase greeted them, extending upwards between two walls as if carved from strange, smooth stone.

"You first," the Russian barked, gesturing to the stairs. Chuck stepped up and Rosa followed him, then the large man filled up the entire space behind. The Russian actually darkened the hallway with his massive frame, and Rosa picked up her pace, pushing closer to Chuck ahead of her as if the massive Russian might accidentally step on her and break her.

At the top of the stairs, they broke left and came to another door in the wall, which Chuck strode towards, reaching it just as it pulled open into a tiny office beyond. Two more thickly built Russians in suit coats ushered them inside, where they were flanked by two others, looking upon an extraordinarily large man sitting at a desk that seemed entirely too small for him. His tree trunk arms rested upon the top of the oak desk, fingers intertwined, his eyes narrow under the wrinkled, bald slope of his forehead. He glared at them as they entered but remained sitting, unmoving, calm, and not even particularly interested in finding out why they were there.

"So, what is this?" the large man asked, turning his palms upward. "Why do you come here and throw names around?"

"I'm sorry?" Rosa asked, a little confused by the question.

He looked at her, narrowing his eyes. "You come to my club here. You throw Stepan's name around, like you're threatening him or something. This is not good idea."

"We're not threatening anyone," Chuck replied. "We just need to talk to someone. About Stepan Federov."

"Federov is of no concern to you. Forget you heard his name."

Rosa looked at him. Many a night went by that she wished she could forget the name Federov. Tonight was not one of those nights.

"I'm afraid his life is in danger," she said.

The man smiled. "No danger. You can trust me on that one. Stepan is safe and sound."

"You know where he is?" Chuck asked.

"I know a lot of things," the man replied. "I am Vasily Sokolov, after all. I don't need to look or listen, these things, they just come to me."

Rosa and Chuck glanced at each other. They had heard the name Sokolov before and knew it had meaning in some of the darker corners of the Springfield criminal network.

"No doubt," Chuck replied, turning back towards the large man. "Can we at least speak with him. We suspect he has some information that might be helpful to us."

Sokolov leaned back on his chair, which groaned under his massive weight, threatening to collapse.

"Tell me, little boy, why should I care what helps you or does not help you? What difference does that make to me?"

Rosa and Chuck glanced at each other, both appearing to make mental calculations on just how much information to reveal to the fat man behind the narrow desk. Rosa took the first chance.

"We have reason to believe that a man with some high-level

connections is looking for him. If he finds out that the Russians are concealing him, it could...it could be trouble."

Vasily leaned forward in his chair again, tenting his fingers and glaring at the two strangers in front of him. His mouth worked, and he tapped his fingertips together, looking at them with a sort of stern wonder.

"No trouble for us," he replied finally. "Trouble, perhaps, for the person looking, yes?"

"Trouble is trouble," replied Rosa.

There was a quiet noise from outside the room. Rosa glanced around and noticed, for the first time, there was a second door here, one near the far-right corner, an unremarkable wooden slab tucked away and almost invisible. Beyond that door there was some kind of argument, raised voices and exclamations.

For a brief moment, Sokolov looked towards the door, as well.

"This isn't what we agreed to!" a voice shouted from beyond the room. "This isn't protection, this is prison!"

Rosa looked at the door through narrow eyes, then looked over at Sokolov. The man didn't give away anything if there was anything to give away. He just smirked and shrugged his shoulders.

"I think it's time for you to leave," Sokolov said, gesturing to the men flanking Rosa and Chuck. "We have nothing more to discuss."

"I beg to differ," replied Rosa.

"Let me go!" the voice shouted from behind the door. There was a slam, the door shook, latched, then burst open, revealing someone standing in the frame of the doorway, fists clenched, eyes wild.

Rosa took a step back, her own eyes widening slightly.

There he was. Standing right in front of them.

It was Stepan Federov. She recognized him from the wallet-sized photograph Capozza had included with the letter. The face had burned itself into her mind.

Rosa couldn't even speak. Her mouth hung open as she glared at the man who looked at her with some strange sense of wonder, a vacant curiosity, but only passing interest.

Vasily pushed himself up from his chair, sending it spinning backwards across the floor, his beefy arms pressed straight downward.

"What is this?" he asked in his abrupt, accent-infused bellow.

"This isn't what I agreed to!" Federov replied. "I haven't seen my son. You can't keep me penned up here like a prisoner!"

"Mr. Federov," Sokolov replied, trying to stay calm. "You came to us, not the other way around. Our only goal is to keep you safe."

"To keep me safe or to use me to fight back against Cap—?"

"Mr. Federov!" Vasily shouted, cutting him off. He gestured to Rosa and Chuck. "We have company. Watch what you say."

Stepan glared at Vasily. He stood all of five foot-ten, skinny build, wearing a plaid shirt and faded blue jeans. His hair was trimmed short, and he had a thin goatee around his narrowed mouth. In this small room, surrounded by massive slabs of Russian bouncers, he looked about as intimidating as a wet paper bag.

"Do I need to call my brother-in-law?" Stepan asked, his voice barely an angry whisper.

Sokolov clenched both fists, curling his fingers on the desk in front of him.

"I'm done," Federov said. "I'm going to get my son, and I'm leaving. I'll figure this out myself."

"That is a very bad idea," Vasily said, stepping back from the desk. "A very, very bad idea."

Stepan shrugged, turning towards the door set in the far wall, where he had entered. It still sat propped open, and the man who had been inside with him stood near it, blocking the way.

"Please, Mr. Federov," the man in front of the door said, stepping towards him. "Please, let's not make this an issue."

Stepan Federov dropped his shoulders slightly, looking defeated. He took a soft, small step forward and pressed his chin to his chest as if he had lost all hope.

Then he ran.

It wasn't so much a run as it was a lurching charge, a sudden forward jump that took everyone in the room by surprise, especially the large man attempting to block his way. Stepan brushed just past him and was gone, through the door, feet slamming on a stairwell just beyond.

"Grab him!" shouted Vasily, and the man by the door was already in motion.

Rosa moved next. She threw an elbow backwards in a straight, piston motion, slamming the peak into the collarbone of the tall man just behind her. He shouted and stumbled slightly, putting some space between him and Rosa. She catapulted herself forward, swiftly intercepting the Russian who was approaching the door. Swinging her hand out in a knife-hand position, she struck the large man in the ribs just under his right arm, and he drew back, snapping his arm close to his body, then pivoting slightly to face her.

He recovered quickly and charged her, arms outstretched, his mouth twisted into a silent roar. Rosa moved in his range of motion, slammed her hip into him, latched onto his arm, and tossed him over her shoulder, sending him slamming and tumbling across the floor, forcing the others to scramble backwards out of the way. Before his motion even stopped, she whirled around and hurled herself through the door, eyeing the narrow stairwell ahead. For a moment she hesitated, looking back, glancing at Chuck through the doorway, then looking at the stairwell ahead. She tensed, glancing back at him again.

"Go," Chuck said. "I got this."

Rosa knew she was out of time and nodded curtly, pushing herself forward. Even as she crested the top of the stairs, she heard the door slam down below. She placed her hands on the railing, and lifted herself of her feet, leaping halfway down the first flight, hitting the platform in a graceful crouch, then turned and repeated the motion, covering six stairs at a time.

As she turned and prepared to leap down the third flight, looking at the narrow exit door down below, she thought for the first time about Chuck Heath. Her breath caught in her throat. He wasn't pounding down the stairs after her, which meant he was cornered upstairs, and that was not a good thing.

She shook that off, thinking Chuck was capable of taking care of himself, and threw herself down the final flight, hitting the pavement below. Her knees buckled, coiling for a moment, then she shot forward, blasting through the exit door and out into the gravel parking lot. Up ahead, she could see the fading shape of Federov running towards the cars, and just beyond the lot, the towering shapes of accompanying factories and warehouses loomed, reaching towards the moon. If he made it into the darkened maze of industrial buildings, he could very well get lost, and if the Russians caught up with him there, it could end even worse.

Rosa accelerated, her feet crackling on the gravel parking lot, sliding sideways between two cars. Ahead, on her right, a flash of headlights signaled an unexpected vehicle approaching as the torpedo of steel and plastic surged out in front of her, blocking her from Federov. She leaped in the air and slid smoothly over the vehicle's hood, ignoring the muffled Russian cursing from inside the car. Landing in a smooth crouch, she ran forward again, keeping her eyes focused on her target, who was weaving in between vehicles himself, continuing to run towards the buildings ahead. A tall chain link fence separated the parking lot from the factories beyond and, already, Rosa could see him desperately trying to scale the fence, though not especially gracefully. A low-profile sports car sat in front of her, headlights glaring, and she looked to see the quickest way around. It was wedged between two other vehicles, barely a hip's width on each side, and she continued dashing forward, leaping, slamming one foot on the hood, then charging straight up the windshield, over the roof, then down the other side, her footfalls echoing in the darkness. Federov's shape was draped over the top of the fence and slowly dropping down behind it, and she swore under her breath. He was almost gone.

Drawing her already ragged breath in, she made one last lurching charge, running towards the fence in four long, swift strides, then jumping, latching her fingers around the top of the crossing metal. Bare links dug into her palms as she clutched the top of the fence, her arm muscles screaming, but she pulled, forcing her legs up and into her chest, then dancing barely across the metal surface and hurtling over in a slick vault, clearing the top and falling on the other side. Bending her knees, she kept moving, and Stepan was just ahead now, she'd made up some serious time, and she was closing. He lunged to his right, running fast, making a break for the dark shadow of a tall factory building, but Rosa cut shorter and ran faster and was right there, right on him, launching herself. She wrapped her arms around his waist and dragged him roughly to the ground. The two bodies entangled and tumbled side over side, limbs crossing and twisting together until they ended up with Rosa straddling Stepan Federov, pinning his shoulders to the grass.

"Where exactly did you think you were going?" she asked in between jagged, catching breaths.

"I...I don't know," he replied honestly. "I don't know what's going on anymore."

"Believe it or not," Rosa said, pulling herself off and standing up. She bent over and extended a hand to him. "I'm trying to help you."

He took her hand and allowed himself to be pulled to his feet. "Tackling me in the dirty grass outside of a Russian nightclub is considered *helping* these days?"

Rosa jerked her head towards the dance club. "Considering the alternative?"

"Point taken."

The two looked at each other, barely able to see in the low light of night, with no streetlights nearby to illuminate them. That was probably for the best as Rosa suspected some of the Russians would probably be out and about, looking for them.

"It looked like they were at least trying to protect you," she said. "Why run?"

"They're keeping me from my son," he replied. "Using him as leverage."

"Leverage? For what?"

Stepan glanced around nervously. "Not here. I don't want to talk about this here." He looked back towards the club. "Was that other guy your friend? Is he still in there?"

Rosa joined his glance, chewing her lip. "Yeah, he was with me.

But, uh, he can handle himself." She knew that was true to a point, but in a closed in room with four huge Russian bouncers? She wasn't so convinced.

Out in the grass, the night was somewhat quiet, with the dull slamming of night club bass a more faded and quiet ambiance. The chase had brought them a distance away from the building, but the loud music still resonated over the still, night air.

"What do we do now?" Federov asked. "Where do we go?"

"Do you know where your son is?"

He nodded slowly. "They're holding him in an apartment. Back in Springfield. That was the last I knew."

"All right. Let's figure out what we can do about that. Until then, we need to get scarce. Not only is Capozza after you, but now the Russians are, too. If we move fast, maybe we can get to your boy before it occurs to them that we might try. Is that something you're comfortable with?"

Stepan shook his head. "Comfortable might be a strong word."

"Fair enough." Rosa looked around, realizing for the first time there might just be a transportation issue to deal with.

"Forget where you parked?"

"No. We brought my friend's car."

She glanced back over her shoulder towards the road they'd entered on, then looked back at Stepan. "Come on. Let's get somewhere where we can get a ride. Uber should take us right into Springfield. It'll help keep us off the radar, too."

Federov nodded and she could see him following her towards the blackened buildings of the warehouses.

CHAPTER 25

It all happened in an instant. Stepan Federov charged from the room and Rosa dashed after him, but not before sending one of the Russian bouncers sprawling.

Chuck Heath tensed his muscles, his eyes darting around at the room full of men far larger and far angrier looking than he was. The door slammed shut, with Rosa vanishing down the stairwell. Chuck stood there, looking at four men slowly gathering around him, with a fifth groaning as he picked himself up off the floor.

"Stepan has stepped out the back door," Vasily Sokolov said, his finger pressed on a call button on the phone on his desk. "Please retrieve him, would you?"

Standing upright, he turned towards Chuck.

"Well, well, what are we going to do with you?" he asked crossing his arms over his chest. "Your friend, she left you here with us. Either she does not care about your fate or she thinks you can defend yourself against all of us." He stepped away from the desk, swinging around it and taking two long strides towards Chuck. Vasily looked down at him, a good foot shorter and at least a hundred pounds lighter.

"Looking at you, I'd say she does not care."

Chuck looked up at Vasily. "I got no beef with you," he said. "We were just looking for Federov. No reason to make this a thing."

Vasily took another step forward, his chest bumping Chuck's. "My friend, this is already a thing."

Chuck looked up into Vasily's eyes. "Come on, man. There's five of you. Just one of me."

Another Russian came up on Chuck's left. "Yes. Five large men against one very tiny, skinny little man. How do you think this is going to end?"

Chuck didn't reply.

"Your friend," Vasily started, "she uses Federov's name. She chases him away from here. Already, our men are looking for them. They will find them, but someone must pay for this."

Chuck took a cautious step back. "Don't look at me, man. I'm broke."

"Not yet," Vasily sneered. "But you will be."

Glancing around, Chuck looked quickly at the five men around him. They could have all been body building brothers, thick shoulders, large, round arms, hair trimmed to a straight buzz in various colors. Sokolov was the outlier, the guy who was much more fat than muscle, but even so, he stood tall and intimidating, looking down at the skinny man, his jaw set and fists clenched.

"Guys, I don't want any trouble," Chuck said, raising his palms.

"Too late." Vasily gestured towards the large man on his right, and one of the bouncers charged towards Chuck. But Chuck anticipated it. He slipped onto the balls of his feet and shuffled backwards, sliding out of the way, then torqueing his hips and driving a clenched fist directly into the bridge of the man's nose. A dull *crack* echoed in the small room, and the man's head snapped back, his feet flying out from under him. Even as the bouncer fell, another lunged at Chuck from behind, but he lurched forward, just out of reach and shot his left leg backwards like a piston. His heel struck the second man in the upper chest, knocking the air from his lungs and sending him stumbling clumsily backwards, his arms pinwheeling.

Vasily moved in himself, surprisingly quick for such a large man, and Chuck twisted, throwing his leg out in a round kick, slamming the shin into the man's ample stomach, stopping him in his tracks. As Vasily doubled over, gasping, a third Russian bouncer lunged. His arms wide, he enveloped Chuck in a massive bear hug, wrapping mammoth biceps around his narrow shoulders. Chuck twisted and tried to slip free, but the embrace tightened, crushing his shoulders together, sending rocket streaks of pain through both arms and down the length of his backbone. He lifted his knee up to his chest and sent it slamming down on the man's left foot, but the hug didn't lessen, and as he was held still for a moment, a fourth large man drove his fist deep into Chuck's midsection. The embrace withdrew, and he stumbled forward, the breath leaving him, his eyes watering and knees going weak. Hands grasped him under his arms, steadying him for a moment, just long enough for the third man to come back at him and slam his fist hard into Chuck's left cheek.

Fireworks exploded in his eyes as his head snapped to the side and the floor came up swiftly towards him, taking up his entire field of vision even as his eyes fogged over. The bright sparks faded into small explosions of pain. His shoulder struck the bare wood floor, reigniting the pain in his arms from the bear hug, and even as he rolled to the side to try and buy some time, feet surrounded him and large figures blocked out the overhead lighting. They looked down on him like giants, waiting for the right time to stomp a village into nothingness.

Even as Chuck stared, the pale light from the ceiling blurred into strange, half-yellow streaks, and darkness worked its way into the corners of his vision as he saw several sets of boots being raised, preparing to kick. Instinctively, he curled into a ball, tensing his muscles, trying to anticipate the powerful blows and, thankfully, he fell into unconsciousness after the first four and didn't even feel the flurry that followed, breaking two ribs, smashing muscle, and bruising bone.

CHAPTER 26

The city of Springfield was a series of white streaks outside the rain spattered window of the dark sedan, the background noise of the busy city phased out by the thick windows of the car. Mitchell Capozza sat in the back seat, glancing out the window at the place he'd called his home for his entire life and, once again, allowed himself to dream that it was his. Not just sporadic middle-class restaurants. Not just a successful real estate development firm, but the whole city. Lock, stock, and barrel.

A dream since his youth, when his father would come home from a double shift at the factory, tired and filthy, working his entire life just to survive one more day. A dream since his dismissive mother tossed dinner on the table to distract her son long enough to take one more drink from the wine glass and one more long drag on the Winston, which seemed to be permanently lodged between her pink lips, pressed together like two pale slugs.

Even as a child, Capozza looked upon these two exhausted, depleted, and vacant shells with disgust and shame, incensed at their lack of awareness of what their own middling education and business acumen had brought upon them. Not just them, but upon him as well.

If it were the last thing he did, he'd succeed where they had failed, if only to prove just how foolish they had been.

Especially his father. His obese, ignorant, drunk father who perceived himself to be so far above young Mitchell and his dreams of success. The elder Capozza who looked down upon him with derision and anger at the fact that he would dream of success rather than work hard with his hands simply to live day to day. Life was work. Life was labor, toil, and aggression. No fancy college degree could replace dirt under the fingernails, and he just could not abide the fact that young Mitchell was working to think and plan his way out of poverty. That's not the way these things worked.

Only, it *had* worked. Capozza had gone to college, he had received a fancy degree, and he'd turned what he learned into a successful business. Shortly before his father's final, fatal heart attack, he'd seen Capital Industries sign its first multi-million-dollar contract, and as his father withered away in a low budget retirement home for those last two years of his life, Mitchell relished every last, painful minute of it. Whenever he wondered just what his parents could have possibly taught him throughout his short and uneventful childhood, he remembered those last years of his father's life and realized they had taught him something very valuable. Succeed in spite of those around you and do whatever you can to spite them on the way to the top.

Sitting in the back of the vehicle, Capozza glanced away from the rain-streaked window, when just ahead, the console phone perched on the back of the center island in front of him chirped three times, a shrill, vocal sound, complimented by strobing light. Bending over slightly, he scooped up the phone and answered it.

"Capozza."

"Mr. Capozza, this is Pietro. We, uhh…there appears to be something going on down at Club Comet."

Capozza squinted. Club Comet wasn't one of his. Why did he care about this? "Club Comet? What does that have to do with me?"

"It's a Russian owned club, sir. We followed Rosa Guzman and her compatriot there tonight."

This got Capozza's attention. "There a Federov connection?"

"We're not sure, sir. What we do know is about fifteen minutes ago, half a dozen Russian bruisers came streaming out of there, combing through the parking lot."

"Looking for someone?"

"Seems that way, yeah."

"Sounds like maybe they know something we don't, huh?"

"I don't know for sure, but neither Guzman or Heath has come out yet, at least not that we've seen."

"All right. We're going to have to push a little on this one, I think," Capozza said. "Watch a little longer, see what you can figure out. I think we're going to have to pay Club Comet a visit."

Pietro was quiet for a few seconds, but finally replied, "Do you think that's a good idea, sir? I wouldn't think we'd want to piss off the Russians. Maybe they were holding him for a reason?"

"Screw their reasons," Capozza hissed. "Who do you have with you?"

"Me, Jerome, and Winston, sir. Just the three of us."

"Get ready, all right? I may need you to go rattle some cages."

"Sir?" Pietro asked. "They've got like a dozen guys in there. I'm not sure I'm comfortable with this."

Capozza scowled and pulled the phone away from his ear, taking a few long, deep breaths. "You're just going to be asking questions. Nothing more, okay? No reason to get all worked up."

"All right, we're here."

Capozza didn't say goodbye, he just leaned forward, pressing the handset into the cradle. The Russians were hiding Federov. Suddenly, he was sure of it.

The question was, what could he do about it?

CHAPTER 27

"I don't like this, Pietro," Jerome said, shaking his head as the three men pushed their way out of the car, easing the doors shut behind them.

"Capozza's orders," Pietro replied, not feeling all that comfortable himself.

"Capozza ain't walking into a den full of the Russian mob," replied Winston.

Pietro turned towards him, holding up the cell phone in his hand. "I've got him on speed dial. Feel free to give him a call and tell him how you feel."

Winston glowered at him, but kept his lips pressed shut. The three men looked out towards the one-time industrial building turned night club. The figures who had emerged from the front door had already dispersed and separated, scattering throughout the parking lot, vanishing among the shadowed cars and night club patrons. They could still make out the vague form of two stocky bouncers by the front door, and the three men glanced at each other as they approached.

Even from ten feet away, in the dim light of the front door, the annoyance sketched onto the faces of the two Russian bouncers was clearly evident. There was a sense of irritated apprehension, glaring at the three men, quite obviously not of their ethnicity and likely not of their crew.

"Not again," one the Russian's exclaimed, rolling his eyes.

The second took a long stride forward, holding his hand out, palm-first. "Okay, just hold it right there. We've already had our fill of unexpected visitors tonight, assholes. What do you want?"

The three men all exchanged bemused glances. "Assholes? Us?" Pietro asked, turning back towards the two bouncers. "We don't want any trouble. We're here representing Mitchell Capozza. We're hoping we can talk with someone in charge."

This time, it was the bouncers' turns to look at each other, then turn back to the three intruders. "Capozza? What the hell do we want with Mitchell Capozza?"

"We believe you may have gotten two other visitors tonight. A man and a woman. We'd like to help you with this situation."

"You've got to be kidding me," one of the Russians said. "Look, we're just trying to run our business here."

"Can you just tell your boss we're here? We're not here to start anything, we just want to talk about the two people who came earlier."

"Un-fucking-believable," sighed the other bouncer, but he turned and walked back into the club, leaving his partner there alone, blocking the door.

"You guys don't know who you're messing with here," the bouncer said, shaking his head. "Seriously. If I were you, I'd just turn and walk away, forget all about those other assholes. It's not worth it."

"It's worth it to our boss," Pietro replied. "If it's worth it to him, it's worth it to us."

The four men stood in silence for a few moments until the other Russian pushed open the door and emerged, gesturing towards the three men. "All right, come here. Be quick."

"Hold up," one of the other men said. "We need to search them."

"Don't touch us," Jerome hissed. "We represent Mitchell Capozza. You don't want to mess with us."

"You think you are going to come in here without us making sure you are unarmed? How stupid do you think we are?"

"You want me to answer that honestly?"

A bouncer took a long stride towards him, coming almost chest to chest, his pock-marked face twisting in an angry grimace, fist clenching.

"Easy," one of the other men said, placing a hand on the bouncer's shoulder. "Just take it easy. We have dozens of armed men in here. They have two. If they bring a pistol, so what, huh? We will just cut them down and be done with it."

The bouncer turned to the other man and opened his mouth to speak but thought better of it.

Pietro looked back at Jerome and Winston, nodding towards them, and they fell in behind him as he followed the bouncers through the front door. As they entered the club, the music was an assault on their senses, a brain-shaking thundering blast of electronic dance music, striking them with an almost physical force as they pushed through a crowd, following the lead of the two Russians, weaving between moving bodies and approaching the bar.

As they neared the bar, a large man maneuvered in from the back, barely fitting through a narrow door near the rear of the bar, then moving out past the bartender and approaching the same section of the counter where the three visitors halted.

"To what do I owe the honor?" Vasily Sokolov asked, looking far less than honored.

Pietro looked at him, noticing a thin sheen of sweat across his forehead and crimson cheeks. He either sprinted downstairs or had just been through some kind of physical exertion.

"Honor's all ours," Pietro replied, smiling.

"Look, I already had to toss two assholes out of this place tonight. I don't want to have to toss three more. Just tell me what the hell you want."

"Stepan Federov," Pietro said, spitting the name as if it were some kind of bitter, rotten fruit.

Sokolov glared at him.

Jerome took a step forward. "Look, we know those other two people who came in tonight. We know they were probably looking for Federov, too. Our boss just wants this to come to a peaceful conclusion."

"Wants *what* to come to a peaceful conclusion?" Sokolov asked. "What exactly do you think is going on here?"

"Our boss has reason to believe that you guys know where Federov might be," replied Jerome.

Vasily laughed. It was a loud, shattering bark of laughter, blowing foul-smelling breath in Jerome's face.

"I have reason to believe your boss can suck my dick," Vasily said, the smile swiftly fading into a narrow, angry line.

Pietro narrowed his eyes. "No need to be disrespectful."

"Disrespectful? You think that's disrespectful? You motherfuckers haven't seen disrespectful."

"Hey, hey, calm down," Jerome said, lifting his hands. "There's no need to get upset."

Vasily's head spun towards him. "Wait. Your boss…this Capozza asshole. He sends five different dirtbags down here to put pressure on us, and you expect us to not get upset? You don't know us very well."

Jerome shrugged. "Fair enough. Look, we didn't come for any trouble, we're just trying to find Stepan Federov. If he's not here, he's not here."

"He's not here," Sokolov barked.

Pietro looked at the group that was slowly forming. Sokolov was now flanked by two more burly Russians while the bouncers had drawn up behind them as well. The crowd of dancers had pulled back slightly as the voices elevated, eyes casually drifting towards them even as bottles clinked and bodies moved to the music. He looked each man in the eye as he surveyed the group, and each man glared back. Everyone in their small group was a rigid board, all tensed muscle and clenched fists, narrowed eyes and set jaws. No flexibility, no one backing down.

"Obviously, we're not getting anywhere here," Jerome said. "Is there someone I can have Mr. Capozza call?"

"Mr. Capozza can go screw himself," Sokolov snarled.

Winston stepped forward. "There's no need for that." He growled. Jerome lifted his arm and pressed his palm against Winston's chest.

"Easy. We don't want any trouble."

"Maybe you don't," Sokolov replied, "but maybe we do. Maybe we're all ready for a little trouble. Maybe you came on the wrong night, huh?"

Jerome smiled and tipped his head forward. "Thanks for your time." He turned to the other two men with him and nodded towards the door. "I think we've heard all we need to, boys."

The three men turned and started walking towards the door.

"What?" Sokolov said, elevating his voice over the din of the music. "That's it? You think you guys can just walk the fuck out of here?"

Winston started to turn, but Jerome pressed his hand to his back and kept him moving forward.

"Tell your asshole boss we have a message for him!" shouted Sokolov. Jerome kept on walking. "Better yet, we have a message to show him!"

The three men were still walking, but Pietro turned, glancing over his shoulder.

"Oh, dammit."

The man just to Vasily's right had an arm extended, fingers wrapped tightly around the contoured handle of a Glock 19 semi-automatic.

"Gun!" he shouted. "God damned gun!"

The Glock thrashed in the Russian's hand as a blast of yellow burst from the barrel, all in slow motion, the noise shattering the slamming drum of the music. Screams exploded from all around them the instant the gun fired, as if it was all some strangely choreographed theatrical event.

Pietro and Jerome lurched and reached into their jackets as Winston started to turn. The bullet struck Winston in the side of the face as he spun around, and his head snapped back, blasting a thin spray of red in a tight arc. Pietro winced as blood sprayed across his cheek, but he didn't linger, removing his hand from his jacket, his own gloved fingers clutching a pistol. He fired three swift times as he backpedaled towards the door. Jerome dropped into a lunging run, ducking his head, his arm angled back with a weapon in it as well, his pistol also rocking in his hand as it fired. The music halted as the staccato fireworks of exchanged gunfire peppered the inside of the club, mixed with screams. Suddenly, all the dancers were runners, scattering in all directions.

The wall by the front door exploded in a shower of plaster and paint as Pietro ducked down and to the left, barely avoiding a 9mm round to the back of the head. He pushed his way out of the door as a second round puckered the metallic surface, rebounding in a shooting spark, then careening out into the empty air outside. He threw himself out into the parking lot with Jerome close behind, feet crunching gravel as a few more scattered pops blasted from inside the club, the sound of whining ricochets signaling near misses.

"Get to the car!" Jerome shouted as they ran low and close to the ground, weaving between parked vehicles. Another quick volley of gunfire burst from their right, from a group of Russians who had been out looking for their previous guests. Sparks raced along the surface of a nearby car, trailing a series of metallic smacks. They picked up their pace and dashed forward, both of them blindly whipping their arms out and rattling off return fire into the darkness, having no idea if they were even coming close to their targets, just hoping no poor suckers were walking around out there. Up ahead, Jerome could see their car, and he surged forward with a renewed energy, overtaking Pietro for a moment.

"I'll drive!" he shouted, already pulling the key out with his slick fingers. Pietro nodded, holding his pistol in two hands, pointed at the ground as they ran.

Ducking, dodging, and running around the front of the car,

Jerome flew the driver's side door open, then hurtled inside as bullets crashed into the door just to his left. A round shattered the driver's side window in a webbed spiral of broken glass. Shoving the key into the ignition, and keeping his head down, he started the car and gunned the engine, looking over just in time to see Pietro throwing himself in the passenger seat. Slamming the car into reverse, Jerome sent the sedan charging backwards, then he pounded the brakes and whirled the wheel, pulling the vehicle into a tight reverse turn until the headlights were spun around and pointed back towards the exit. Up ahead, shadowed figures emerged, arms raised. More gunfire briefly lit the darkness ahead. The two men kept their heads down as small holes crawled their way up the windshield and Jerome quickly punched the car into first and pounded down the accelerator, the rear tires spitting rooster tails of gravel behind them. For a frightening moment, the vehicle started to drift left before the tires caught again and sent the vehicle thundering forward, straight into the bursts of gunfire.

"Head down!" Jerome shouted as he pushed the pedal all the way to the floor. Above him the windshield starred, popped, and blew inward under a volley of gunfire, but it only lasted seconds before the car was upon the small group. The shadows scattered, but not quickly enough and the vehicle lurched under the impact of a few slow-moving gunmen, who were tossed roughly aside. The right headlight shattered, and the hood crumpled as a twisting body cartwheeled over the vehicle. Breaking through the group, the sounds of gunfire were now behind them, and Jerome guided the vehicle out into the street outside, floored the accelerator again, and sent the car roaring into the darkness.

CHAPTER 28

"Are you sure they don't know about this place?" Rosa asked as she watched the small car fade into the darkness. The Uber driver had brought them within two blocks of Federov's requested destination, then dropped them off on the sidewalk so they could advance on foot, just in case.

"They don't know. This place is why they were holding me down at the night club. They've been trying to figure out where it is for a week."

The two of them walked along the sidewalk, flanked by thickening trees with houses peeking through the crowded leaves, looking down upon them from over the top of the foliage. Small, square, backlit eyes glared down on them from all directions, watchful brick and shingle sentries curious about these intruders making their way through this nice neighborhood.

Rosa glanced back at Stepan. "You trusted the Russians in the first place, but didn't trust them with this? Why?"

"Family ties," Federov replied. "My wife's family. I didn't know what else to do."

"Oh, you're married?" Rosa asked. Her heart skipped for a

moment, a bright blossom of hope flowering inside of her. Had she been wrong? Was this man not the one she thought he was?

"I am," he started, then paused. "Well, I used to be."

Inside, she felt the blossoming flower of hope, drying, cracked and withered, sucking a small piece of her soul down with it. She felt a lump press forward in her throat, and she choked it down with a muffled cough, looking away so she wouldn't have to see his eyes.

Rosa nodded beside him as they walked, shrouded in darkness just under the lip of the streetlights casting a glow upon the road to their left. It was a two-lane street, but not heavily traveled in this somewhat quiet and quaint college community. Downtown Springfield was only twelve miles from here, but bracketed with trees and million-dollar homes, it might have well been on another coast.

"So why is Capozza after you?" Rosa asked. "I mean, you realize he's after you, right?"

"Of course. I didn't realize he was going to sic a bounty hunter on me, but…"

Rosa chuckled. "I prefer Fugitive Recovery Agent."

Stepan looked over at her, a crooked smile on his face. "I'm not a fugitive."

"And I haven't recovered you yet."

For a brief moment, they walked in silence before Federov spoke up.

"Listen, if you're being paid to bring me in, why are we even doing this? Why didn't you just knock my ass out and bring me in? A hell of a lot quicker and less painful, probably for both of us."

Rosa drew in a breath. "Like you said, you're not a fugitive."

Up ahead, the road veered towards the right, the curved asphalt concealed by a fresh throng of trees growing out from beyond the normal line.

"House is up around the corner, then down a few more streets," Stepan said.

"Then talk fast," Rosa replied. "Or I will knock your ass out and bring you in."

Federov stopped walking, reaching out, and grasping Rosa's left shoulder. He squeezed gently, and she took the hint, halting her forward progress.

"I don't know if you know this, but Mitchell Capozza is a criminal."

Rosa looked at him. "I figured he did some questionable things, but criminal seems extreme."

"It's not. He's been bribing and paying his way to the top for decades, and now that it's become clear his normal methods aren't getting him far enough, he's ratcheted it up even more."

"Bribery? Is that what this is about?"

"It goes much further than that," Federov replied. "I've heard stories. Families being forced out. Perpetuated violence on the streets to raise crime rates simply to draft more beneficial business deals."

"What?" Rosa asked. "Like actual violence?"

Federov nodded. "Actual violence. Email exchanges cataloged and identified, then corroborated with newspaper stories. Bank transactions."

"And you have proof of all this?"

"Gigabytes worth. I was the Director of Information Technology for Capital Industries for five years."

"Jesus."

"Yeah. I'm ashamed to say I looked the other direction for most of those five years. Until I couldn't."

Rosa leaned to the side, peeking around the bushes and looking down towards the large, two-story house sitting at the end of the street, wide and tall and costing more money than she'd make in fifty years.

"So, you have evidence?"

Federov nodded but said nothing.

"Look," Rosa said, "I know you have no reason to trust me. I know you have every reason to doubt me. I can't tell you to feel any different. I'm a stranger to you and the smart thing would be for you to tell me to go to hell and move on."

Federov looked at her through narrow eyes, seemingly unmoved by her argument.

"You've got to think of your son," she said. "Consider your options. Mainly the fact that you don't have any options. I am your one and best."

"I understand," he replied. "I do. I get it. I just don't particularly like it."

"You don't have to like it, but if I'm going to help you, I need to know what you know, or I'm going to stumble into something that will get us all killed."

Federov nodded reluctantly, but finally spoke. "There's an external hard drive hidden in the house. I need to get that and my son and get the hell out of Dodge."

"I told you I'd help get your son," Rosa replied. "I still have a contract to worry about here."

"Jesus Christ," Federov replied. "He will kill me."

"Watch out," Rosa whispered, pressing her palm to his chest and pushing him back. A car came up the street, headlights splashing across the sidewalk just as they backed into the bushes behind them. It rolled slowly by, then passed down the road, not even turning.

Rosa released the breath she'd been holding and stepped back out onto the sidewalk, Federov close behind her. She jerked her head towards the house as a signal they should continue.

They took several steps before she spoke again.

"So what does your ex-wife think about all of this?" she asked. She knew how this conversation was going to go, she was painfully aware, but felt compelled to have it anyway. In spite of everything she knew was about to happen, she felt that spark of optimism flare inside, a low and flickering candlelight, battling against the breeze.

"Uh, she died," Federov replied. "Over ten years ago."

"Oh," Rosa replied quietly. "Sorry." And with those words, the candle blew out, a snuff of wind snapping the weak flame into smoke and ash.

He didn't reply, he just picked up his pace slightly walking towards the house and Rosa had to quicken her own to keep up. The house grew larger ahead of them, Rosa realizing just how big it really was, taking up a lot that was likely meant for two smaller houses. The driveway extended up towards a two-car garage, and a dark van was parked in the driveway. It was a white house with an ornate front porch, lined with two rows of windows, most of them with the curtains pulled. Nice, plush bushes littered the front lawn and larger, equally full and elaborate trees flanked the backyard, creating a natural, beautiful perimeter, cast in the low light of moonlight.

Stepan Federov stopped walking, his momentum halted on the sidewalk as he looked out towards the house. He held his hand out, palm facing Rosa as an indication to stop.

"What is it?" she asked.

Federov didn't continue forward, but he did shuffle slightly to the right, shrouding himself in the trees to the right of the sidewalk. Rosa repeated the motion, more than a little concerned about his sudden decision to conceal himself.

"Stepan!" she barked in a barely hushed whisper.

His head snapped around. "Sorry." He turned again and looked back towards the house. "That's not their van."

Rosa's eyes narrowed, focused on the vehicle in the parking lot. She couldn't quite make out the license plate and couldn't tell if anyone was actually sitting inside. Looking over the large house, she noticed again that the curtains were all drawn over every one of the countless windows, and that the lights were on in almost every room in the house.

"Who owns this place?" she asked.

"It belongs to my uncle. An uncle on my side, not my wife's. An uncle the Russians don't know. My father was from Russia, my mother was born in the United States. This is her brother's house."

Rosa dropped to a knee, supporting herself with one hand and trying to get a good angle on the house. She looked at the curtain-covered windows, trying to visualize what might be happening behind them, but no shapes moved and nothing was visible.

Purely by instinct, she reached behind her to the small of her back but felt only empty air instead of the familiar contour of her Ruger in its slim, leather holster.

"Crap," she whispered.

Federov kneeled down next to her. "What do you think?"

"I think your son and your uncle might be in deep trouble."

Federov stood, pressing his palms to his head. "No, no, no, no," he stammered over and over again. "Why did I do this? Why? I should have just ignored it. Why did I open this can of worms?"

Rosa stood and turned, placing a calming hand on the man's shoulder. "Relax. Don't make a scene. Be quiet and let me think."

Federov paced nervously back and forth, taking quick, ragged breaths, on the verge of hyperventilating, the sound escalating in the cool air around them.

Rosa turned back towards him. "Okay. Calm down. Stay here, okay? I'm going to go check some things out. I'll be back."

"What are you going to do?" Federov asked anxiously. "Don't do anything risky."

Rosa shook her head. "I won't do anything that puts your boy in danger, I promise. I'm just going to go check something out, okay? That's it."

Federov nodded, his head bobbing with a rapid, unconscious rhythm.

Rosa patted him lightly on the leg but stayed low to the ground and propelled herself across the paved road at a low run, her feet quietly scuffing across the pavement. Within seconds, she was at the black van, pulling herself upright and pressing her shoulders flat against the edged surface of the back of the van, the cool metal smooth through the thin material of her shirt. Glancing down, she looked at the license plate and confirmed it was from the state of Connecticut, which only seemed to reinforce concerns that it might have been sent here by the Russians. She couldn't hear any noises coming from the house, but there was a very low pattern of dance music that seemed to be coming from the van itself, a mildly thumping bass she could feel against her back, even if she couldn't hear it clearly.

She shuffled to her right, keeping tight to the van, then leaned around the corner of the vehicle, looking up the driveway, but nobody was there. Dropping low, she duck-walked along the side of the van, looking up into the driver's side rearview mirror, seeing if she could get an angle on the person in the driver's seat if there was someone. She took another step, then another, her shoulder staying tight to the metal, her body moving slowly and silently alongside the blind surface of the vehicle, which sat between her and the main section of the house.

Extending her arm, she latched her fingers into the handle of the car door.

This could go one of three ways. She could either try and open it and would find that it was locked, and this whole thing could be blown wide open. Or it could be unlocked, and she could move just fast enough to pull this off.

Or it could be unlocked, and she wouldn't be quite fast enough, and the thing would be blown wide open anyway.

She promised nothing would happen to Federov's son. In her heart, she believed the Russians held family very close and if his wife was truly a member of the Russian mob's family, they would never hurt her only child.

Her orphaned child.

Inside the stroller, a baby screamed.

Rosa closed her eyes and sucked in a quiet breath. Not here. Not now. Push past that. This isn't the time or the place.

She could feel her heart racing, the thumping beat accelerating to the point where her breath caught and sweat started forming at the base of her neck. The panic was starting to slowly set in. The sharp knife of fear digging deep into her lungs, rooting around, digging into her insides. She was going to lose her cool if she didn't act fast.

Curling her fingers, Rosa drew in another deep, steady breath then hooked and lifted in one smooth, swift motion. The door handle popped open and the latch released, the driver's side door easing open.

"What the hell?" the thick, accented voice said from inside the van. Just as his head turned, Rosa moved in, launching from a crouch into a swiveling spin, reaching into the van and locking her fists around the loose cloth of the man's jacket. With the van parked, he had unhooked his seat belt, and when she pulled, her momentum managed to drag him from the seat, his eyes widening in a way that would have been funny had her life, and the lives of others, not depended on it.

Continuing her spin, she hurled him over her bent hip, slamming him down back first on the paved driveway, his lips bursting open and his eyes flying shut. He coughed out one ragged exclamation that Rosa couldn't understand, but then she moved in and drilled her elbow into his forehead, pinning his cranium between bone and concrete with a dull *crack*. After one swift strike, he lay still. Rosa hefted herself over his prone body, looking back into the rest of the van, hoping nobody else was inside. Blessedly, the vehicle was empty, and her racing heart settled.

Not wasting any time, she grasped him around his arm pits and dragged him from where he was, softly kicking the door shut and maneuvering him towards the back of the van, then shoving him backwards into an awkward seated position, leaning back against the metal hide of the vehicle, his head lolling to one side.

She rifled through his coat, and her fingers closed around a trademark piece of molded rubber and smiling, she pulled out an automatic pistol, a Glock 19 by the looks. In a few quick moves, she popped out the magazine and checked the rounds, verifying that it was fully loaded with one in the chamber ready to rock.

But was she ready to rock? Was she prepared to storm into the house with a loaded pistol and risk the life of an eleven-year-old boy? This van was a decent size, there could be five or six people in that house. What the hell was she getting herself into.

Walking around the van, Rosa signaled to Stepan to come over, but stay low to the ground. He obeyed, shuffling across the street on bent knees, half-running and half-stumbling awkwardly until he came to a stop just behind the van, joining her and the unconscious

Russian beside her. His eyes fixated on her right hand, clutched around the Glock she'd retrieved from the Russian van driver.

"What the hell are you going to do?" he asked in a hushed whisper. "My son is in there! My aunt and uncle are in there!"

Rosa looked at him through narrowed eyes. "You don't want to hear this, Stepan, but chances are your aunt and uncle are already dead."

His eyes grew wide, and his lips quivered slightly.

"Your son, the Russians are very much about family. If your wife is...if your wife was a member of their family, they'll treat your son that way, too. I don't believe his life is in danger."

"It will be if you storm in there and start shooting up the place!"

"That's not the plan."

"Then what the hell do you have that thing for?"

Rosa leaned to her right in a crouch, peering around the side of the vehicle, then turned back towards him. "I need to protect myself."

"Jesus," Federov muttered, shaking his head. "Jesus, Jesus, Jesus. Why did I do this?"

Rosa pressed a palm to his shoulder. "Because it was the right thing to do. Don't forget that."

"If something happens to my son—"

"Nothing will," Rosa said. "I'm going to go in there, and I'm going to grab that hard drive, and grab your kid, and I'll be back in fifteen minutes."

"Then what happens?" Federov asked, looking at her closely. "You turn me over to Capozza? Hang us out to dry?"

The truth was Rosa hadn't thought that far ahead. In her mind, this case was pretty open and shut. Capozza was paying her to bring Federov in, she was going to bring Federov in. It wasn't her problem.

Even knowing her history with his family. Even knowing what had happened to his wife, she honestly thought she could hand him over with a clean conscience and not think twice. She closed her eyes for a moment, picturing the numbers in the contract. Thinking for a minute about how that could potentially change her life. Get her a new office, or even better, score herself an actual apartment. The number on that contract was life changing.

But was it worth a life ending?

She clenched her fingers around the handle of the pistol and rested her thumb on the safety. The weapon felt heavy, but well balanced in her firm grasp. While she preferred her Ruger these days, she'd certainly spent plenty of time around the Glock and was more than comfortable with that pistol. She suspected she was just about to find out exactly how comfortable she truly felt.

"Fifteen minutes," she reiterated, nodding towards him. "Stay here. Do not move, no matter what. I will come to you."

He nodded. "There's a door in the back of the garage. It's always unlocked. You can get into the house from there."

"Anything else?"

"Garage is attached to a kitchen, which opens up to a large living area. Big television set. Hallway from the living room leads to three rooms on the other side, two guest bedrooms, and an office."

"Thanks."

Federov nodded, and she nodded back, then rose to a half-crouch, twisted around the corner of the van, and charged towards the garage. Slipping just to the left of the house, she ran close to the side wall, halting near the rear corner. Taking a moment to pause, she leaned around the corner and verified that nobody was lurking around back there, then pushed forward, half-running, half-crouching towards a narrow rear door.

As she reached it, she tested the doorknob, which turned freely in her hand, then she pushed it open and slunk inside, dropping low in the darkened room, pressing herself back into a corner to let her eyes get adjusted. Crouching low, she drew in deep, regular breaths, calming her nerves. She had certainly faced more daunting odds in Afghanistan, but that felt like a long time ago and in a whole different world. She also had backup and there wasn't an innocent eleven-year-old boy at the mercy of her actions.

Closing her eyes, she focused on what she could hear, which wasn't much. The low rattle of some random television show echoed from within the house, the volume up just a little bit loud, but no surrounding conversation could be heard. Steady pressure was audible with the occasional creak of floorboards, some coming from up above her and deeper towards the inside of the house. She pictured the house in her mind and saw the two floors, with a row of four windows looking out over the front lawn. From the sounds of the floorboards, there was at least someone on that second floor, probably near the front of the house.

She leaned slightly and wrapped her hand around the doorknob, then twisted and pressed slowly forward, easing the door open into a small, square mud room, lined with pale gray granite tile. Moving into the mudroom with the Glock held towards the floor, she pushed the door closed behind her with a quiet click. The television was louder inside the house, and the creaking floorboards were even more audible above her. Rosa took careful steps into the house, her practiced feet balancing cautiously as she moved, step overstep, pistol clutched between two firm hands, arms locked in a straight line. She looked through the quiet, dark kitchen and the living room beyond was fully lit, the wide screen television set sitting on a stand in the far corner with some random show on display.

Her eyes passed over it, roaming to other corners of the wide living room, the floor covered in thick white carpeting, a long, pale couch taking up much of the floor space, flanked by a pair of recliners. She could see where the wall split into a hallway across the floor, but the hallway was dark and no shadows moved inside. In spite of this, she walked gingerly across the floor, navigating around the couch and between one of the recliners, walking in a straight line towards the hall. To her left, near the rear of the house, a set of stairs ran to the top level and again, as she moved forward, a floorboard creaked above her head. Beyond the gibberish on the television, she hadn't heard a single voice. Progressing down the hallway, she slowly peeked in each room, verifying that nothing moved inside. Once she had investigated each one in darkness, she flipped on a light in the office, which was the farthest room down the hall. Bookshelves lined the wall, and a dark wood desk sat facing the door with an ancient looking Macintosh computer perched on top. On its face, things looked completely ordinary, but as she stepped forward, the distinctive smell of spent blood tinged her nostrils. It had a unique and familiar soaked copper smell, and when she stepped around the desk, she saw the man crumpled on the floor in an almost fetal position. For the first time, she saw that the books behind the desk had been splattered in a wide arc of crimson, and it appeared as if the man had been shot in the forehead as he sat at his desk, spinning back and tumbling out of the chair, likely dead before he even hit the ground.

"Dammit," she whispered to herself. Judging by the man's age, she figured he must have been the uncle. Stepan was going to take this one hard. Rosa turned off the light and exited the office, looking both ways, her weapon facing the floor. Veering right she eased her way into one the guest bedrooms and flipped on the light, but the room was completely empty. She walked around the bed, weapon at the ready, but the floor was empty and the room quiet.

Turning off the light, she crept across the hall and into the second bedroom, reaching in and flipping on the light switch there. The scatter spray of red across the white blanket struck her like a fist, and she took a step backwards, turning away slightly at the stark difference in color painted before her. Taking careful steps into the room, she walked around the bed and saw the older woman face down on the floor on the other side of the wide bed. A thick collection of red blood was pooled underneath her, already mostly soaked into the carpeted floor, both arms splayed out at odd angles.

Rosa closed her eyes and shook her head, turning away to walk towards the door, weapon still aimed at the floor. She turned off the light and slipped out of the room, her eyes scanning the living room again.

"Who the hell are you?" the voice took her completely by surprise. Rosa snapped her head up and swung it around, and across the living room, a man was exiting the stairwell, his foot falls muffled by the thick carpet of the stairs. He was tall and wide, his hair not much more than thick stubble. His voice was slow and steady, but soaked with a distinctive accent, and as he started reaching into his loose coat, Rosa jerked her arms up, the pistol cradled in a two-handed grasp.

"Don't do it," she said.

He froze, his fingers slightly opened near the shoulder holster he had revealed.

"I'm a good shot," Rosa said in a quiet voice.

"Everyone in the house will hear it," he replied, choosing his words carefully.

"I can live with that."

"Gregor, what is going on?" a second voice asked, and Rosa shifted. The man started coming down the stairs, another tall and broad-shouldered man with dirty blond hair.

"What the hell?" he asked, his eyes widening when he saw her.

Rosa twisted and pointed the pistol at him, then shifted and pointed it back at Gregor, trying to keep them both covered.

"How many others are here?" she demanded. "Where are they?"

"You dumb woman!" the man at the top of the stairs replied. "You cannot cover us both."

Gregor, standing at the bottom of the staircase jerked, thrusting his hand deeper into his coat and clutching at the pistol that was inches from his fingers. Rosa shifted, but the man already had the pistol in his hand and was pulling it up into firing position.

Instinct took over. Rosa twitched right and squeezed the trigger, double tap, pumping two rounds into his center mass. Gunshots echoed loudly in the quiet house, and the man tumbled backwards, hitting the stair rail with his lower back, and tipping over backwards, spilling off the stairs clumsily. As he fell, Rosa lunged to the right, gunfire echoing from the top of the stairwell, blasting tufts of carpeting up into the air at her feet.

"Jorge! I'm here to help!" she shouted above the gunshots, then planted her foot and turned, lifting the weapon and squeezing off a trio of shots towards the shape at the top of the stairs.

Pungent smoke filled the air, and she backpedaled towards the hallway, the man on the second level adjusting his aim and firing again. Plaster and paint exploded from the wall to her left as four round holes punctured the surface, rippling out through spider web cracks. Pale chips of dried paint scattered across the floor as Rosa pressed herself tight to the wall of the hallway, aimed and fired another three shots. Her stolen pistol had fifteen rounds, and by her count she had fired eight, so she would have to be careful. Up at the stop of the stairs, the tall man drew back behind a wall, which burst apart under her brief but aggressive barrage. Taking advantage of the momentary reprieve of return fire, she surged forward, running across the floor and towards the stairwell. She leaped up three steps in one jump and as the man at the top came around from cover to return fire, she had already drawn within six feet of him, her pistol lifted and centered on his torso. He gasped in surprise, tried to compensate for her new location, but three shots struck him in the upper chest and carried him backwards until he slammed against the wall behind him, exhaled, and slumped to the floor.

Still running up the stairs, Rosa reached up and grasped the waist high wall at the top and jumped, vaulting cleanly over it, twisting, and landing on the second floor in a low crouch, her pistol at the ready. The second floor was silent.

"Jorge?" she called out in a soft voice. "Come on out, Jorge, I'm a friend!"

She walked forward, crossing one foot over the other and staying low, looking down the wide hallway ahead of her. It led all the way down to the other end of the house, with rooms scattered upon each side.

Setting one more step ahead a blur of motion caught her eye, and she spun, her finger touching the trigger. She drew in her breath and tensed every muscle in her arms, hands, and fingers, the pistol leveled and straight, homed in on the swiftly moving shape.

Jorge's eyes went wide and his hands lifted. "Behind me!" he shouted quickly.

Rosa twisted.

"You little jerk!" a large man lunged from the room, arms outstretched and reaching for the young boy. Rosa pulled the trigger twice, but he lurched left, letting the two bullets smash into the doorframe behind him. Lunging forward, he barreled into Rosa, knocking her backwards, then as she scrambled to the ground, he slipped a long combat knife from a sheath, flipping it around into an attack position.

"You bring gun to a knife fight, little girl. Sam, he doesn't play with guns!" Sam charged, arcing his knife strike, and Guzman barely backed away, wincing as the blade nicked her left arm. She glanced behind her, pushing Jorge gently backwards against the bed, then leaped back towards Sam the knife streaking, missing her stomach by inches.

"Sam, you're pretty good with that thing," Rosa said, sliding to the left to avoid another stab. The Russian twisted and hacked back towards her but missed again.

His lips curled and he hissed, charging towards her, his massive bulk barging through the doorway. Rosa turned aside and the man plowed face-first into a mirror mounted on the wall, shattering the glass. Grunting and shouting, he stumbled back and she moved forward, hacking at his wrist, knocking the knife away.

"No you don't!" he yelled at her and whirled a ham-sized fist in a straight jab, but she was already ducking underneath the strike and sweeping the knife from the thick carpet. As his arm passed over her, she arced up and left with the blade, burying it deep behind his left pectoral muscle. Shouting, he stumbled backwards, reaching for the handle of the knife, his fingers flexing, but he never quite got a hold of it before the life left him and he toppled to the carpeted hallway beyond the bedroom.

Rosa looked back at her other hand, still clutching the pistol and looked at the young boy, his face a mask of fear and confusion.

"Don't look at him," she said quietly, stepping between the dead Russian and the young boy. "How many others?"

His lips quivered, but he didn't answer. She gestured towards him hurriedly, telling him to run towards her, and he jumped from the rug and hurtled her way.

"Don't move!" the voice came from down the hall and two more men appeared, their own pistols in hand. Rosa scooped up Jorge around his waist and lifted him, nearly tossing him over the waist high wall at the top of the stairs. Depositing him on the carpeted stairwell, she watched him scramble down the stairs as she ducked low, barely avoiding a cascade of gunfire shattering the stairwell wall just ahead of her. From her almost kneeling position she squeezed off a burst of return fire while shuffling backwards, then curling around the wall and charging down the stairs herself as more blasts echoed behind her.

"Run, Jorge! Go out through the garage!"

He turned and dashed through the kitchen, Rosa close behind as footsteps crashed down the stairwell after them. Bursting through the door into the garage, the young boy turned right, opened the back door and ran out onto the grass, Rosa coming up next to him in a clumsy backwards shuffle, pistol raised and ready.

"Stepan!" she screamed into the night air. "Start the van!"

One of the Russians emerged, and she fired twice before her weapon clicked empty. He jerked backwards, but the bullets slammed off the door frame, careening out into the darkness.

"Damn!" she shouted, then turned and ran around the house, charging towards the van. She could see the vague shape of Federov in the driver's seat, fiddling with the ignition. To her left, the garage door began to slide open.

"Get in, Jorge!" she shouted. "Quick, quick!"

The boy yanked open the passenger door, then threw himself inside, scrambling between the front seats to work his way towards the back. The garage door rose up halfway and one of the gunmen ducked down, slipping under the door and out into the driveway. He lifted his pistol and fired, and Rosa instinctively dashed left, bullets crashing into the metal surface of the van just to her right, sparks dancing in a strange haphazard gait.

Grabbing the door with her free hand, Rosa yanked, pulling herself around and nearly throwing herself inside as two more shots banged off the door and a third shattered the window, but managed to miss everyone.

"Gun it!" she shouted, barely holding on to the side of the van, still trying to pull the door closed behind her. Stepan slammed the van into reverse, cranked the steering wheel, and send the large black vehicle hurtling backwards, narrowly missing the unconscious form of the former driver lying prone in the driveway. More shots crashed against the front of the van, the short-sloped hood, and the metal grill, but amid the blasting sparks of ricochets, the boxy vehicle spun around and surged forward, leaving the large house behind.

"My aunt and uncle?" Stepan asked frantically, his head lowered as two more metallic bangs echoed near the van's rear.

"I'm sorry," Rosa replied. She didn't need to say any more.

Stepan's head whipped towards her. "What about the hard drive? Did you get the hard drive?"

Rosa's eyes went wide. She had been so focused on Jorge that she hadn't thought to grab anything else. The crushing weight of disappointment settled in her chest, and she leaned back against the passenger seat, a deep and thick fog overcoming her.

"I've got it, dad."

She whipped her head to the left. Jorge was leaning in from the backseat and holding a strange black shape in his left hand.

"I kept it safe like you said."

"Good boy," Stepan replied. "That's my good boy." Rosa could see the glistening of tears in his eyes just starting to form, a look of unadulterated pride on his face.

She wanted to feel good about it. She desperately wanted to sit in the passenger seat, safe and sound, and be happy.

But she couldn't. She could pretend to be, but she wouldn't be. Yes, she might have saved the boy's life, but he still had no mother and Stepan Federov still had no wife.

Dalia Federov was dead, and Rosa had killed her, and whatever she did from now on would never, ever change that fact.

CHAPTER 29

"What?" Vasily Sokolov asked, barking into the phone in his hand. "Are you kidding me with this?"

Sitting at his desk, he looked over the small office. It sat empty except for his large frame at the desk, which seemed a size or two too small for the large man. He pushed himself to a standing position, the curled cord of the phone handset pulling taught.

"We just found him! Now we lost him again?" He listened for a moment, shaking his head softly. "You say it was a girl? A girl did this? Capozza's fucking girl? I'll cut his fucking head off and put it on my wall."

Vasily nodded as the man on the other end of the phone spoke.

"I got it. We'll send out the hounds."

He set the handset down and pressed the intercom button.

"We need all hands on deck, got it? Leave one man down there. The rest of you, meet me in my office."

Sokolov lowered himself back down into his chair, pressing his fingers together.

CHAPTER 30

Chuck's shoulders were aching, but not as much as his ribs. He lay prone on the concrete floor of the basement, his entire body sore from the previous beating. Looking up around him the collection of four rugged looking Russians had been a persistent presence over the past several hours, but he'd heard some kind of announcement in the speaker system down here in the basement and now some of them looked to be packing up to leave.

The floor was filthy and uneven, as if a pile of loosely packed rocks had been poured over with cheap cement, and the walls were a grimy, gray slate. Exposed pipes ran along the ceiling, several of them dripping regular spatters of water down onto the rough floor. Crates and boxes were stacked around, especially wedged into the darkened corners. Only a few well-placed dangling light bulbs lit the small room and Chuck could barely make out the different men roaming around. One thing was clear, though, most of those roaming men were separating from the group and heading to the metal door which led to the staircase they had brought him down a few hours ago.

Murmured voices spoke from one of the far corners, the men all gathered to talk about something, then four of the five men peeled away, opened the door, and vanished up the stairwell, leaving Chuck laying on the floor with a single guard ten feet away. He lifted his head slightly, looking over at the last man remaining, a dark-haired brute of a guy, a good stack over six feet tall, wearing a blue shirt stretched over bulging muscle. He wore no jacket, content to have the shoulder holster pulled tight over his barrel chest, fully revealing the automatic pistol stuffed inside. His rounded face was covered in a thick, dark beard and as soon as his friends left, he turned and walked over near to where Chuck lay.

"You awake, asshole?" he asked. Chuck lay still. "Hey!" he shouted, jabbing the steel toe of a thick boot into Chuck's ribs.

Chuck groaned and curled tight.

"Your little bitch friend messed with the wrong people," the man growled. "You'll be seeing her soon, when you're both in hell."

Chuck stirred a little, his eyes opening and sliding so he could see the man better. His muscles tensed as he slightly adjusted his position on the floor.

The Russian noticed. "What are you doing, huh? You scrawny little puke. You going to try something with me?" Crouching down low, the massive man with tree trunk legs rested his elbows on his knees and sneered at the prone form of Chuck Heath. "You think now that I'm the only one here that maybe you can take me?"

Chuck curled tighter, bringing his knees up into his chest and groaning, but shifted his weight, just a little.

"I think maybe my kid sister, she hits harder than you."

Chuck mumbled something.

"What's that?" the Russian asked, leaning in.

Chuck turned slightly, glaring up at him. "You want to find out?"

"I'll break you," the large man replied, but he remained crouched. Meanwhile, Chuck had shifted his weight to his right hip, lifting his left leg slightly off the ground. As the man leaned forward, he torqued his hips and swept his left leg up in a tight, swift arc. His sneakered foot slammed the Russian in the right cheek, whipping his head painfully to the left. Continuing the momentum of his own leg sweep, Chuck spun around on his shoulders, twirled, and struggled to come up onto his feet in a haggard fighting stance. Swift stabs of sharp pain dug at his side, slowing his movements.

With barely a hesitation, the guard recovered and lunged towards him, lips parted, his white teeth visible through specs of blood in his gums and on his lips.

"That's the last mistake you'll ever make!"

He swung a massive fist in a straight piston, but Chuck was already sliding to the left, sending the punch just past his right shoulder, glancing harmlessly. The skinny man followed up with a rocket left to the Russian's jaw, then launched a right haymaker deep into the large man's solar plexus, knocking the wind from his considerable lungs. Stumbling slightly, the man in the blue shirt recovered quickly and charged forward again, but Chuck was still well-prepared.

He stepped into his charge, his leg coiled, then released, slamming a heel into the side of the man's knee. It didn't break, but it jarred clumsily to the left, sending him sprawling forward, and Chuck countered the forward momentum with another vicious right punch, catching him under the chin. His head snapped back, and he toppled backwards, hands clutching for some kind of nonexistent handhold to stop his fall. As he was hitting the ground, both shoulders slamming against solid concrete, Chuck was already leaping above him and running across the uneven floor of the basement towards the door. Even as the Russian rolled over and screamed after him, his muscular legs had carried him up the stairwell, to the right, and out the back door into the grass. Moonlight was still the only source of illumination and it took him a quick second to get his bearings, but he saw his car sitting in the parking lot, one of only a few left, and he took off towards it, his feet sliding slightly on the wet grass. Behind him he heard the exit door slam open.

"Stop!" shouted the Russian, his voice somewhat muffled with his swollen lips. Chuck didn't stop.

Two gunshots rang out swift and sharp, and as he ran, he thought he heard the distinct whine of passing bullets, but he couldn't tell how close they'd come. All he knew was that his car was only twenty yards away, and then he was right there on top of it. Skidding to his knees on the gravel driveway, he reached into his shoe for a spare key and as three more shots sprang off the hood amid a series of bright sparking ricochets, he threw open the door and lunged inside. Slamming the key into the ignition, he fired up the sedan, threw it into reverse and throttled backwards out of his space even as more shots pounded into the American steel of the vehicle.

Moments later, ducked in the driver's seat, Chuck guided the car out of the lot, squinting through swollen eyes, and drove towards the highway to head back home.

CHAPTER 31

It would be great to hear Katie Godsoe's voice again. One of the few constants from her time in Afghanistan, Katie G. had been an intelligence analyst that Rosa had spent a considerable amount of time with, both in her infantry position as well as her role in Military Police and security. In a war full of men, Rosa gravitated towards the other females, and in Katie she found a connection. For years they spoke almost every day, talked about life, love, the Army. Everything. Rosa was always hesitant to call someone a friend, because every time she did, they vanished. Yet, she had considered Katie a friend, though to be fair, it was more a friend of convenience, and she relished their conversations in ways that she did for few others. They'd touched base a few months ago on an especially hairy situation, and Rosa had found out that Katie was working with the National Security Agency out of an office in central Massachusetts. They hadn't had a chance to get together again since then, but the more Rosa thought about all of the moving pieces for this case, the more she thought Katie needed to be involved. As the image of Katie faded from her mind, the grayscale memories began working their way in from the corners. Fresh and raw, they came to her again as if she had just dreamt them moments ago instead of in the dead of night.

She could never quite remember how long it took before she got the word. Was it weeks? Months? Had it been years?

As always with these memories, everything came back to her in various shades of gray. No longer living on the streets with the Blades, Rosa was now an inhabitant of the Springfield Juvenile Reform Institute, a sterile and bland building that was better than prison, though not much. She shared a room with two other girls and while she was allowed some moderate freedoms, compared to life on the streets, she might as well have been behind bars.

She'd followed the case religiously. Switch had been accused of negligent homicide in the death of Dalia Federov, a young mother who did have family connections to the Russian mob, but on that particular day was just an innocent bystander taking a walk with her young baby in a stroller. She had planned to meet with her cousin and walk with him when he left his first shift job, then have dinner with him and his family. Her husband at the time was a network engineer for a local technical services company and was working a weekend shift so rather than stay in the house alone, she was going to spend some time with family.

But a gang ambush broke out, and she was caught in the crossfire.

Police confirmed that the .320 caliber pistol that was found clutched in Switch's hand was the murder weapon, and he confessed to attempting to defend himself when one of the Russians shot him in the leg and threatened to kill him. Switch's entire defense was built around the fact that he was only trying to defend himself, but the overwhelming evidence that the Blades had started the ambush to begin with was just too much for the defense lawyer to overcome, not that he tried all that hard.

Switch was sent away. Sent away for a long time, and Rosa more or less got off. She was sentenced to two years in juvenile detention for her potential role in the ambush, but essentially escaped clean and clear, a fact that had weighed on her, even at that young age. She went to bed every night with the memory of firing the weapon etched in her mind. The vision of Dalia Federov laying in the street, draped under a pile of her own clothes, a lifeless shell where a vibrant young mother used to be.

And from the stroller a baby screamed.

It had taken less than a year, of that fact she was certain. Razor came to see her. She was allowed certain visitation rights, and Razor came during one of those Wednesday windows to visit, starting off with some small talk first.

How was she doing? What was it like in here? Did she have any plans for after she got out?

Oh, and by the way, the Russians ambushed Switch in prison and stabbed him 23 times.

Switch was dead. Less than a year behind bars and the Russians had gotten to him.

It was her fault.

He was like a brother to her, the only mentor she ever had in her life, the only person in the world who had ever truly cared for her. The only person who would have even considered sacrificing something for her. And Switch had sacrificed everything.

He had to have known. He had to have been aware that the death of an innocent family member of the Russian mob would solicit fatal vengeance, yet still he grabbed the pistol from Rosa's uncertain hand and made sure his fingerprints were the only ones that could ever be found on it. He saved her future and likely saved her life with that one move.

Rosa looked at Razor as he delivered the news, a vacant, wide-eyed stare, not quite comprehending what he was saying. Was this real life? Was she really just stuck in this glorified college dorm while Switch had laid in a concrete tomb, bleeding out from twenty-three stab wounds. So not only was the death of Dalia Federov on her conscience, but so was the death of the only real family member she'd ever known? How would she ever live with that?

Somehow, she had.

Somehow, here, over ten years later, she was still breathing. Still living.

If you could call it that.

She wasn't sure she could call it that, but she did. Breathing was living, and she was breathing, that much was true. She woke up every morning, she went through the motions, she did all the things a living person should be doing.

But was this life?

Was the weight of two deaths on your soul truly living?

And if she did manage to save the dead woman's son and her husband, would that somehow fix what had already been done?

Would she even be able to save them?

Should she?

Their lives had been ruined already, thanks to her and the Blades. Nothing would ever be the same. How much value was she really adding by extending their lives at this point? Should she just turn them in, collect the contract money and move on to the next job?

How could she?

Stepan and Jorge were innocents. Even worse, Stepan was trying to stop a criminal from dramatically impacting the lives of other innocents, how could Rosa even think of doing anything to stop that from happening?

That contract, though. The money there could change her life. But what kind of money was it? How dirty? How soaked with blood? If she took the job, took the contract, and blinded herself to the fate of these two people, was she really any better than Capozza himself? Mitchell Capozza, a complete and total slumlord piece of crap. Was she just as bad as he was?

No, no she wasn't. Not anymore. Part of her thought the Army had fixed that. It had beaten that selfishness out of her. Made her a better person.

Not better enough to stay in the Army forever, but maybe just better enough? What did that even mean?

She'd killed an innocent woman. Someone else had taken the blame, and that someone else was dead, too. How could she even dream of rectifying that? What chance did she ever have of living a normal life with that kind of guilt hanging over her, glued to her, clinging to her limbs, dragging her down. Could she ever live her life again, knowing these things?

She decided she probably couldn't. But she owed Stepan and Jorge some measure of justice. Some measure of protection.

Mitchell Capozza could go screw himself. She wouldn't pile more tragedy upon the Federovs, she owed them that much, anyway.

Rosa drew in a long shaky breath, pressing her back against the metal hide of the van, her eyes lowered towards the ground. The phone was a cold slab against her ear, the rhythmic bleat of ring tone echoing from the earpiece.

"Hello?" said a tired voice on the other end.

"Katie?" Rosa asked back. "Is this Katie G.?"

"This is Katie Godsoe," the voice replied, clarifying as awakening settled over her.

"Katie, this is Rosa. Rosa Guzman."

"Goose?"

"Yeah. Goose. How have things been?"

"Good," the voice replied. "They've been good. Good to hear from you."

"Yeah, you too."

"What can I help with?"

Rosa closed her eyes, trying not to be drawn back into her past life, thrust back into the cloudy memories, not of her inner-city gang life this time, but of her time in Afghanistan. Her time serving in the military, times of complete and utter boredom book-ended by frantic life and death. She hadn't made many friends over there, and she hadn't had many good memories, but Katie Godsoe had given her both.

"You still work with the State department?" Rosa asked.

"Yeah, I do," she replied, her voice hardening on the other end. "It's only been a few months since we spoke. But I'll be honest, I'm not sure I like this train of conversation, Rosa."

"I know, Katie, I know, and I'm sorry. I'm in a bit of hot water here."

"Okay," Godsoe replied. "What do you need?"

"I need you to tell me a little bit about Vasily Sokolov. He's a regional Russian mafia leader in the northeast."

"Jesus, Rosa, what are you into?"

"Nothing good."

"Okay. I need you to give me some time with this. Can I call you back at this number?"

"Yeah, that's fine, Katie. And thank you."

"Don't thank me yet, you may not like what I've got to say. Talk to you soon."

Rosa clicked the phone off, standing in the darkness and wondering just how she got where she was and marveling at how a single stupid decision was going to control the rest of her life. The last time she'd seen Katie, she'd told her to reach out with anything she needed, but Rosa knew, deep down, that was a courtesy more than anything. She hoped what she was asking her friend to do wasn't going to cause serious issues for both of them.

CHAPTER 32

Guiding the sedan around the corner and deeper into his neighborhood, Chuck glared out through his swollen eyes. It had been an adventure navigating his way up from Hartford, though most of the travel had been on a relatively straight stretch of Interstate. He squinted at the strange car parked in the street outside his apartment building, a four-door American-made vehicle that he couldn't quite get a clear look of in the dim light of late night, which was slowly shifting into early morning.

As he neared the vehicle, the shape became clearer, not just the shape of the vehicle, but the unique attachment stretched across the roof. A bar of police lights.

"Dammit," he whispered inside his empty car as he pressed forward. From where he was, he could see the front door of the apartment building open and three darkened figures huddled there talking. Was that who he thought it was?

His headlights splashed across the trio, and he could see the vague shape of the police officer turn towards them, holding her hand over her face to block the unexpected light. Chuck pulled the car over and eased the engine off. As the headlights faded, he saw his brothers Prentiss and Travis speaking with the female officer, and the worst possible scenario ran through his mind.

"Chuck?" asked Prentiss as his older brother pushed his way out of the driver's seat, stepping out onto the sidewalk. "Is that you?"

"Yeah," Chuck replied, stepping towards them, his walk little more than a pained half-shuffle. In the darkness, his face was draped in shadow, but as he approached, he stepped into the faded circle of pale light from the streetlight above.

"What the hell!" shouted Travis, stepping forward to catch up with Prentiss. As Chuck stepped out into the light, they could see the state of his face, the thick and swollen face, shifted jaw, and twisted nose. Both eyes were swollen, the right one nearly completely shut, but the left one at least had a narrow viewpoint, the white of his eye slightly visible. His dark face was stained darker with dried blood, and the T-shirt he wore was discolored slightly around the neckline.

"You should see the other guy," Chuck replied through puffed and cracked lips. He tried to smile, but his jaw hurt too much.

The female cop stepped forward, a look of compassion on her face. "Christ, Chuck, what the hell happened?"

He realized for the first time that it was Helen Bondalewski. "It's a long story," he said, shaking his head.

"Jeez, Chuck, we were freaked out over here. We called Helen because you hadn't come home. You always come home."

Chuck stepped forward and wrapped Prentiss in a tight hug. "I'm all right, bro, okay? Rough night, but I'm okay."

"Not to interrupt this family reunion," Helen said, "but I need you to tell me what happened and who did this."

Chuck reached and grabbed Travis in his left arm as well, and in spite of his tough teenage façade, the younger brother moved into the embrace, allowing himself to be held tight.

"Nobody did it," Chuck replied. "Fell down some stairs. Smacked my face on a door. You name it, it happened. It was just a simple accident."

She glowered at him. "Dammit, Chuck, don't pull that."

"I can't talk about it, Helen, I'm sorry. Trust me."

Officer Bondalewski glanced over to his brothers, then gestured for Chuck to walk over towards the police car with her, and he obediently followed.

"Chuck, there is something going down," she whispered. "Reports of a gunfight down at a night club in Hartford, with bodies at the scene. Shots fired and at least three corpses at an upscale house in Longmeadow, like ten miles from here."

Chuck's eyes widened slightly.

"In both cases, the Russians look to be in the middle of it."

"What's that got to do with me?" Chuck asked.

"I know you and Rosa have been looking into Stepan Federov. I don't think it's a coincidence."

Chuck shrugged. "I don't know nothing about nothing," he said.

"Come on," Helen almost snarled. "If this does have something to do with you and Rosa, you're going to be dead before morning. Let us help you."

Looking at her, Chuck grimaced slightly, his nose a sudden spark of pain. But he didn't talk.

Helen shook her head. "If you are mixed up in this and the Russians find out where you live, it could be Prentiss and Travis who end up in the crossfire. Think about that for a minute."

Chuck did. In actuality, he'd been thinking about it the entire drive back up to Springfield. But he also realized that they'd never taken his wallet, they'd never looked at an identification, hell they'd never even asked his name. There was no way they could possibly know who he was or where he lived, and at this point, they were much more focused on Capozza than him. He thought his brothers were safe.

"Officer Bondalewski, I appreciate your concern," he said, trying to sound genuine. "But I believe the situation is under control."

She glared at him, an even more narrow and tighter glare than previously. "I've got a handful of dead bodies that beg to disagree, Heath. So, help me, if your brothers add to the body count, I will personally see to it that you take the rap."

"You won't have to," Chuck replied through tight lips. "If my brothers get caught in anything, it'll have to be over my dead body."

"Let's all hope not."

Helen looked at him for another few seconds, adjusting the angle of her view, checking his face all over.

"Doesn't look like anything's broken, but you should get looked at. They messed you up good."

Chuck nodded. "I'll do that."

"Call me if anything changes, you got that?"

Chuck nodded again.

"Just answer me one question," Helen said as she started to walk away. "Is Capozza mixed up in this somehow? Is this going to turn into a turf war? Because a lot of innocent people could get hurt."

Glancing around briefly, he turned his attention back to the officer directly. "One way or another, this is going to fall in Capozza's lap," he said quietly. "We don't know what yet, but something is going down. Or something has gone down."

"Do me a favor," Helen said. "Don't try to go up against him yourself. If you get evidence, bring it to the police. Let us deal with him. You and Rosa have been through enough."

"Fair deal."

Officer Bondalewski nodded and turned away, walking towards the police car. She tipped her hat, slipped in the driver's seat and, moments later, was nothing more than two fading red taillights in the darkness.

CHAPTER 33

The phone blared in the darkness of Mitchell Capozza's bedroom, an elaborate and lavishly decorated master, with a king-sized bed, an ornate mahogany dresser and deep red velvet curtains to block out the outside world.

Struggling to pull himself from slumber, Capozza rolled to his right, tangled up in the sheets and blankets, working to free himself and reach the end table where the handset shrilled like an angry bird. Lunging across the covers, he grasped the handset and thumbed the answer button, rolling back over and pulling the handset to his ear.

"Hello?" he asked, his voice thick and slow with sleep.

"Mr. Capozza," the voice said on the other end.

"Pietro?"

"Yes, sir."

"What time is it?"

"Sir, there was an incident at the club tonight. At the Russian's place."

Capozza pressed his head back into the lush pillow, tightening his eyes further. He remembered now.

"What happened?" he asked, not really wanting to know but

feeling like he had to ask.

"They didn't take kindly to our line of questioning. Connected the dots with us and Guzman pretty quickly."

Capozza pushed himself up to his elbows, his eyes opening. "Okay?"

"They opened fire on us, sir."

His eyes widened, and he levered himself even more upright, swinging his legs up and around, sitting upright on the bed. "What did you say?"

"They fired on us. Winston is dead, sir."

"Jesus Christ!"

"Jerome and I made it out okay, but we've been driving back roads for the past ninety minutes to make sure we weren't being tailed."

"Why would they do this?"

"I don't know, sir. Federov is a hot commodity from the sounds of things."

"God dammit! Are the police involved?"

"I don't see how they couldn't be. There were dozens of people in the club at the time."

Capozza sighed deeply, closing his eyes again. "Okay. Come back. We'll regroup and decide what to do next."

"We're on the way back now, Mr. Capozza."

"Good. I'll let the gate know. See you soon." Capozza clicked the phone dead and sat on the bed, staring out into the darkened room. Selectman Gregg's voice resonated in his ears, the vague threat for funding and the reality of his situation. The Russians were undoubtedly angry. Did they know Capozza had initiated this inquiry?

Placing his hands on his knees, he stood shakily to his feet, looking at the clock and shaking his head. Rage was boiling inside of him, a barely covered pot of red water, the lid rattling and shaking, threatening to spill over. He clenched his fists tight, veins bulging in his forearms, his eyes squinting closed so tight they pulled at the skin on his forehead. His teeth hurt with his anger, but he kept it inside, he didn't let it out. He would have to soon.

CHAPTER 34

Not too far away, a dark colored van navigated some of the same streets that Officer Bondalewski patrolled on a daily basis. Through these parts of inner city Springfield, the streets were narrow and clogged with cars parked on both sides. The rundown vehicles created an artificial steel blockade between the potholed streets and the ramshackle multi-level buildings, a collection of broken infrastructure, bent metal, and hole-punched concrete that mirrored the fragile day to day life of the inhabitants of this corner of the city. Like their surroundings, their lives were often broken and only barely repaired, enough to keep moving, but not enough to truly thrive.

Rosa was behind the steering wheel now, having let Stepan take a break to spend some time with his son, and she eased the wheel to the right, taking a sharp turn down a darkened street. Standing sentry at the entrance to the dwindling road was a pair of streetlights, bulbs dim against the already dark sky, failing in their only true responsibilities.

Stepan looked up from the back seat, his eyes widening slightly.

"Where are we going?" he asked. His voice had an uneasy edge.

"To a friend's," Rosa replied, hoping that this was really true.

Around them the tall buildings looked down with dark, scornful eyes, accusing her, as if the buildings themselves knew what she had done and what it had cost them.

When Switch had gone to prison for her, it decimated the Blades. For the past ten years they'd barely been holding on, losing most of their tenuous grasp on Springfield territories and mostly withdrawing into smaller clusters. The diehards had drifted to other parts of the country to join stronger groups and Springfield itself now just housed a scattering of members, many of which blamed Switch for trying to take on the Russians and failing. Those who didn't blame Switch were angry and vengeful.

Johnny "Razor" Rodriguez was Switch's brother, and in spite of the Blades falling apart around him, he refused to leave the city that had been their home for their entire lives. For several of the last ten plus years he'd worked to try and keep their weak foothold in Springfield intact, but had mostly given up the fight. Rosa leaned forward, looking out the windshield, squinting through the low moonlight to look at the buildings on her left.

Carefully, she eased the van towards the sidewalk, managed to find a blank patch of pavement, and pulled the large, boxy vehicle into it, settling it into place just behind a torn-up Ford station wagon. The streets were empty and dark, with only a small handful of lights on in various windows in the buildings surrounding them.

"Are you sure we should be driving this van?" Stepan asked, looking around at the inside of the vehicle. "What if they have GPS? What if someone recognizes it?"

Rosa shrugged. "No OnStar," she replied, pointing to the ceiling. "This is the Russian mafia, not some global spy agency. I've been dealing with them for years, they are surprisingly low tech. Prefer to invest their money in weapons, not gadgets. Plus, we're over in gang territory here. Nobody's going to recognize us."

"If you say so," Stepan replied, then looked out his own window. "Your friend live here?" Jorge laid down in the backseat, his head resting on his father's lap.

Rosa nodded. "Last I knew, yeah."

She opened the driver's side door with a lingering squeak that sounded much louder in the quiet night and stepped out onto the sidewalk. Leaning back in, she looked at Stepan. "Lock the doors. Stay in here with your boy. I'll be right back."

"Are you sure about this?" he asked.

Rosa looked around. "Honestly? No. But we have Capozza on one side and the Russians on the other. We're kind of out of options."

Federov cast his eyes downward, looking at the face of the young boy asleep in his lap. Thinking of the faces of his aunt and uncle. "Why did I do this?" he asked the empty air inside the van.

Rosa looked at him. "Because you're a good man," she replied quietly. "We'll get through this, okay?"

The phone thrummed in her pocket, a low and persistent vibration, drawing her attention.

"Guzman," Rosa said, plucking the phone from her pocket.

"Rosa, this is Katie."

"Thanks for calling back."

"What friends are for, right?"

"What do you have for me?"

"Not a lot. Vasily Sokolov is a nasty son of a bitch, but according to official records, he's completely legal."

"How can he be both?"

"He's got a paper trail three miles long. Lots of known associates. Former known associates, if you get my meaning. A metric ton of connections to morally questionable businesses, but somehow, he manages to keep his hands clean. I've got nothing I can do from a legal angle."

"What kinds of friends does he have in Western Mass?"

Rosa could hear fingers clacking on a keyboard, and the wheel of the mouse whirling.

"He's got friends. Can I tell you how many? No. But the Russian mob is crawling all over Springfield and West Springfield, all the way down the 91 corridor, south of Hartford. A few known scattered throughout, so you know there are plenty of unknown wedged in between."

"So, I'm screwed then?" Rosa asked.

"If you're making them mad like you used to make Sergeant Walsh mad, then yeah, you're pretty screwed. I know making friends and influencing people is one of your specialties."

"Kicking a girl when she's down. I get it."

"Oh, chill out, Goose. If I can't harass you in the face of certain death, who can?"

"All right. Thanks, Katie. I may reach out if I need something else, is that okay?"

"Be sure you use my private line, all right? If my boss knew I was handing out this information, that would be very bad for business if you get my meaning."

"I get it," Rosa said. "Sorry to put you in a tough spot."

"I'm happy to help a friend, all right? Stay safe."

"You, too." Rosa disconnected the call as Stepan stepped closer to her, his eyes narrowed.

"That...did not sound good."

"Let's not worry about it right now," Rosa replied. "We need to focus on the safety of you and your son."

Federov looked at her and nodded softly. She nodded back, then pulled out of the car and eased the door closed, waiting for it to click locked. It did.

In truth, no matter how confident Rosa tried to sound, she was having some concerns herself. Federov had valiant reasons to do what we did. He was trying to fight for the side of good, trying to prevent more than one vicious crime from occurring. What was she doing? Trying desperately to somehow account for the pathetic nastiness of her past? Grasping for some small shred of hope that by helping the Federovs now it might somehow make up for practically tearing their family apart then?

Maybe they wouldn't even be in this position now if she hadn't done what she did. Maybe they'd have a whole different life in a whole different place, worry free and happy.

She closed her eyes, trying to force that thought from her head. She couldn't change what had happened. All she could do was look forward.

But every time she looked forward, she saw that contract from Mitchell Capozza. She saw those zeroes and envisioned a life where she didn't have to live in her office in squalor and where maybe she could actually move out of this neighborhood imprisonment that she could never seem to escape no matter how far she traveled.

Then she got angry with herself. Furious, really, for even considering hanging Federov and his son out to dry. That wasn't even an option. She couldn't let it be an option. She'd taken Stepan's wife, Jorge's mother, she'd taken her from them, she couldn't take this from them, too. She couldn't let Capozza take this from them.

Drawing in a breath, she walked up the long, concrete stairs to the apartment building and pushed through the double front doors. Inside was a small square lobby area with wall-mounted mailboxes on the left and the building manager's office on the right. Straight ahead was another set of stairs with a metal railing crawling up the levels in a zig-zag pattern. Just to the left of the stairs was a narrow doorway leading to an equally narrow hall, which curled around the perimeter of the building, leading to several first-floor apartments.

Razor's place was on the third floor.

Fighting back the strange sense of *deja vu*, Rosa ran up the stairs, taking two at a time, ignoring the barking pain in her legs from being on the run all day without much time to sit and take a breath. In moments she came up around the third level and exited onto the platform, easing open the metal door and emerging into the thin hallway. A few of the ceiling lights still worked, and the corridor was at least somewhat illuminated to the point of revealing the scattered trash on the floor, the stained walls and cracked plaster. She walked the hall, took a left, and stood in front of Razor's apartment, the door standing flat and plain, daring her to knock. Even Razor was likely asleep at this time of night, but Rosa couldn't afford to wait until the sun rose, she needed to find a place now.

Curling her knuckles, she punched the door three quick times, the knocks echoing uncomfortably loudly in the sparse hallway. She was certain she'd wake the entire third floor, especially once the first series of knocks didn't rouse him, and she lifted her fist to rap again.

Halfway through the second series, she heard shuffling inside.

"The hell is this?" the voice came from behind the door. Good old Johnny, as blunt as always.

"It's me," Rosa replied. "Rosa. Rosa Guzman." She kept her voice a low whisper, but hopefully loud enough to carry through the thin wooden door.

There was a moment of silence on the other end.

"Goose?" he asked quietly, somewhat incredulously.

"Yeah," she replied. "It's Goose."

Behind the door several metal scrapes indicated latches being unhooked and locks disengaging, and a few seconds later, the door creaked open, revealing Razor's tired but astonished expression. He kept the door open, but did not let her in.

"What the hell are you doing here, Rosa?" he asked.

"I've got nowhere else to go, Johnny. Can I come in? Please? Just for a second?"

Razor leaned out of his opened apartment and looked down the hallway, then turned and looked down towards the other end. Satisfied that the hall was empty, he pressed his hand to Goose's back and pulled her inside, then shut the door behind them both.

His apartment was just like she'd remembered it from all those years ago. The same ratty furniture, the unusually large and expensive television set cabled up to several video game systems, even as trash littered the floor and the chairs looked as if they'd been pulled from dumpsters. The priorities of a twenty something year-old were eminently clear.

It took her a few moments to recognize the other man in the apartment. He was thin, with close cropped brown hair, hunched over a threadbare card table in the corner of the kitchen. Rosa's eyes passed right over him at first, leaned over on some strange contraption on the table, cutting away at some kind of fabric.

"Hey, Goose," the man said.

Rosa stopped and glanced back, eyes narrowing. "I know you?"

He smiled, and recognition settled upon her, seeing the tooth-filled grin.

"Chris?" she asked. "Chris Polansky?"

He stood from the table and walked over, and she met him halfway, giving him a quick, but affectionate embrace. In her crew, Chris had been unique. Where most of her brothers and sisters had lineage going back to Puerto Rico, Mexico, and many other locations South of the border, Polansky was local, through and through, local to the point where his nickname had been "Gringo" among Rosa's group.

Rosa had formed a bond with Gringo way back, the two of them with a common interest in Star Wars, something that made most of Goose's friends roll their eyes. Shortly after meeting Polansky, they'd watched the whole trilogy together in a single night and spent most of the weekend talking through all their opinions and perspectives on the film franchise.

"So, you seen Rogue One yet?" Polansky asked, cracking a smile.

"Well, duh," Rosa replied. "Saw it in West Springfield opening night. The place with the bad ass sound system."

Polansky smiled thinly. "Yeah, good stuff, huh?"

Rosa saw that familiar look in Polansky's eyes and her own smile faltered. She saw a lot of herself in him. He had been involved in his own fair share of violent situations in his younger years and like her, they'd left a mark. Not a visible mark, no outward scars or obvious damage done, but inside, where things were more wet and raw and not so easily healed.

"You doing better these days?" Rosa asked in a quiet voice, trying to say it in a way that Razor wouldn't hear. Razor was one of the macho tough guys of the group, he didn't always understand those less visible scars.

Chris nodded, his smile broadening a bit. "Yeah, Goose, I think I am. Been a long road, but I really think I am."

Guzman stepped towards him and slapped him lightly on the shoulder, her eyes fixated on the fabric bunched up on the table.

"How's the shoulder holding up?" she asked. Polansky had been caught in the crossfire of a nasty situation a short while ago, and after spending some time in the hospital, was officially on the mend.

"It's doing okay," he replied, smiling, apparently happy that she remembered.

"What are you working on there?" she asked, leaning in to look at what he was sewing.

Polansky's cheeks flushed a light crimson. "Oh, that? It…it's a costume. There's a comic convention in Worcester next month and a bunch of my friends are going."

"That's pretty bad ass," Rosa replied, nodding. She lifted the dark gray cloth and examined it. "You're pretty good. I'll let you know next time I tear a hole in my jeans, huh?"

Polansky laughed. "Yeah, yeah. I'll be your seamstress, it's all good."

"We done talkin' about sewing and dressin' up in costumes?" Razor asked, his voice as narrow and sharp as the needle Chris was using.

"Yeah," Rosa replied. "Back to business." She turned from Chris and heard him sitting back down in the chair as she moved closer to Razor to continue their business conversation.

"Goose, this ain't a good idea," he said. He was wearing a white tank top, draped over his well-toned muscles, a veritable canvas of tattoos visible on nearly every part of his shoulders, arms and chest. There was a thin swath of dark hair on his head.

"There are some Blades that still aren't crazy about you working with the cops. You've got some serious bad mojo with some of the guys here."

"I know. I can't help that," she replied. "I need to make a living, Johnny. Nothing else seems to work."

"We'd take you back," he said. "I could convince some of the others to vouch for you. I think they'd overlook what you've been doing."

"I'm not interested in that, Johnny. That life isn't for me anymore. It hasn't been since Switch…" she didn't finish. She couldn't finish.

Razor shook his head. "Shit happens, Goose. Switch got a raw deal, but that's part of the life, okay? We could use your help, you always had a good head on your shoulders."

"That's not why I'm here."

"Why are you here then?"

Rosa walked past him towards the couch and settled herself down on it, with Razor following close behind, joining her there on the torn and stained sofa.

She leaned forward, putting her elbows on her knees. "I'm in some trouble."

Johnny leaned back, spreading his arms on the back cushion and looked at her. "What kind of trouble?"

"I took a contract. A private one," she added, glancing over at Johnny so he wouldn't think she was talking about helping the cops. "And, well, it kind of pissed off the Russians."

"Jesus Christo," Johnny said, shaking his head. "Not the people you want to piss off, sis."

"That's not the worst of it," she added. "The guy who gave me the contract is connected, too. Connected deep."

Razor looked at her, eyes narrowing.

"He's going to kill this guy and probably his son, too, if I turn them over. They've got some dirt on him."

Johnny shrugged. "So? Deal is a deal, Goose."

Rosa pushed herself up from the couch. "Not an option, Razor. I'm not going to do that."

"Okay, so what am I supposed to do about that?"

"I need a place. Just for a little while. A place off the radar."

Johnny stood up and turned away, pressing his hands to his hips. "So, you want to get us in the middle of this, too?"

"No!" Rosa exclaimed. "No, not at all. I just need a place to crash for a few days. It doesn't have to track back to the Blades."

Razor stood, arms on his hips, looking away from her.

"Johnny, I wouldn't come to you if it wasn't important."

He turned towards her. "You're not exactly a friend of the Blades these days either," he replied. "If anyone else finds out that I helped you, it could get both of us in the crap."

"I know."

"Stay here," he replied, walking from the living room into one of the smaller rooms flanking it. Rosa heard him rummaging around for a few moments, then he emerged, a key chain in his hand. He fumbled through some keys as he walked towards her, then glanced up at her and tossed a pair of keys connected to a single ring. Rosa snapped the keys out of midair.

"We've got a place. It's nothing special, but we keep it for any leaders who might come in from New York or Chicago."

Rosa turned the keys over in her hands.

"Obviously, it's not getting used much these days," he finished.

Rosa looked over at him, sensing the disappointment in his voice. "Johnny, I'm sorry. I wouldn't come to you if I thought I had any other choice."

"Place is in Westfield," he said. "Just off 90. Address is on the keys."

Rosa looked down at the keys again, surprised by a sudden fog in her vision, a streak of tears brimming.

She didn't look back up at Razor, she just kept looking at the keys. "Thank you, Johnny. Really. I know you're taking a risk."

He stepped forward and placed a firm hand on her shoulder. "You're still Blades, Goose. You're still family. At least to me. Switch would have wanted this."

Rosa stood up and embraced him, engulfing each other and holding for a few moments. It was a rare moment of emotion for both of them and felt a little strange inside the chaos of the trash strewn room.

"Be careful, *chica*," Razor said, stepping back, keeping hands on both of her shoulders.

"You too," Rosa replied, wiping her eyes. "Thanks again."

Rosa walked from the room, back down the hall, and made her way down the zig zag stairwell, pushing her way out into the cool, night air. The van remained parked at the side of the road, windows dark as silent and empty looking as the street around it.

Approaching the van, she reached forward and tapped on the

driver's side window lightly, trying not to surprise Stepan and Jorge. She saw Stepan lean over from the backseat and look nervously, then reach over the driver's seat and unlock the door so she could get inside.

"Glad you're back," he said quietly.

As she settled into the driver's seat, she glanced back towards him. "I got us a place," she said. "We'll get through this, okay?"

He nodded slowly, then leaned back in the backseat, adjusting Jorge's resting head and closed his eyes as if he might actually be able to rest his mind enough to sleep. Rosa started the engine and pulled away, guiding the large, dark vehicle out of the city and towards the Massachusetts Turnpike.

CHAPTER 35

The Mass Turnpike was dark and quiet and the van rolled along, blending in with the dim light and empty air around it. There were no other cars on the road at this hour, which suited Rosa just fine considering their current situation.

She glanced in the rearview mirror, seeing Jorge slumped over in the backseat, fast asleep, the taught seatbelt the only thing keeping him upright. Stepan had moved to the passenger seat, but his eyes were open, staring mindlessly out the windshield.

"Raising him on your own must be tough," Rosa said in a quiet voice, just something to break the silence.

He turned slightly to look at her. "Not as hard as it could be. He's a great kid."

"Seems like it."

"Lots of kids, they lose their mom, they get resentful. He doesn't seem that way. He was only a baby when she died, but still. It would have been easy for him to be angry."

Rosa chewed her lip but kept driving.

"His mom was shot and killed. Gang violence, just some random thing."

"I..." Rosa caught her breath but tried to keep it subtle. "I'm sorry to hear that."

Federov shrugged. "It was a long time ago."

For a few moments, the car continued on in silence, neither person eager to continue the conversation.

"I still think about her every day," Federov finally said. "But I've accepted our roles in life." He turned in the seat, craning his neck to look at his sleeping son. "But I can't let anything happen to him. That is something I will not accept."

"So, tell me more about this evidence," Rosa said.

Stepan looked at her again, more than a little mistrustful. "I haven't forgotten why you tracked me down," he said through pursed lips. "He hired you. You're not on my side on this."

"Fair enough," Rosa replied. "But I disagree. I think it's pretty obvious I've made a choice here. One that isn't necessarily healthy for me."

Federov turned back to look out the windshield. "There's a large construction project planned. River front property that is currently occupied by low income housing."

"Yeah, I think I know where you're talking about."

"He's appealed to the select board several times, gone to countless planning meetings, but no matter what he does or how many palms he's greased, he can't seem to get clearance to relocate and build there."

Rosa nodded.

"So, he actually considered a side deal. An outside contract."

"What kind of outside contract?"

Federov glanced over at her, once again a look of mistrust creasing the skin at the corners of his eyes.

"I don't know all the details, but supposedly there was a plan to start a fire. He was working with an underground organization that specializes in insurance fraud contracts. They can start these fires that leave no trace, or even worse that look as if they were started naturally or by faulty equipment."

"Are you kidding me?"

Federov shook his head. "And he had the building inspector, selectman and fire marshal all lined up to place the blame on the landlord for inadequate repairs and fire safety equipment. He was 100% prepared to start a fire in an occupied building to get the property owner put out of business, then sweep in and take it over."

"How many families live there?"

"Somewhere around ten. Maybe twelve."

"Jesus."

"Yeah. That's the guy you're working for, Rosa. That's Mitchell Capozza."

"And you have the evidence of this?"

Federov looked at her again. "I overheard a conversation several months ago that didn't sit well with me. Since then I've been secretly archiving and exporting all his email conversations. Things were heating up, so I backed them up to the external hard drive and took off. It felt like he might have been catching on to me."

Rosa looked over at him momentarily, then returned her eyes to the road, the two headlights shining on the dark pavement. The sign for the Westfield exit emerged from the darkness up ahead.

"Yeah, I think that's a fair bet."

"So, knowing the connections that Dalia had, I went to her family for protection. But once they heard the dirt was on Capozza, they got a little too aggressive for my liking."

"They have a beef with him?"

"No idea, but he's a big player. They probably figure any leverage they have on him is good for business. But that's not what this is about."

Rosa eased the car off the turnpike and onto the off ramp. She dealt with the toll booth then pushed forward slowly.

"Why not go to the police directly?" she asked.

"Capozza is connected," Federov replied. "Connected to everything. He's got some high-level cops in his pocket, and I've got it all on that hard drive. I go to the cops, I end up handed back to him on a silver platter."

"Christ."

"Yeah, that about sums it up."

"So, what are we going to do?"

Federov looked over at her. "Well, I was hoping you had some magic answer."

Rosa chuckled. "You obviously don't know me real well. If I have magic, it's only the shittiest kind. I don't exactly have a stellar track record."

Stepan gestured to the center console where the Glock pistol sat. "You know your way around that thing pretty well by the sounds of it."

"Didn't have much of a choice. Rough childhood, United States Army once I was eighteen. It kind of comes with the territory."

"How long did you serve?"

"Almost eight years."

"What happened? Had enough?"

Rosa blinked hard at the bluntness of the question and didn't answer. That comment was actually closer to the truth than she liked to admit, though the full story was a lot more complicated.

"Not really into talking about that time of my life," she replied thinly.

"Sorry."

"We all have demons."

Rosa stared off into the night as the van continued onward. For some reason, her thoughts drifted to Lenny Goff, the man who owned People Finders. The man who started the business, developed the relationships and made it what it was.

What would he have done? Would he have thrown Stepan and Jorge to the wolves for a quick buck? Honestly, would he have taken the job to begin with? Capozza had his hands in a lot of pockets, including the pockets of the police department, and suddenly Rosa found herself wondering just what had forced Lenny out and why. He'd been a career cop, working vice, making waves, and making a real difference. What would make him give up all of that?

"Jorge is the most important thing," Stepan said suddenly from the passenger's seat. "If you can get him to safety, I'll go with you. I'll turn myself into Capozza, as long as Jorge is free and clear. You get your money, he gets safe. Everyone wins."

Rosa looked over at him. "Except you."

"I don't matter," he said. "I'm the one that caused this mess. I should be the one to fix it."

She kept driving. How could she tell him at this point that no, she had caused this whole mess? She was the one that set this ball in motion ten years ago when she killed his wife. How could she tell him that at this point?

She couldn't.

"We're in this together, like it or not," she replied. "There's no guarantee he'd let Jorge live even if he got you. We can't take that chance."

"Isn't it my decision?"

"With the lives of the people who live in that apartment at stake? No, you can't make that call alone."

He leaned back, resting his head on the seat, closing his eyes.

"Let's sleep on it," Rosa said. "We'll figure out our next steps in the morning."

Stepan didn't reply. The rest of the ride was quiet, the van humming along the narrow roads of Westfield, Rosa following the path her phone was taking her. Pushing the van right, they pulled into a small driveway with a simple one-floor ranch and attached garage. It was a quiet road, the nearest neighbor several hundred yards away, and looked to be the perfect place to set up shop and not get noticed. All Rosa could think about right now, though, was getting some sleep. She didn't care what kind of bed or couch was inside, she needed to set her head down, let her mind relax, and grab some shut eye. Like she said, they could figure out the rest in the morning.

CHAPTER 36

"A night of unexpected violence has left several people dead and at least two wounded in what appear to be connected incidents in Hartford and Longmeadow," the voice said in its typical newscaster monotone from the small television on the kitchen counter.

Rosa cast a glance towards the television, though she didn't really want to, and continued cracking eggs into a small glass bowl on the counter in front of her. She'd risked a quick trip to the convenience store down the street this morning, hoping that nobody would be there at that time of morning, and she'd been in luck. Returning to their new permanent residence with eggs, milk, bread and a few other essentials had given her one small slice of normalcy in the midst of forty-eight hours of chaos and uncertainty.

She had a hard time digging through the events of the past two days, her mind drifting one minute, then focusing intently on isolated incidents the next minute. Hour to hour she was in a hazy trance, but at those key moments in time, those moments usually punctuated by gunfire and blood, she could see and remember all too clearly.

Stepan Federov had praised her acumen with a pistol and while she knew he meant it to be a compliment, it wasn't something she was necessarily comfortable with. Her entire life had been one on the scant edges of bloodshed and violence, and while she allowed herself to be consumed by that world when it suited her, she didn't embrace it. She didn't long for it.

Growing up among the Springfield gang scene, she had to learn to defend herself, both with or without a weapon, and she had. Both Switch and Razor brought her up hard, weaned on Muay Thai kickboxing and firearms training. Her only brief experience with firearms in an actual combat situation was the ill-fated gunfight that landed Switch in prison, but after a brief stay at juvenile detention, she ended up in the Army and only served to further hone her skills there.

Rosa's mind drifted as she thought about her time in the Army. The years spent with the 91st Battalion both in Fort Drum and over in Afghanistan. She'd formed bonds there, met people she thought she'd know and learn from for the rest of her life. She was crafting a career path for herself.

Like all good things in her life, it was destined to come to a horrible end. A painful end. And end with bloodshed and misery just like nearly every single punctuating moment in her life.

"What's for breakfast?"

Rosa turned just as Jorge Federov walked into the small kitchen. He was still wearing the blue jeans and T-shirt he was wearing the previous night (at some point they'd have to venture out to get clothes at least), and he was rubbing the sleep from his young eyes. His hair was tightly curled on top of his head, slightly messed from a night of restless sleep.

"Morning," Rosa said. "Just making some eggs. Do you want some?"

Jorge nodded in that way that kids do, when they're not sure they know you enough to actually speak to you.

"How do you want them?"

"Scrambled."

"You got it." She turned towards the counter and cracked another egg, then opened the fridge to retrieve some milk.

"You sleep okay?" she asked as he walked past her and lifted himself into a wooden chair at the small circular table just next to the kitchen. It was a dining room in name only, mostly just extra kitchen floor space that happened to fit a place to sit.

He nodded again, wordlessly.

The fork clanked against the glass bowl as she stirred, mixing the milk and eggs into a swirling whirlpool of yellow and white. Reaching down towards her feet, she retrieved a frying pan, removed it, and plopped it down on the stove top.

"How you feeling?" she asked.

Jorge looked at her and shrugged mildly. "'Bout what?"

"About what happened last night. Are you doing okay?"

He nodded again.

She fixed him with an uncertain glare.

"I didn't really know them," he said quietly. "My aunt and uncle. Never met them besides this week."

Rosa nodded. "They were still family, though, right?"

Jorge acknowledged this fact.

"I'm sorry I had to do what I did last night," Rosa said. "To the people in the house. I don't like to do that."

Jorge sat quietly for a brief moment, then looked up at her. "I'm glad you did."

Blue flame snapped under the Teflon-coated pan and Rosa dropped in a small pat of butter, which sizzled, releasing bubbles and smoke. Waiting a moment, she spilled the white and yellow mixture into the pan, which joined the butter and sputtered some more while she waited for it to solidify.

"I'm sorry about your mom, too," she said, not even looking at Jorge this time. Keeping her eyes down, focused on the eggs.

Jorge didn't reply. She noticed for the first time that he had some kind of smart phone device in his hand, an old iPhone by the looks of it, and he was playing a game with it.

"We got wi-fi in here?" she asked, bending over to look at his phone.

Jorge nodded again, his apparent default mode of communication. "Unsecured even," he reported.

Rosa nodded and moved back to the pan, slipping a spatula into the mixture and folding the eggs, then adjusting and repeating the motion again. The sizzling and smoking continued, and she started stirring.

"Want anything to drink?" she asked. He shook his head in the negative. This was going to be a long few days.

Few days? Was that what this was going to be? Did she have any hope that resolution was coming sooner than that? Or even that soon? The more this went on the more she wondered if this would be a longer, more drawn out event than that. Maybe a few days? Maybe a week? A month? She didn't even want to consider anything further out than that. The longer it took the more chance they'd have to find them, and if they found them, this whole thing would be over before it even began.

"Breakfast smells good," Stepan Federov said as he entered the kitchen himself. He looked considerably more awake than his son had when he came in.

"Morning, Dad," Jorge said quietly.

Rosa nodded towards him but focused most of her attention on the frying pan of eggs in front of her.

"Rosa's making me eggs," Jorge finished.

"Enough for everyone if you want some," she said.

"Sounds great." He ran a hand over his thin, dark hair, looking at the empty counter tops. His eyes widened. "Oh God," he said quietly.

Rosa spun around. "What?" she asked, panic evident in her voice.

"I don't see a coffee maker."

"Jesus Christ," Rosa replied, putting a hand to her chest. "It's in the cabinet down there. I didn't set it up yet."

Stepan took a step forward and leaned over, prying open a cabinet door, then pulling out the familiar shape of the Mr. Coffee.

"Oh, thank goodness," he said as he maneuvered it up onto the counter.

"I'm glad at least one of our crises are solved," Rosa said, rolling her eyes.

Just to her right, Stepan pulled out some coffee grounds and mixed them up, filled the coffee maker with water and started it brewing. The rich, thick smell of coffee mingled with the fading smell of cooking eggs and made a blend of breakfast smells that for one brief moment almost made her forget their current situation. For a second, life seemed normal and intact. They weren't on the run, their lives weren't hanging in some precarious balance, hiding from the two most powerful groups within a hundred-mile radius. They were just people cooking breakfast with no worries in the world.

"Pour me a cup?" Rosa asked and Stepan nodded. She flipped off the burner and flopped the scrambled eggs onto a small plate, then moved over, scraping it onto the table in front of Jorge. "Eat up, kid," she said. Pushing past Federov she opened the fridge and retrieved the milk again.

The kitchen was beyond small, barely fitting her and him both. Its smallness was representative of the rest of the house as well, just enough real estate for the bare essentials with no extra space to move. Two bedrooms, one that he and Jorge had slept in and one that she had slept in, a single bathroom, a small living room and the combination kitchen/dining room. Just the bare bones.

Could she live here for a month? No, she wasn't sure she could. Hopefully, she wouldn't have to. Her office attached room certainly wasn't the shining example of spacious room and functionality, but it was just her, and her alone, which was how she was used to living. This instant family situation wasn't exactly her cup of tea.

She cracked four more eggs, mixed the milk and started them cooking.

"Can you watch these?" she asked, looking at Federov. "I need to make a phone call."

Stepan looked over at her and nodded. "Sure. I've got it."

Rosa turned and walked away from the kitchen into the living room, then navigated down the hall towards her bedroom. She pulled the cell phone from her pocket and punched a saved number.

The phone rang a handful of times, then clicked open.

"Hello?" The voice was tired, a bit sluggish, but immediately recognizable.

"Chuck?" Rosa asked, surprised. "You're home?"

"Hey, Goose," he replied. "Yeah. I made it back early this morning."

"Thank God," Rosa sighed. "I'm so sorry we left you, Chuck. I feel like shit, man."

"I had it all under control like always. No harm no foul."

"You sure?"

"They roughed me up some, but I'll live. Got back, saw my brothers, even chatted up Officer Bondalewski a little bit."

"Oh?"

"Shit's going to hit the fan. We weren't the last ones to visit the club last night."

"I heard. It's all over the news this morning."

"Great."

"So, what did Helen say?"

"Not much besides the Russians are pissed. Mostly pissed at Capozza, but they think we work for him, so, you can imagine."

Rosa sat down on the bed, letting the weight of the previous night take her down into the soft surface, her shoulders drooping. So, the Russians think she works for Capozza, but meanwhile she's screwing Capozza over, and he's probably after her, too. Most of her Blades buddies think she's working for the cops. She was quickly running out of places to turn.

"Goose? You there?" Chuck asked.

"Yeah," she replied. "I'm here. I just...I don't know what to do, man."

"I know. Me neither. All I can do is lay low. Lucky for us I don't think those Russian jerks looked at my identification or anything while I was there. I don't think they know me from Adam."

"Good. Let's keep it that way."

"You need to be off the grid, too," Chuck replied. "Where are you?"

"I pulled a few strings with one of the few Blades who will still talk to me. He set me up with something, but it's very temporary."

"Then we have to figure this out quick."

"That's one of the few things I'm certain of."

Chuck didn't reply for a few moments and the line was silent as they both tried to work through some things. He was the first to come back on the line.

"Let me think on a few things. Give me the day, let's see if we can come up with anything brilliant. I'll call you if I think of something, you do the same, okay? If neither of us has something lined up tomorrow, I'll meet you where you are and we'll do some brainstorming in person. Sound okay?"

"I'm good with that, Chuck."

"All right."

"Chuck," she said just before he could hang up. "I really am sorry, okay? You deserved better."

"It's all good, Goose. Guy and his kid were first priority. Speaking of which, you guys have the kid, too, I assume?"

"Yeah, we do," Rosa replied. "Everyone's together."

"All right. Good. Talk later."

Rosa hung up all at once guilty and thankful for the man she'd been lucky enough to partner with. It could, after all, have gone much differently.

CHAPTER 37

It was a strange feeling, standing up on top of the skeleton structure, nothing more than a vague rectangle of iron beams, attached wood planks and roughed in sheet rock walls to shield from the wind three stories up in the air. From his vantage point up on the top floor, Mitchell Capozza could see the meandering Connecticut River, twisting its way down through the city, ducking under the Memorial Bridge and winding on South towards the state it was named after.

On this top floor there was actual walls and windows, though sheets of plastic whipped about as the wind picked up, slapping the air and reminding anyone who happened to be there that this was still an unfinished project, there was still plenty of work to do here.

Capozza turned as the plastic whipped again, scowling at the stark reminder of this project. His crown jewel of Capital Industries. A towering office building overlooking the river, which had already started accumulating a waiting list of clientele eager to sign leases and put their stake in this prime real estate.

Walking over towards the plastic, Capozza looked through his smart phone, scrolling through the various messages from the banks, the real estate agencies, the swift and constant reminders of how much he'd overextended to construct this masterwork, and how much of his reputation, money, and livelihood was riding on this, He'd spent a decade greasing the right palms, coaxing the right zoning ordinances and putting all the pieces in play to get this building constructed.

Veering off from where the plastic sheet rattled, he walked towards the second window, a wall-sized behemoth of double-paned glass looking proudly over a smaller tenement building less than a block away. A cast off from decades' past, worn brick and sporadic broken glass. A shabby reminder of the lingering elements of low income neighborhoods that had stretched out here towards the river. An outlier that belonged back within the city proper not out here where the upper class ruled the day.

His office building would redefine the term upper class. Leveraging his entire bankroll, Capozza had envisioned a world where the Capital Galleria would host dozens of prestige businesses, a small mall of stores and a food court, and would be a destination location for residents of Western Massachusetts all up and down the Connecticut. The newly renovated Basketball Hall of Fame was within sight of this top floor view, and he could already envision current and past NBA stars roaming the halls of his building, admiring the decor and wondering how they could get a piece of the action. The Select board had promised him considerations as they came up for vote, some buried proclamations that would offer relocation plans for the inhabitants of the small building next door. Ways to get the families to move amicably and legally.

But one by one, they all fell through. One by one, his promises dropped off, an around the same time as his cash reserves began to dry up, the members of the local board of selectmen suddenly seemed less and less eager to help.

So here he was.

The Capital Galleria was well under way, but until that building went down, he had no options for expansion.

In the public eye, he had accepted his fate and had relegated the Galleria to simply being an office building, to not including the food court and cutting the shops in half. He had made several presentations to the city and in each one was disappointed, but still committed to making a state of the art home for area businesses.

Under the covers, though, he was far from satisfied.

He dialed a number on the phone.

"This is Hunger," the voice said on the other end.

"Hi, Russ, this is Mitch," Capozza replied.

The voice on the other end was silent for a moment, but Capozza could hear some shuffling, then a door shut. "This isn't a great time, Mitch."

"Is it ever?"

"What can I do for you?"

Mitchell Capozza looked out the window, relishing the eagerness in the voice of Captain Russ Hunger, one of the many police captains of the city of Springfield.

"Have you heard anything about Federov?" Capozza asked.

"Nothing yet. One of our officers brought up his name a day or two ago, but that's it."

"Oh?"

"Yeah. Bondalewski. I'm not sure what her connection is, but she's got no leads or anything. It's a dead end, whatever it is."

"Good. I want to find Federov before any of your blue shirts do."

"Understood."

"I'm at the site now, Captain."

"How's it coming along?"

"So far so good," he replied, but he returned to the side window and looked out over the rundown building. "But we've got to do something about that housing complex."

"We've had this discussion, Mitch. I can't be a part of anything overt. It's too obvious."

"Yes, I understand. You've made that perfectly clear," Capozza snapped. "But you also cashed my last check pretty quickly."

Hunger sucked in a breath and let it out slow and steady, as if slowly letting the air out of an overinflated balloon.

"I assume you recall our agreement," Hunger replied. "If something should happen, we can spin this. But you've got to be very careful."

"My middle name," Capozza replied. "I didn't get this far without being careful."

"What about the fire marshal?"

"He's on board."

"I'm still a little concerned about this," Captain Hunger said. "You've been on the record, several times, looking to rezone that area. Now, on the verge of finishing construction of the main building, the place is going to burn down?"

"The evidence will be irrefutable," Capozza replied.

"None of that matters if you don't find Federov."

Capozza sneered at the phone, though the police captain couldn't see it. "Don't forget, Russ, that data has email communications between you and me. Very compromising communications. If it comes to light, I won't be the only one going down."

"I am well aware of that, Mitch," Hunger replied. "We're on the same side here, let's not forget that."

"We are on the same page," Capozza said. "Give this thing six months and it'll be all over."

"Hopefully without one or all of us in prison. They don't take kindly to cops in prison."

"You worry too much."

"Says the man who has his entire bankroll invested in this project. Maybe you don't worry enough. Not to mention this stuff with the Russians. We've got a war brewing, Mitch. A war you do not want to start. It's a war you will not win."

Capozza stood, thinking about those words. He didn't start this war. He didn't ask for this war. The Russians were bringing it to him. Federov was the one that went running to them, he was the one to blame here, not Capozza. And why hadn't he heard from Rosa Guzman?

"Good day, Captain Hunger," Capozza replied, his voice thin. As he pressed the hang up button, the plastic sheeting shifted again, and he turned, but this time, two well-dressed men pushed their way through the sheet, the man in front lifting his arm high, pressing the sheet up like a surgery curtain.

Jerome stepped in first, Pietro close behind, the two men wearing suits and coats, baggy and draped over their large frames, concealing any holsters or weapons that might be pulled tight across their chests beneath. There was still a lingering look of shock and exhaustion on their faces as they pushed through the plastic sheet and approached him, footsteps echoing in the vast, empty space of the top floor.

"Sorry to hear about Winston," Capozza said quietly before they even reached him. "Have you heard anything from the police?"

Jerome shook his head. "The Russians will keep it quiet, I'm sure."

"Do you think anyone at the club might have ID'd you?"

Pietro shook his head. "It was dark and loud. Once the gunfire started, nobody was looking at our faces. Winston will get identified for sure, but I see no reason to worry about it leading back here."

Capozza nodded. "So, what happened?"

Jerome looked at him, his face a little too stern, Capozza thought. "We went to the club like you asked. Mentioned Federov. Apparently, someone else beat us there, and they weren't crazy about our line of questioning. Next thing we know, they're trying to put caps in our ass."

"And they knew I sent you?"

Pietro nodded. "Oh yeah, they knew all right. I'd watch my back, Mr. Capozza. For whatever reason, Federov has a guardian angel watching out for him. A whole mob worth."

"Dammit."

"One thing you probably want to know," Jerome continued. "Sounds like Rosa might have gotten her hands on him. On Federov."

Capozza narrowed his eyes at them. "What makes you say that?"

"The Russians seemed pretty pissed. And if you're following the news, there was that home invasion in Longmeadow."

"What about it?"

"House was owned by Federov's aunt and uncle. Two of the bodies recovered were Russians."

Capozza's eyes went wide and his fists clenched. "What?"

Pietro nodded in confirmation of Jerome's news brief.

"So why hasn't she called me if she has him?" Capozza inquired, turning around and walking back towards the window.

"Your guess is as good as mine, boss," Pietro replied. "But I'm pretty sure she either has him or knows where he is."

Capozza nodded gently. "We need to find them."

"You think maybe she changed her mind about helping you?"

"She doesn't get that choice," Capozza snarled. "There is no changing her mind about this."

Pietro and Jerome glanced at each other, then Pietro looked back towards Capozza. "So, what now?"

"Get Dennis on the phone. I want my car here in half an hour. We need to get a group together and figure out where Guzman is and what the hell she thinks she's doing."

"I'm on it," Jerome replied. He turned and walked away, slipping a phone from his pocket. Pietro followed him, leaving Mitchell Capozza standing alone in his top floor penthouse, bracketed windows, fluttering plastic sheets a physical manifestation of his current emotional state.

Fragile and very, very exposed.

CHAPTER 38

*E*ven happier memories seemed to be broadcast from an old projector, flickering and dimly lit, the whole world cast in this strange shade of yellowed gray.

Rosa's memory was clear on this, if somewhat discolored, of walking from her beat up car to the front door of the single floor building. The single floor building that had now become so familiar to her. The single floor building that had essentially become her home.

That day was the first day she'd really seen it, even though it was in her neighborhood, basically a few blocks away from where she grew up. It was the kind of indistinguishable gray and brick structure that could have been occupied by any number of businesses, but she knew which one resided there now, and she knew who owned it.

People Finders.

The ad had run in the newspaper the day before, an ad looking for some additional help running the business. Contracts were coming in hot and heavy and the current operator couldn't keep up with all the work, so he was looking for some part time help. Rosa felt drawn to the place.

She knocked on the door, a trio of quick taps, banging on the metal surface, echoing on the quiet streets.

"Come in," said the voice from inside. "We're open!"

Rosa eased the door open and slipped in, letting it bang shut behind her. She came into a wide room, mostly square shaped with worn out hardwood floors, the walls all but covered with an assortment of various filing cabinets. On the far side was a desk with swivel chair, and the man sat in the chair, his feet propped up on the desk, a laptop sitting precariously on his legs as he tapped away on the keyboard.

His hair was medium length and dirty blond, the same color as his thick, rambling bush of a beard, both of which covered a face that looked as if it might have been chiseled and handsome ten years ago, but now was starting to wither and soften with age.

Everything except the eyes. His eyes were sharp and alert, two gleaming knife blades, shooting up and pointing directly at Rosa as she entered, a manila folder in her hand with some paper stuffed inside.

"Help you?" he asked, pulling his feet from the desk and leaning forward slightly, setting the laptop down gently.

"I, umm... I saw the ad," she said quietly, looking around the office, suddenly not sure what she was getting into.

"Oh yeah?" he asked. Leaning forward further, his low budget button-up shirt wrinkled and twisted with each movement. Rosa could see the hint of muscle bulge underneath the loose-fitting cloth, his sleeve pulling tight around the bicep.

"Yeah," she replied. "I'm from the neighborhood. Know my way around."

He nodded towards the folder in her hand. "Can I see? I just interviewed a guy who seems really good but let me see what you've got."

Rosa took a nervous step forward, handing the folder over, and the man retrieved it, spreading it open, and pulling out the makeshift resume. He leaned back again, returning his sneakered feet to the top of the desk and ran a finger down the paper as he read.

"Rosa Guzman?" he said, then glanced up at her. "Goose Guzman?"

She nodded softly.

"Seem to remember you joined up," he said, going back to the paper.

Rosa looked at him curiously. He caught her glance and smirked.

"Sorry. I try and keep tabs on all the kids from the neighborhood. Especially the ones who get out. I thought you'd gotten out."

"Me too."

"What happened?"

Rosa drew in a deep breath. "I'm not sure I'm ready to talk about that a whole lot yet," she said, looking at him cautiously. "I mean, unless that means I don't get the job. I'd just... I'd rather not right now."

The man nodded.

"You hung with Carlos, right?" he asked, not looking up from the paper.

"Yeah. He was like a brother to me."

"Switch was a good kid," he said. "Damn shame what happened to him in prison."

Rosa dipped her chin slightly but didn't reply.

"No felonies on your record?" he asked.

"No. I was in Juvenile Hall for a bit but never charged with anything."

"Good." He snapped the folder closed, withdrew his feet again and leaned forward. "So why are you here? What are you looking for exactly?"

Rosa looked at him. "What do you mean?"

He smiled gently. "This gig isn't for everyone. There's a unique mindset that wants to get into this kind of work. Unfortunately, there's a thin line between the folks who want to really do good work and the folks who are just looking for a cheap adrenaline rush."

"I've had enough adrenaline rushes in my life," Rosa replied, shaking her head. "I've got military experience, I know a lot of the locals, just seems like a good fit. I definitely need the money."

The man chuckled.

"What's so funny?" Rosa asked, her hard shell softening somewhat.

"Nothing. You just sound exactly like the last guy I interviewed. He's been around the block, has military experience, needs the cash. Mirror images of each other."

Rosa didn't answer. Even as she had walked up to the building, she wasn't convinced she desperately wanted this job, it just seemed like a good way to earn some extra cash, that was all. It's not like she'd always wanted to be a bounty hunter when she grew up or anything.

"If he's the better fit, I'm cool with that," she said. "No harm, no foul."

"I never said that," the man replied. He leaned back again, looking at her. "How would you feel about splitting time?"

Rosa shrugged.

"With three of us, I might be able to fit in a couple extra contracts. You and Chuck split some time, see how things go for a little while, make sure this is all going to work out? You guys get some extra cash in your pockets, I get some of the pressure off, everyone's happy."

"I'm good with that if you are. And if he is."

"I'll call and bounce the idea off him. He seemed like an understanding guy."

Rosa smiled and nodded. "Sounds good."

The man stood and extended his hand. "By the way, name's Lenny. Lenny Goff. This business is my baby, it's not easy for me to share it, so let's all play nice, okay?"

Rosa nodded. "Yeah. I'm good with that."

"Great," Lenny replied, easing himself back down into his chair. "I need to run some background checks and give Chuck a call, but you should hear from me tomorrow."

"Great," Rosa replied, a true and legitimate smile on her face. It had been a long time since she'd felt really happy. This seemed like a step in that direction.

And it had been. At least for a while.

But as with everything in Rosa's life, what seemed like a step towards happiness generally ended in smoke and blood.

CHAPTER 39

The clouds crowded in the sky, bathing the city below in a strange mid-afternoon dusk. In this part of downtown Springfield, traffic was sparse and Mitchell Capozza's long, black Cadillac navigated a turn a few blocks away from the construction site. The looming partially complete structure was visible from the road, flanked by dark clouds, and Dennis looked at the building from the driver's seat.

He'd worked for Capital Industries for a decade and a half and had been Capozza's personal driver for eight of those years. There were days that the job wore him down, but his boss was mostly calm and reasonable, and he paid really damn well. Dennis himself could almost afford a Cadillac not too far less extravagant than this one, though without the bulletproof windows and reinforced armor plating.

Dennis chuckled as he thought about all the additions to the vehicle. It seemed as if Capozza looked for reasons to overspend, certain fancy accoutrements that he didn't really need, but put him one more step towards the upper-class crowd that he so desperately wanted to be a part of. Glancing in the rearview mirror, Dennis eased the vehicle around a corner, keeping the building in view. The street was narrow, barely a two-lane road and was surrounded by rows of buildings, though many were uninhabited. This area of Springfield was growing quickly abandoned as the upper echelon clientele withdrew deeper downtown and the lower tier businesses couldn't quite afford a spot so close to the hustle and bustle of the center of the city. This street led down that strange middle ground, a border between the class conflicts, a place separating the two, but completely uninhabited even from the folks in the middle.

As Dennis picked up speed, he heard a sudden screech of tires from up ahead and eased on the brakes, but before he could react another dark car burst from a street up ahead and to the left, bouncing over the sidewalk, striking the pavement, and pulling up perpendicular to his vehicle, blocking the road entirely.

Dennis glared at the vehicle, slamming on his brakes and bringing the Cadillac into a crooked forty-five-degree spin just as a second car ejected itself from a road just behind him, swerved in and pulled across the street behind him. Dennis whipped his head around, seeing the two cars and immediately knew something was about to go down.

"Damn," he said quietly to himself, seeing that there were several shadowed heads in each car, and they were rustling around inside as if preparing to burst out. "The Russians."

Dennis cut the engine, pulling the keys out and tossing them down onto the passenger side floorboards. Reaching back and around the seat, he retrieved a weapon from a sheath on the back of the passenger seat. A Heckler & Koch HK416 D10RAS, the automatic rifle was modified with a 10.4-inch barrel with mounted scope, RIS foregrip, and carried the standard 5.56mm NATO rounds. Along with being Capozza's personal driver, Dennis was ex-military and well-trained in the use of firearms. Dennis had always thought Capozza was overprotective, after all he'd never been important enough for anyone to try and kidnap or kill, but as his hand wrapped around the pistol grip of the 416, he was glad that he had his background.

Doors flew open in the car ahead and three men exited, all of them with pistols clasped tightly in their two-hand grips. Dennis shifted slightly and saw that doors were also opening on the car behind him and four more men had emerged out onto the vacant street. The Russians weren't messing around, and they probably thought Capozza was in the car.

A series of rapid pops signaled a small barrage of pistol shots stitching bullet holes in an upward angle on the front windshield. Purely by reflex, Dennis drew back and down, though the reinforced glass repelled the bullets effectively. More echoing pounds signaled gunfire coming from the rear and Capozza's driver remained huddled down towards the steering wheel as he retrieved a pair of spare magazines and stuffed them in his jacket pockets. All around him the car was jostling with the peppering of small arms fire, though none of the bullets were going in, as of yet.

That wouldn't last long.

Reinforced glass generally stopped a volley or two of gunfire, but a consistent, steady stream of offense would eventually smash through and start causing some real damage. Seven against one was not good odds.

Dennis hunched towards the driver's side door and looped his fingers around the handle as his other hand tightened around the contoured grip of the H&K.

For a brief moment, the volley halted as several of the Russians stopped to reload, and Dennis jerked back his fingers, popping open the door handle, then he lunged with his shoulder, forcing the door to swing open out into the darkened air. Within seconds he was out on the pavement with the weapon pressed tightly to his shoulder, his opposite hand clutched around the supporting front foregrip. Using the door has temporary shelter he swung the weapon up and into the gap between the window and the windshield, took careful aim and pulled the trigger, the weapon rattling a series of rapid fire gunshots. One of the Russians shouted and stumbled backwards, and even before he hit the ground, Dennis adjusted and fired again. The side window of one of the doors exploded and the man hiding behind it pinwheeled, throwing his weapon into the air as he fell backwards.

Gunfire exploded behind him, and he dropped slightly as sparks danced across the metal roof of the Caddy, then swung up and around behind him rattling off another series of shots. A third Russian grunted and stumbled backwards, but three others behind him began drifting left to get better trajectory. Dennis adjusted again to regain his aim, but the remaining man in front of him leveled his Glock and fired six times in quick succession. Two shots struck Dennis in his right shoulder, slamming him back against the roof of the car and loosening his grip slightly on the weapon. He shouted, shifted his weapon to the other hand, and came back up around to return fire, but the three Russians from behind were now in perfect position.

All at once the four remaining men unloaded with their pistols, blanketing Dennis in 9mm gunfire, and he thrashed as the rounds struck him. Many drilled into his Kevlar protected torso, but at least two rounds punched through the vest and a deadly third struck him just under the chin, shattering his jawbone, then careening up into his spinal cord.

Dennis dropped the weapon, stumbled, then collapsed onto the pavement like a puppet with his strings cut. For a moment, silence overtook the streets, a deafening lack of gunfire as smoke lingered, floating like a strange ephemeral fog. Carefully, the Russians progressed forward, taking turns moving, then flanking, and moving again, making sure nobody else was in the car with a powerful automatic weapon.

One of the men signaled as he moved towards the back of the car, making a motion towards the back door. He hooked his fingers around the handle as he looked at his teammates, and they moved in around him, weapons drawn. Gesturing with his own pistol he counted three, then popped the handle and opened the door, everyone around him bringing their pistols around, prepared to destroy anything within.

The backseat was empty.

"Capozza's not here," the man remarked, his accented voice laced with rage. He turned towards the other men. "Get the bodies. Load them in the car. Let's get out of here before the police show up."

Already in the distance, the distinctive warble of sirens had started to bellow, but the Russian assassins were quick and by the time the police arrived, the cars were gone, leaving a dead man and a bullet-ridden Cadillac in their wake.

CHAPTER 40

Mitchell Capozza looked up into the pink sky, the sun shrouded by thickening clouds as the light of dusk settled around the construction yard. He rubbed a hand through his closely cropped graying beard, turning and looking over the horizon, south towards the Connecticut River, the back up north, trying hard not to focus his attention on the low-income housing within the shadow of his new office building for fear that someone would somehow sense his plans and find him guilty.

Glancing at his watch, he squinted and flexed his fingers.

Where was Dennis?

He'd called him over an hour ago, and it hadn't seemed like he was too far away.

Behind him, the plastic sheeting shuffled, and he turned, mouth open, prepared to admonish his driver for his lateness, but it wasn't Dennis who walked in, it was Pietro.

"What are you doing back here?" Capozza asked. "You're supposed to be out looking for Guzman."

Just as he finished speaking, his phone thrummed in his chest pocket, a consistent humming vibration, pushing down on his chest muscle protected only by a layer of nicely woven fabric. Pietro started to reply, but Capozza lifted a single finger in a silencing gesture and scooped the phone out.

"Mitchell Capozza," he said quietly, pressing the narrow rectangle to his ear.

"Mitch, it's Russ again."

"Do we need to have this conversation again?" Capozza asked, his cheeks flushing.

"No, listen."

Capozza hesitated. Something about the tone of the police captain's voice caught his attention. There was an edge there.

"I'm listening," he said.

"There's been an incident. A gunfight downtown, about three blocks from where you are."

"Okay?"

"It looks like your car was ambushed. We don't have a good feel for the number of assailants or any specific details, but we found your vehicle and the driver."

Capozza straightened, his fingers curling tight around the phone. "What?"

"Yeah. Dennis is dead, Mitch. Shot several times, looks like 9mm rounds."

"No."

"The car is a mess. By the looks of the shell casings and some other evidence found at the scene, your boy put up quite a fight but was eventually outnumbered and outgunned."

"God dammit!" Capozza yelled. "Who did this?"

"We don't know. Our evidence team just arrived at the scene. I think it's safe to assume that the Russians had something to do with it."

Capozza closed his eyes and drew in a deep, lingering breath. He exhaled long and hard, then repeated the motion, willing himself to calm down. Slowing his heart rate and relaxing his muscles he unclenched his tightly closed left fist, then slowly closed it again, then opened it again. Pietro could actually see him trying to force his way into calmness as he walked that thin line between normalcy and unbridled rage.

"When you know something, make sure I know it, too, okay, Russ?"

"Of course," Captain Hunger replied. "We're on it."

"You know what depends on this."

"I do."

Capozza removed the phone and thumbed it off, holding it in his fist. Pietro could see the veins stand out on the back of his hand and run up into his forearm like a wandering river of blood just under a thin crust of skin. He was certain that if the phone didn't have a titanium backbone, he would have crushed it in his grasp.

"Are you here to tell me the same thing?" Capozza asked, not even looking up. "Dennis is dead? The Russians ambushed him like this is some kind of goddamned third world country?"

"Yes, sir," Pietro replied. "We tried to get eyes on the scene, but the cops were everywhere."

Capozza nodded, then finally looked over at him. "Who do we know around here?" he asked. "Who can we leverage?"

"How do you mean?"

"I'm not going to stand for this, Pietro. I'm not going to sit here and do nothing while one of my closest confidants is gunned down in the fucking street!" His cheeks were deep crimson underneath the thin beard, and his forehead darkened to a light purple tinge.

"Sir, the Russian mob has hundreds of foot soldiers in Western New England alone. There is no group we can leverage who would be big enough to stand up to them."

Capozza stood there, his face still three shades darker than the rest of him, his fist wrapped around the phone in some kind of desperate death grip.

"The Blades are still scattered to the wind," Pietro continued. "The old school Mafia isn't playing around with Springfield anymore. They've moved on to bigger and better places. I don't know what to tell you, sir."

"What about contractors? I've been working with some ex-military guys who run private security."

Now it was Pietro's turn to slowly exhale, to consciously attempt to deflate the boiling conflict inside of him.

"Mr. Capozza, the Russians outnumber us and outgun us. We cannot go up against them, we just don't have the manpower or the firepower. Maybe it's time we rethink this strategy. Maybe we can convince them to help us with the Federov problem? Cut them in on the deal or something?"

Capozza raised his head slowly and steadily, his face twisting into an almost unrecognizable scowl of disgust.

"Did you say cut them in?" he asked in a low hiss. "Get in bed with the Russians? The men who just killed my driver in cold blood?"

Pietro lifted his hands as a sign of peace. "I didn't say I agree with that perspective, sir, but I'm having a hard time finding another way around it. I'm afraid we poked a hornet's nest with this one...and there's no way to put the hornets back in their hive."

Capozza smirked at him, a sideways, crooked smile that chilled Pietro to places deep inside of him that he didn't know he had.

"Then we burn the hive, Pietro. We burn it into ash."

Capozza turned from him again, lacing his fingers behind his back, taking two steps towards the wall-sized window, looking out onto the river. The river that carried so many through so much of New England. The river that would finally take him from his place in the upper echelon of middle class to the true upper-class stature where he belonged. Take him to the place his father said he'd never go.

The clouds pushed closer together, further blocking out the setting sun and the sky shifted from pink to purple, preparing for the oncoming night.

CHAPTER 41

"What do you mean take the day off?" Rosa asked, that small, tin voice in the back of her memory as she slowly drifted off to sleep.

Lenny Goff leaned back in the creaking swivel chair, lacing his fingers behind his head. His shabby loafers were crossed on top of the worn wooden desk.

"Both of you guys. Take the day. Paid. My little gift to you for all of your hard work."

Rosa narrowed her eyes at him, then glanced over to Chuck who had the same strange look on his face.

"I don't get it," Chuck said. "Work's been coming in. Things are going well, aren't they?"

Lenny unlaced his fingers and gestured to them. "Yeah. You guys both got your fugitive recovery licenses. Contracts have doubled. We're doing good. That's why you deserve a vacation day."

"Are you closing up for the day?" Rosa asked, pulling her red jacket back over her narrow shoulders and shrugging it on.

"Not sure yet," Lenny replied. "We'll see."

"Whatever," Chuck said, pulling his own coat on over his slender, but muscular frame. He and Rosa turned and walked back out the front door, glancing back and waving casually to Lenny, who nodded towards him, his face suddenly stone serious. Rosa stopped for a moment.

"Everything all right, Lenny?" she asked again, staring at him from the stairway before the front door.

He smiled thinly. "We're good, Goose," he replied.

He didn't look good. Chuck continued on and Rosa fell in beside him. "So, what's the plan, Chuck?" she asked. "Want to grab a bite to eat or something?"

"Why not?" he replied. "Great little coffee shop around the corner."

They rounded the building and approached the small restaurant, placed their orders and sat in a corner, trying to find some separation between them and the slowly filling clientele.

"I don't think we ever really talked," Chuck said, tipping his coffee to his lips.

Rosa smirked at him. "We got stuff to talk about?"

He chuckled. "We've been working together a year already. You're ex-Army, right?"

"91st out of Fort Drum. Spent some time in Kabul and Baghlan."

"Why'd you leave?"

She looked up at him from her coffee cup, her eyes a pair of thin ovals. Tipping the mug back she took a long, steaming sip.

"That was a tough time of my life, Chuck," she replied. "I don't like to rehash it if I can help it."

"I get it," he replied. "I was in military intelligence myself. Though I ended up in Iraq, not Afghanistan, preparation for, then clean up after the troop withdrawal."

"Tough spot," Rosa replied. "So, what are you doing back?"

Chuck took another swig of coffee, set down his cup, then picked up the breakfast sandwich and tore a piece out of it. "My mom died. Car crash. Left my two brothers to fend for themselves. I had to jump through a bunch of hoops but ended up being able to shift some service hours stateside and wind down over time. Gave me a chance to look after Prentiss and Travis."

"I'm sorry," Rosa said. She felt a small pang of guilt over her fierce resistance to discuss her discharge. In the grand scheme of things, it felt less…personal than what Chuck had gone through, though no less traumatic.

"How did you end up with Lenny?" Chuck asked.

"Just saw the ad. I had my military experience, I know these streets inside and out. Seemed to make sense. He remembered me from being around the block."

"Funny that we never crossed paths before," Chuck said, looking at her.

"All I knew back then was the Blades. I didn't really mingle with any other crowd beyond them."

Chuck nodded.

"So, you didn't have any run ins with the Blades? You were in the neighborhood, right?"

"Sort of. Mom worked hard to try and keep us away from that sort of thing. I was a geek. Spent most of my time in school or in the computer lab. I had no interest in the streets."

"Good."

"Travis, though. Travis is a live wire. He kept mom busy…he's going to keep me busy. Prentiss is a good kid, though. I'm hoping he'll help."

"I give you all the credit in the world."

Chuck shook his head. "Don't. Just doing what I have to do."

"Lots of guys I know wouldn't even do that."

Chuck shrugged. "I find ways to get my release."

"Yeah? You're a gym rat, right? I think I heard you talking to Lenny about that once."

"Yep. Do a lot of lifting. Boxing. Kickboxing. Whatever I can do to forget life for a bit and take my frustrations out at the same time. Kickboxing helps."

"I'm with you. Switch…uhh… Carlos, he was like a brother to me. Put me through the ringer when I was growing up. He knew a couple of guys who taught a lot of us Muay Thai, basic street level self-defense. Stuff like that."

"Nice. Seems like you've got a good head on your shoulders, Goose. What are you doing as a low rent bounty hunter in this armpit city?"

Rosa smiled lamely. "What's that line in the Godfather...every time I think I'm out, they pull me back in?"

"Who pulls you back in? Family?"

"No. No family."

"Friends?"

She glanced up at him. "I dislike people in general. Don't have many of those either."

"So why?"

Rosa looked around the small coffee shop, eyes lingering on several of the patrons as she moved from seat to seat and booth to booth.

"I don't know. Because I know what to expect here? Because every time I try something new and exciting it blows up in my face? At least in this place I know where I stand and what my limitations are. I'm not tempted to think outside my comfort zone."

"Sounds like an awful way to live."

"There are worse alternatives."

Chuck looked at her, his eyes narrowing. "Sure you don't want to talk about Afghanistan? I served, too. I've seen the look. You've got that look. The look of someone who has seen something horrible that they can barely explain to themselves, much less to anyone else." He drank his coffee and took another bite of his breakfast sandwich. "I've been there, Goose. Maybe I will understand."

Rosa dipped her head and took a bite of her own breakfast. "I don't know. I didn't see anything worse than anyone else. Our situation just blew up and someone had to take the fall."

"That someone was you?"

"Yeah."

"Was it fair?"

Rosa squeezed her lips shut and shook her head.

"Couldn't fight it? Didn't want to?"

"Not worth it. It's just karma," she replied, drinking again.

"Karma doesn't just get the bad people," she smirked up at Chuck who nodded his agreement.

The day went on. In Rosa's half-asleep memories it went on nearly forever, clouds slowly drifting through the sky, the sun crawling up towards noon, the hustle and bustle of pedestrians outside cruising at double-speed like some sort of time lapse.

She'd gone up to the counter for her second coffee and was walking back to the table where Chuck sat, nursing his own second cup, their breakfast sandwiches long since gone, the only remains some scattered crumbs among the crumpled foil wrappers. The blur of motion took her by surprise, the *whoosh* of white and blue, followed closely by the time delay bark of echoing siren. The police car roared past them, then hung a tight left just after the coffee shop, the horn blaring and warble continuing, sounding remarkably close.

Chuck glanced over his shoulder, to see where the car went. "That seems close," he said.

Rosa leaned over, trying to glance through the window, and she could see a pair of police cars, not just one, parked in a strange pointed V-shape in the road just a block away.

The road that led to People Finders.

"Let's go," she said quietly, a tight, hard nugget forming deep in her guts. "Something's wrong."

Chuck stood and followed as she was already headed towards the door, then the two of them banked left and broke into a run, trotting towards the police cars, past them and angled for the familiar office building that sat there on the side of the road, looking normal and undisturbed.

Undisturbed except for the uniformed police officer standing outside the front door. Undisturbed except for the whipping red and blue lights flashing along the surface of the outside wall.

Rosa pressed forward, approaching the small stairway to the front door. "What's going on?" she asked.

The officer stepped forward, holding up a firm hand. "Crime scene, ma'am," he said. "Please step away."

"We work here," Chuck replied. "Our boss is in there."

The officer held his hand up but dropped all fingers except his index finger, signaling them to hold on a moment. He leaned around to his right and barked into the open front door.

"Hey, we've got people outside who might know the vic!"

"Vic?" Rosa asked. "Victim? What happened here? What's going on?"

Another uniformed officer appeared at the front door. "Can I get your names?" he asked, gesturing them to take a few steps backwards.

"Rosa Guzman."

"Charles Heath."

"Okay. Come over here for a minute, will you?" the officer replied, taking a few steps past them. They followed.

"Delivery man stopped by with a package. Front door was open, so he stepped inside. Victim was found on the floor, multiple gunshot wounds to the torso and head."

"What?" Rosa asked. She could feel tears starting to dig at the corners of her eyes. "No, no, no," she said, shaking her head.

"We were just at the coffee shop," Chuck protested. "We didn't hear anything."

"Looks like a professional hit," the officer replied. "Quick and quiet."

Rosa ducked her head and pushed her hand through her short hair.

"Do you know of any enemies that Mr. Goff might have had?" the officer asked, glancing around as if waiting for someone more prepared to ask these questions to show up.

Chuck leaned back against the chain link fence that ran the perimeter of the grounds behind him. It sagged slightly under his weight.

Rosa brought herself up right, looking at the cop. "I'm sure he had his fair share. He made a living as a cop, then as a bounty hunter. Those are two professions that are pretty sure to create enemies, aren't they?"

"Anything specific? Any recent contracts?"

Rosa shook her head. "He was adamant that Chuck and I take today off, which struck us as pretty strange."

The officer narrowed his eyes at her. "Do you think that he might have suspected something?"

Rosa shrugged. "No idea."

"He suspected something," Chuck interjected. "I'm sure of it."

The cop looked over towards him. "Any ideas who might have orchestrated this?"

Chuck shook his head. "None."

Rosa stood, looking towards the building. The building that no longer seemed like a building, but instead like a tomb. Lenny Goff lay in there, his lifeless corpse on the wooden floor where they'd been standing a few hours before, blood pooled and staining. Would she ever set foot in there again? Did she even have a job?

Was anything good in her life ever going to end in something besides bullets and death?

Even as she fell into a deep slumber, the memories of that day fading from her conscious mind and the knowledge that Stepan and Jorge were safe in the next room, even then she wondered the same thing about this chapter in her life. She couldn't see an end-point without violence. She couldn't see a finish line without gunfire or corpses. She couldn't see the light at the end of this tunnel that wasn't an oncoming train.

Then she slept. Blissfully, she slept.

CHAPTER 42

*H*ad it really been less than twenty-four hours?

Rosa stared up at the ceiling in the spare bedroom, her eyes fixated on the bizarre popcorn pattern of the rough, white material, trying to think of a time and place where she didn't feel so trapped, penned in, and alone. Stepan and Jorge were in the next room over, Jorge absorbed in his iPhone as he had been all day long, perfectly content to be trapped within these four small walls with no connection to the outside world.

Rosa, to her credit, had attempted to be busy to start the day, going to the local grocery store and fixing everyone breakfast, then doing some perimeter walks to get a good idea of the layout of the property. She'd cleaned the house and done some basic security inside, making sure every window and door was locked and dragging some heavy objects to the front and rear doors, so they could be barricaded quickly should the need arise.

Razor had been like family to her, almost as close as Switch himself, but at the end of the day, he was still a gang kid and as much as she needed the safety and security of an off the grid place to crash, she wasn't sure he could really be trusted for too long. Once every window and door was checked, then checked again, she walked every hall and checked every room, registering the house's layout to her memory, crafting the floor plan in her head, complete with assault and defense scenarios. She felt dangerously exposed here. They'd been in such a rush to get off the grid she hadn't had time to collect any weapons, so all she had was the Russian's Glock 19 she'd stolen the previous night and even that pistol had dreadfully few bullets for it. At some point tonight, she'd call Chuck and see about meeting up to collect her Ruger and maybe some other more potent weaponry as well, but for now she felt nearly defenseless.

In reality, she could have called Chuck and gotten him to come right over, but she still felt bad about ditching him at the Russian nightclub and honestly, as much trouble as she was in, felt like he needed a bit of a break from the life and death struggle. Let him spend some time with his brothers, zone out a little bit and separate himself from this whole thing. That's what she'd want to do.

If she had any real brothers. If the closest thing she'd ever had to a brother wasn't in the ground.

Even after all these years, she still wasn't sure what was worse, the fact that she killed an innocent woman with her careless gunfire, the fact that she'd let the person closest to her take the hit for what she'd done, or the fact that Switch had been executed in prison by a fellow inmate less than a year after being convicted. Those three elements came together to frame the worst time of Guzman's life, a defining turning point over eighteen months that would create the woman she was and decide the woman she would ever be. Those were events she would never forget and never get over, and events she never wanted to revisit as long as she lived.

Only now, with Stepan and Jorge in this house with her, she was in a constant state of revisiting. An unending, persistent mode of recollection, small pinprick knives of bad memories relentlessly stabbing at her, reminding her, focusing her pain.

In some small ways she still relished that pain. She still clutched those moments in her fist and held tight, wanting to remember what happened and use that as fuel for shaping her morality going forward. It was something that did not kill her, and thus made her stronger, but the constant practical reminder, seeing Dalia's husband and son constantly for the past twenty-four hours, she worried that it was a little too much. Granted, being able to wallow in this moment in her life allowed her some leeway to forget some of the other things that had happened to her, especially those tragic events in Afghanistan, but at some point, she would have liked to have gone a full day without being thrust back into that world of violence and blood.

Her phone vibrated, a rattling shake on the wooden nightstand, moving the smooth gadget sideways across the smooth surface like a strange crab walking along the beach. Rosa pulled herself up into a seated position and reached over, plucking the phone from the table and pressing it to her ear.

"Hello?"

"Rosa, this is Helen Bondalewski."

"Helen, how's it going?" Rosa asked tentatively. Helen wouldn't be calling her unless something was going poorly.

"Not real well, to be honest."

Rosa swung her legs off the bed, and scrunched forward, her breath quickening a little. "What's up?"

"Things with the Russians are escalating quickly. Earlier this afternoon, there was a gunfight in the streets of Springfield. In broad daylight. Mitchell Capozza's personal driver and bodyguard was executed."

"Jesus Christ," Rosa mumbled. "What about Capozza?"

"He wasn't in the car. We believe he's being moved to a safe location."

Rosa found herself slightly disappointed. Capozza being dead would solve a lot of their problems.

"So, you think this has something to do with Federov?"

"I do. As you know, Capozza sent some goons to the club last night, which turned into violence, as well, and then there was the home invasion in Longmeadow. This is getting really ugly really quickly and Federov is at the middle of all of it."

"Any ideas where he is?" Rosa asked, not wanting to tip her hand.

At least not yet. She still wasn't sure how many people within the Springfield Police could be trusted, though she felt like Helen at least was one of them.

"Not yet, but we're working a few leads."

"Okay. What do you need from me?"

"You should be aware that Federov will be on the evening news tonight. In just a few minutes. We couldn't hold them off any longer, especially after his aunt and uncle were killed last night. This is turning into a thing. A big thing."

"Not good," Rosa replied.

"Sorry, but I think you need to back this one down a bit, Goose."

Rosa smiled. Helen didn't call her by her nickname very often. It added a little edge of friendly sisterhood. She kind of liked it.

"Last thing I want is to get in the middle of a Russia versus Capozza gang war," she said. "No matter how well the contract pays."

"Good," Helen replied. "Try to stay out of it, okay?"

"You know me, always staying out of trouble," Rosa replied. Helen did know her, and Helen knew staying out of trouble was one of the few things Rosa Guzman was not good at.

Officer Bondalewski's voice hesitated on the other side as if she was chewing on something. Thinking something through. "Are you trying to tell me something?" she asked curiously.

Rosa looked up from her lap, her eyes fixating on the wall ahead of her, only a few feet ahead of her, then she looked over at the wall to her right, then the wall to her left. The walls all seemed to be so close and it actually felt as if they were slowly pressing towards her, shrinking the room, closing her in. The breath caught in her lungs as she imagined the huge world outside looming around her, bearing down on this small house and the fragile people within. Behind every tree and hidden in every dark corner was an enemy, and they were in the last stronghold against those enemy forces, concealed for the moment, but way too easily discovered.

"Rosa, are you okay?" Helen asked. "You're breathing heavy."

"Yeah, I'm fine," she replied. "I'm good. Sorry."

"Is everything all right? I'm here to help if you need it."

She trusted Officer Bondalewski. She'd known her for a decade and had met her on the worst day of her life. But she didn't know how many others she could trust, and if Helen didn't suspect...if she didn't know who was on her side, this whole thing could go bad.

Very, very bad.

"I'm fine, Helen, really," Rosa said. "Just a rough couple of days. A little freaked out about this situation."

"I get it," the officer replied. "It's okay. I'm only a phone call away if it gets to be too much."

"I know. Thanks."

"Be careful."

They hung up at the same time, burying the small room in a thick cushion of silence. Rosa sat on the bed, staring at the wall, her eyes glazing over and the white surface slowly shifting into a light blur. She stared at the phone in her hand, the useless rectangle of glass, metal, and plastic, a conduit to call nobody. A doorway to a world she could not enter for fear of ambush. This wasn't a house, it was a cage.

A hand tapped at her closed door lightly, a methodical pattern of quiet rapping. Her heart jumped slightly, and she drew in a quick, but silent breath.

"Everything okay?" the voice said from the other side of the door. "I heard talking."

"Come on in," Rosa replied, slowing her breathing. Stepan Federov pushed open the door and came in.

"What was that about?" he asked.

"Don't worry about it," Rosa replied.

Federov rolled his eyes. "I don't have time to do anything but worry stuck in here, Rosa. Talk to me."

She leaned back on the bed slightly, putting her hands behind her to stabilize. Seeming to slowly chew on her words, she looked up at him.

"Things are getting heated outside. The guy who hired me has ruffled the Russians' feathers and, well, they're ruffling back."

"What do you mean?"

"More violence, Stepan. More dead bodies. Is that what you want to hear?"

"Of course not!"

"I know, and I'm sorry to be the one to tell you, but it's the truth. They're looking for you and looking hard."

"What can we do? How can I fix this?" Federov slowly eased the door closed behind him so as not to alert his son to their conversation. He leaned back on the door, the strength appearing to go out of his legs completely.

"I'm not sure you can," Rosa replied honestly. "Things may have gone too far already."

"So why don't we just go to the police? Let's go to the police and hand this over and just be done with it."

Rosa shook her head. "I'm not sure that's an option. Capozza's in deep with everyone, including law enforcement."

Federov looked around the room as if the answer to his questions might be found within the tiny space he and Rosa currently occupied. "Then what exactly are we supposed to do? Just sit here and hide? Forever?"

"You want honesty, Stepan? You want me to be honest here?"

"Yes!"

"I don't know what we're supposed to do, okay? I'm not sure where to turn or what to do next. The entire God damned world is shooting at each other out there, and all I know is right now, we're safe here. That's all I know and all I'm banking on. Keeping you and Jorge alive. That's all I got."

Federov pressed his forehead into his hands and dropped down on the bed next to her. He wasn't crying but seemed to be on the verge.

"Look, Stepan. I know it doesn't feel like it, but you did the right thing. You did the only thing you could do. It's up to us to figure out what to do next, and believe me, we will. I just need a little more time."

He looked up at her. "How much time do you think we have,

really? How much longer do we think we've got before the Russians find out where we are? Or worse, until Capozza finds out?"

"We've got some time," she replied, though she didn't truly believe it. "I have to think we've got some time."

"I hope you're right, I really do."

Rosa stood, pressing her hand to his back to ease him up into a standing position.

"I'm right, okay? It's getting late. We were all up early. Why don't you and Jorge think about hitting the sack. We'll get some sleep and try to come at this fresh tomorrow. How does that sound?"

Federov nodded. He removed his hands, and she saw just how pale his face was. Completely and utterly drained of life. Walking as if his bones weighed a metric ton, he pried open the door and rounded the hallway towards the room that he and Jorge shared. She could almost taste the desperation and the uncertainty as it wafted from his wake. It was a thick, musky, pungent smell and it clung to everything around them.

Rosa had been honest with him, she didn't know what to do next. But she hadn't been quite honest about how much time she thought they had. She needed him to be patient, but in truth, she felt vulnerable here. Exposed. In the crosshairs. It was just a matter of time now, they just had to try to stay one step ahead.

Sleep would help. She hoped so, anyway. Recently, sleep only brought dreams and memories.

Bad ones.

At this point, that was a chance she had to take.

CHAPTER 43

The echoing slam came from somewhere, but Rosa couldn't quite figure out where. Slowly, hand over hand, she crawled her way up out of her deep and thorough slumber, feeling as if her brain was crawling up through thick custard. Every motion was met with resistance, every thought towards the light of the surface was obscured by layers of congealed gelatin. Even as she blinked her eyes, trying to chase away the creeping darkness, trying to pierce through the light of day.

It wasn't just her muscles feeling like they were caught in the swamp, her brain couldn't process the sound she was hearing with her surroundings. The closed in walls and vacant square of light coming through her window. This strange bedroom that was far too small and confined to be hers. Light walls, light ceilings, plain furniture, it was all so damned strange to her, even as the rapid-fire slamming wrapped its fingers around her and forced her to emerge from her deep slumber.

Slamming, who was slamming? Was it slamming? Or knocking?

As she struggled with a constant battle against sleep, she swung her legs up and around, sitting on the bed, a surge of dizziness washing her brain in a confused swarm. Her head pounded with a need for more rest, but the bone-on-metal banging wouldn't allow it.

"Rosa?" a frantic voice echoed from the hallway beyond her door. "Rosa! Someone's at the door!"

"I know," she mumbled as she clamored to her feet. "I know, get in your room!"

She heard Stepan's footsteps thump down the carpeted hall and retreat back into the bedroom as she pulled on her jeans and dropped the sweatshirt over herself. Sliding open the single drawer on the nightstand, she withdrew the Glock 19, recalling that it only had a handful of rounds, and slipped it into her waistband at the small of her back.

Emerging from the hallway leading to the two bedrooms, she crossed the living room floor, making her way around the small couch towards a rectangular window. Even as she crossed, more loud metallic *whams* resounded from the front door, the unique sound of fist on metal screen.

"Hey! Goose! Open up!"

It was someone who knew her at least. Was it Razor?

Taking a cautious step towards the front window, blanketed by the thin, white curtain, she slipped the pistol free of her waistband and pressed the barrel into the cloth and slowly pushed it aside, glancing out into the front yard. A busted up white hatchback sat in the driveway, perpendicular to the black van, blocking its exit, pock marked with batches of rust, a dent in the rear and torn off bumper. She leaned further out to look down the wall, and she could see four young men hovering outside the front door. They wore the familiar colors of the Blades but as she focused on their faces and tried to get a good view of their body shapes, she couldn't recognize any of them.

Razor.

Had Razor sold her out? She found it hard to believe, but the evidence was right here. The young man in the lead raised his hand into a fist.

"Goose!" he shouted, loud and long. He slammed his hand down, banging the metal door three times in quick succession. "Goose, get out here!"

Her heart raced. The Glock was cool against the flesh of her lower back, but felt very, very heavy, weighing down her entire body.

They had come for her. And even worse, they had come for them.

CHAPTER 44

"We're not messing around, Goose! We know you're there, *chica*!"

Rosa backed away from the front window, letting the curtain slide back in place. She slid the pistol from her waist band and ejected the magazine, counting to see how many rounds she actually had. Six was the answer. Too few by a lot.

"Who is it?" Stepan asked, peering out from the hallway, his hand pressed to the curve of the wall. "Are they calling to you?"

Rosa turned and nodded. "Yeah. But they're no friends of mine. Just get back in the room and keep Jorge calm, okay? I'll have to see how we can fix this."

His eyes flashed to the pistol in her hand, then back up to her face.

"Don't worry," she said. "I won't use this unless I absolutely have to."

He shook his head. "I hate guns," he whispered and went back into the hallway, shutting the door to the bedroom behind him.

"You and me both," Rosa replied. Giving Stepan a few minutes to get settled in the bedroom, she turned and walked towards the front door, her heart racing. Back first against the door, she pressed her left cheek against the smooth surface and shouted through the wood to the men outside.

"What do you guys want?"

"Just let us in, Goose, okay? We can talk inside."

"I'm not going to do that."

"Come on! Razor sent us, okay? We're supposed to come check on you."

"Well, consider me checked on. I'm good to go."

"That's not how this works!"

Rosa lifted her cell phone from her pocket and thumbed a number, then put the phone to her ear.

"Chuck, this is Rosa," she said when the voice answered. "We've got trouble."

"What kind of trouble?"

"I don't know why, but I've got some dudes from the Blades here. They say Razor sent them, but I'm not buying it. They're feeling pretty aggressive."

"Okay, give me your address," he replied. "I'm on my way."

Rosa recited the Westfield address to him, over the phone, and he acknowledged each part.

"Chuck, bring my Ruger, okay?"

"Never leave home without it."

Rosa hung up just as another flurry of slams echoed on the door.

"Open this door or we're going to open it for you!"

"That's not a game you want to play!"

The sharp raps of fist on metal stopped. It was silent for a few heartbeats. Rosa clasped her hands around the pistol and held it towards the floor at her hip, her hands shaking somewhat, her finger hovering around the trigger. Outside the metal screen door was pried open and pressed flush against the side of the house.

She wasn't prepared for the next metallic bang. It wasn't the sharp, rapid smack of fist on door, it was a deep crashing slam, a shoulder-shattering blast of someone charging forward and sending themselves crashing into the front door. She saw the wood give and bow as the body struck it. Hinges screamed. Outside she heard the shuffle of feet backing up, pausing, then surging forward again, slamming back into the wooden door, and again it bowed. The sound echoed throughout the entire living room and back behind her, Rosa thought she heard Jorge cry out in fear.

"God dammit," she swore, taking a step back. "I'm armed!" she shouted towards the door.

The next crash was the loud, dull slam followed by a sharp splintering crack. Where the hinges met the faux wood, the door split and burst, jagged edges thrusting out from the smooth, wooden surface, snapping and spewing splinters.

Rosa took three steps backwards as the front door spun inward like a drunken ballerina, one of the metal hinges breaking free and cartwheeling through the air in slow motion. Rosa's eyes fixated on the glint of metal, her view drawn from the door, just for that split second in time.

Bodies filled the frame of the door as a large, broad-shouldered man in a white tank top and yellow bandana charged into the living room pistol in hand. He was flanked closely by two more men of equal size and heft.

Rosa halted her backwards momentum and instead lunged forward, slamming her heel into the knee of the lead man, stopping his momentum and altering his sense of balance. As he lurched clumsily, she broke off, and lashed out with her right hand, fist clenched tight around the pistol, slamming the Glock butt first into the second man's right temple. She backpedaled as the third man pushed forward, but she raised her knee tight to her chest and shot it forward like a piston, pounding the bottom of her foot high into his chest, stopping his progress and throwing him back hard like a bag full of rocks. As he fell back out of the front doorway and down the steps, the first man corrected his fall and lumbered towards her, swinging wildly. She effortlessly parried his punch, moved into his range and drove her knife hand into his throat, stealing his breath for a moment.

As he coughed and stumbled, she twisted and drove the butt of the pistol into the crown of his head, splitting the thin skin there, drawing a gout of blood immediately. She stood in the center of the entry way, the three large men scattered around the floor around her.

"I can do this all day," she said through ragged breaths, turning at the waist and surveying her carnage. To her right, the guy started to climb to his feet, his pistol still gripped in his sweat slicked left hand.

Rosa swiveled at the hip lifting her weapon into firing position. "Don't fucking move!"

"Easy, Goose, easy," he mumbled.

"I don't know you." She growled. "You don't get to call me Goose."

"I don't know. That's just what Razor called you. That's all I know!"

"So, what do you want?"

"We just want the guy and his kid. Just let us take them and we'll leave you the hell alone."

"Why would I do that?"

"Because if you don't give him to us, the Russians will be here next. They'll just kill your ass and take them anyway."

Rosa glared down at him. "Do the Russians know where we are?"

"I don't know anything! Honest!"

"Did you assholes tell the Russians where we are?"

"I just know Razor was working some angles. They showed a lot of money. Seemed to know who you were and what crew you hung out with."

Things were starting to fall together. Rosa glanced out through the now empty front door. Things were making sense. Razor cuts a deal with the Russians, throws them under the bus, then sends his own goons in to snag them first and sell for even more cash. It's exactly the type of thing that Razor would do...she just never thought he'd do it to *her*.

They had to get out of here and now.

"Stepan!" she shouted, turning back over her shoulder. "Jorge! We need to move! Right now!"

The door burst open and the two nearly fell out into the hallway.

"Come on!" Rosa shouted, jerking her head towards the door. "The Russians are on the way. We're out of time."

Stepan held up for a moment. "They'll protect me. Maybe I'm safer if I stay with them? We can make this work!"

"We don't have time for this!" Rosa shouted. "At this point, they'll take any leverage they can get against Capozza. They have no attachment to you, trust me on this."

"But I'm their family," he said. "We're their family."

Rosa nodded towards Jorge. "Jorge is their family, yes. You and me? We're cattle. They will execute us, take the evidence, and who knows what will happen to your son."

Stepan looked around at the bodies on the floor, the men were moving and started to try and stand back up.

"We are out of time," Rosa reiterated. "Let's go!"

Tires screeched out in the road, a long and shrill rubber peeling skid.

"God dammit!" Rosa shouted, turning and running towards the front window. "We're too late."

The man behind her started to stand. She twisted and kicked back, striking him hard in the face with the sole of her shoe, snapping his head back. He slumped to the ground and his pistol thumped onto the carpeted floor. Rosa swung down and scooped it up, checked the model, it was a Heckler & Koch P30L, then pushed her stolen Glock back into her waistband at the small of her back. Moving over to the second Blade, who remained unconscious, she grabbed his pistol and compared it to the first, then ejected the mag of 9mm ammunition and slid it into her pocket. Repeating the motion with the third fallen gang member, she returned to the front window, this latest pistol clamped in tight fingers.

Out in the road, a blue hatchback was parked half on the front lawn and four men emerged from it, all dressed in T-shirts and jeans. Three of them held pistols, one of them had an automatic rifle held across his chest, and they started making their way towards the house. Seeing the front door busted open, they must have figured the Blades had already made their way in and broken the spirit of all who were inside.

The man with the automatic weapon was in a black T-shirt, a brown shoulder holster pulled tight around his barrel chest. He pressed the stock into his shoulder and lifted the weapon, moving into the point position as the pistol wielders spread out at his flanks.

Rosa spun towards the other two in the living room. "Get down!"

The sound came from all around them. Out in the front lawn, the man in the black T-shirt lifted his automatic weapon and hauled back on the trigger, roaring off a seemingly endless staccato rattle of gunfire. Front windows exploded inward, glass shearing the air above their heads as Rosa and Stepan hit the floor. Jorge pulled back into the hallway, his eyes widening. Bullets pounded into the outside walls and some blasted through plaster and wood, spraying into the living room, scattering tiny debris all over the carpeted floor in strange cascading patterns.

For a moment, the gunfire lapsed, and Rosa moved, figuring it was time for him to reload. Throwing herself up onto her knees and moving towards the blown out front window she saw the three men with pistols coming out around the man as he ejected his magazine and prepared to load a fresh one. Wasting no time, Rosa lifted her P30, aimed, and squeezed off two shots. Both shots struck the man with the rifle in the upper chest, and he shuffled backwards, spun awkwardly, and dove face first into the ground. As he thrashed, the men around him lifted their weapons and began firing back, driving Rosa to take immediate cover back behind the wall underneath the shattered window.

"Still trust them?" she barked back at Stepan as he looked up at her from his stomach, wood, plaster, and glass scattered all around him.

He shook his head.

Outside sporadic pops of echoing gunfire and more bangs of bullets on house walls kept their heads down. Rosa shuffled to her left towards the open space where the door used to be and sprang up into a firing stance, swiveling around the edge of the wall, weapon raised. She rattled off a quick series of shots, then yelled back to Stepan.

"Grab Jorge! We need to move!"

"There's men out there! With guns!"

"More will be coming!"

Stepan looked back and gestured towards Jorge, calling him over to him. At first the young boy shook his head nervously and stayed put, his muscles rigid.

"Come on! She's going to get us out of this!"

Jorge's eyes darted. Another pair of gunshots popped in the distance, then there was momentary silence, and the boy threw himself forward into a sprint. Stepan extended his arms and drew him into a massive bear hug, picking him up and carrying him from the living room into the entry way where Rosa stood, back to the wall. A few shots rang out, slapping wood from the door frame just to her left.

"You got the hard drive?" she asked, looking Stepan in the eyes.

He nodded and reached his arm around Jorge's waist, patting his chest pocket. "Right here."

"Okay. Can you run with him in your arms?"

He nodded.

Rosa looked down at her pistol and popped out the mag, exchanging it with the full one in her right pocket. Pressing her back against the door frame, she bent her arm, holding the weapon close to her with two hands.

"Get ready," she said. "When I open fire, head towards the van at full speed and get you and Jorge inside. I'll be right behind you."

Stepan nodded.

Four more shots rang out, three of them humming through the open rectangle and shattering against the wall deep inside the house, spraying sheet rock dust.

"Let's do this," she said, and spun around, pistol elevated. She squeezed off a rapid series of several shots and the minute the first crack of her pistol sounded, Stepan lunged forward behind her, out the open door and off the porch towards the van's driver's side. One of the Russian gunmen yelled and spun backwards while the other two scattered, grabbing cover, and Rosa glanced over towards Stepan then took off herself, coming up close behind him and his son. A scattering of return fire danced over the short, sloped hood of the black van, sparks bursting just to Rosa's left as she dashed around the edge of the snub-nosed vehicle.

"Are you in?" she screamed as she came around towards the driver's side, her hand already pressed deep in her pocket, closing around the keys.

"We're in!" screamed Stepan, his voice echoing in the empty darkness of the rear of the large vehicle.

Ducking her head, she swung around the opened driver's side door as one of the gunmen emerged from around the rear, his gun raised and firing. Rosa threw herself to the left as the window exploded just to her right and returned fire, clustering a pair of shots directly in the chest of the gunman. He flew backwards as she pushed herself into the driver's seat, jamming the keys in the ignition and twisting to fire up the engine. Rosa pulled herself up into the driver's seat as echoing bangs from the other side of the vehicle signaled the last Russian desperately trying to somehow stop them. Clutching the shifting lever on the steering column, Rosa slammed the car in reverse.

"Hold onto something back there!" she shouted and stomped on the gas pedal, sending the dark vehicle lurching backwards with a sudden, aggressive jolt. The tires caught on the pavement and screeched, then catapulted the van backwards, heading straight for the beat up white hatchback that had been parked there to block it in.

The last Russian gunman ran across the lawn, weapon raised, and fired at them, his pistol barking in his hand, spewing sparks and smoke, bullets rattling along the passenger side door. Rosa tensed her muscles as she looked in the rearview mirror and the van barreled into the hatchback with a shattering smash, breaking glass and crumpling the metal and plastic hybrid material of the vehicle.

Flat, square, and made of American steel, the van won the battle, spinning and tossing the smaller wagon aside into a lazy half circle in the road, the van screaming out among spraying glass and broken plastic. Spinning the steering wheel wildly, she went with the momentum of the vehicle behind her and brought the van into a tight left reverse turn, slamming on the brakes and bringing the large, boxy vehicle back around, then punched the accelerator and screamed forward, leaving black smears on the pavement behind them. Four more rapid gunshots followed, bullets smacking into the thick hide of the rear of the van and careening off into nothingness.

CHAPTER 45

Chuck thumbed the phone off, slipped it in his pocket and navigated around the scattered dumbbells in his bedroom. Swiftly pacing towards his dresser, he slid open the top drawer and reached deep in the back, withdrawing a locked metal box. He pressed a key from his key chain into the small padlock and unhooked it, then opened the top of the case and withdrew a Beretta 9mm pistol and a handful of magazines, setting them all out on the bed. Moving quickly, but as quietly as possible, he pulled out a pair of dark blue cargo pants from the third drawer down and pulled them over his narrow legs, then stood and speed-walked over to his closet.

"Prentiss!" he called, moving deeper into the closet. "Come on out, man."

"What the hell, bro?" he asked, coming into his brother's bedroom, looking at him kneeling in the closet. "What's going on?"

"No big," Chuck replied. "Just a contract. Don't get worked up."

"Dude, don't get worked up? You don't always wear that junk during one of your recovery contracts."

"Just need a little extra protection, that's all."

He pushed a thick stack of clothing over to the left, digging deep into the right-hand side of his closet, fishing around until he put his hands on the familiar surface of what he was looking for. With practiced, quick precision he drew out the Kevlar vest and swung it over his arms, fastening it in place around his chest and stomach. Reaching back into the closet, he pulled out a black vest of a thinner and more tactical nature, web stitched shoulder straps, a thin covering for the chest and several stacked pouches around the lower torso. Raising his arms, he dropped that down over his shoulders as well, then picked up the magazines from his bed and started sliding them down into the pouches around his torso. Wrapped up inside the vest was a thigh holster and strap which he removed and fastened around his right leg.

Prentiss looked at him, unconvinced.

"Just keep an eye on Travis tonight, okay? I'm not sure how late I'll be."

Afternoon was on the verge of its first appearance of the day, the sun high and bright in the sky, its light baking in through the open windows around them.

"Be careful, all right?" Prentiss asked. "Like really careful?"

Chuck picked up the pistol, checked that magazine as well, then slipped it into the holster, sliding it in place, then flopping over the leather strap and buttoning that down as well.

As a fugitive recovery agent, Chuck Heath made sure he had the equipment he needed, especially for particularly dangerous engagements. Something told him this engagement would qualify.

"Always, bro," Chuck replied. He stepped towards his brother and wrapped him in an uncharacteristic embrace. They broke it off and Chuck turned towards the other bedroom.

"Travis, you here?"

"Yeah!" he shouted from the other room.

"Listen to Prentiss, okay? I'm going out, maybe until late. No bull, got it?"

"Got it!"

Chuck looked over at Prentiss and shrugged. "I'll call you in a little bit, okay? Nothing to worry about."

"Are you telling me that or trying to convince yourself?"

Chuck smirked and slapped a hand on Prentiss' shoulder. Without another word, he turned, walked around the couch, out the door and towards the staircase to the front door.

He guided his sedan from the curb and turned left down a side street, his eyes alert for any sign of motion anywhere around him. If Officer Bondalewski was right, the Russians were out in force and while he had told his brothers and her that they didn't even know who he was, he couldn't be certain of that fact. His car had been sitting in their club parking lot for several hours, and while it was mixed in with plenty of others, that didn't guarantee anything.

Moments later the sedan passed the familiar coffee shop on the left and neared the road leading towards the People Finder's office. Chuck flipped the blinker and slowed to make a turn but corrected almost immediately. As he neared the turn off, he noticed a dark car parked in front of the building and two men talking near the front door. Men he didn't recognize. Men who reminded him distinctly of the unfriendly Russians he'd run into a couple of nights back. Steering back into a straight path, he touched his face gently, rubbing his fingers over the still swollen cheekbone. He could see quite a bit better now than previously, and his face looked a lot better than it had two nights ago, but there was still some tenderness there. Some evidence of a beating. Glancing at the clock on the car's dashboard, Chuck chewed his lip. This was going to get hairy, there was no doubt in his mind, and Rosa was in it deep. He had her Ruger in the glove compartment, but there were some things in the office that he needed, too.

"Dammit," he said under his breath and eased the car to the left, bringing it to a rest against the curb just past the entrance to the office building. The chain link fence ran parallel to the front of the building, then took a sharp right, creating an artificial perimeter around the small, one-story office, creating a driveway into a parking lot of sorts right in front of the squat building. There was no sign advertising what it did, but anyone in the neighborhood knew well enough. They'd all known Lenny Goff, and between Rosa and Chuck they knew the majority of the locals as well. It might as we have been a family business.

If Chuck and Rosa hadn't suspected Lenny knew he was in trouble when the police arrived that day over a year ago, the note and legal documents found afterward would have confirmed it. He'd left the business to the two of them, split both ways. Technically Rosa owned 51% of it, which was fine with Chuck, he had no desire to maintain a majority ownership, but Lenny was clearly feeling the heat and had made sure his business was in good hands should anything happen to him.

Something had happened to him. Maybe one day they'd figure out exactly what.

Chuck eased out of the driver's side door and slammed it behind him as he walked down the sidewalk towards the entrance. He'd have to worry about that later. There were bigger fish to fry right now. Chuck tugged at his black sweatshirt making sure it covered his Kevlar vest entirely. He'd removed the tactical half and left it in his car.

Pulling the hood up over his head, he stuffed his hands in his pockets and shuffled across the parking lot towards the parked car, glancing up from under the hood, verifying that the two men had spotted him.

The first man had a slender, but muscular build, clearly visible underneath his sparse tank top. He wore black wind pants and bright green Nike sneakers. The man behind him wore a gray T-shirt and blue jeans with a dark blue baseball hat cocked backwards on his head. Pulled tight across his gray shirt was a brown, leather shoulder holster.

"Hey!" the man in the tank top shouted in his thick accent. "What are you doing here, kid?"

Chuck looked up with a glossed over haze in his eyes. "Say what, man?"

The second Russian came up next to the first. "Come on, kid, you don't belong here. Move along."

Chuck looked over at the building. "This is that People Finder place, right? I need some people found, assholes."

The Russians looked at each other, both smirking. The one in the tank top turned back to him, hardening his face into a stone grimace.

"Don't be stupid you scrawny little piece of crap. There's nothing for you here, just move along, okay?"

Chuck took another step forward. "Where's Lenny? He here? Guy owes me some money."

The second Russian moved in, reaching across his chest towards the holster hanging under his left arm. Chuck's eyes darted from one man to the other, and he took one more step to move into their personal space, then thrust his left hand out, pinning the man's arm to his chest so it couldn't move. Tank top guy narrowed his eyes and lifted his arms to grab at him. Chuck pivoted and swung his right elbow out, striking the man in the bridge of the nose and sending him stumbling backwards.

"You son of a—" the second man in the T-shirt started to say, but Chuck torqued and drove his fist forward into his jaw, then drew it back quickly, moved his other hand and drove the fist into his solar plexus. Two quick punches and the Russian dropped into a heap on the concrete. The muscular man in the tank top had recovered and charged forward, blood streaming from his twisted nose. Chuck spun around and kept spinning, slipping out of his way, then drove his arm up in a rigid straight line, catching him under the chin with a reverse knife hand. His head whipped back and his feet flew out from under him, driving him backwards, dropping him onto the pavement on the back of his head.

He groaned and rolled over, motionless.

Chuck looked around, making sure there were no other men sneaking around outside the building, then he advanced slowly and quietly towards the front door. They wouldn't be out for long, he had to get in and get out and get gone.

Taking a careful stride up the stairs, he leaned forward and hooked his fingers around the handle of the front door, slowly turning. Pulling it open towards him, he eased sideways into the entrance, taking it especially slow and steady, his eyes darting to the various corners of the People Finders office. He could feel the pistol flush and hard against his right thigh, but he always hated using the weapon unless he absolutely had to. Slowly closing the door behind him, he took a single step into the main office, file cabinets standing firm along the perimeter and the familiar wood desk near the back wall. It looked exactly the same as it had when he'd come in for that first interview and, for a moment, he thought he saw the faded spirit of Lenny Goff sitting there, feet perched up on top of the desk, his eyes dancing and lips parted in his trademark smirk.

But it was just a memory. The office appeared empty.

Appearances could be deceiving.

The floor creaked just slightly, the slightest shift of pressure from one place to another, like something heavy being lifted or a person taking a quiet step.

Chuck turned to the right, towards the small kitchen area offset from the main office, essentially just a refrigerator and a few cabinets. A third Russian was there, his pistol leveled, his eyes wild, but focused. Chuck moved.

Shifting his weight, he lowered himself slightly, then lunged forward just as the man's Glock kicked off a roaring gunshot in the tight quarters, the bursting spark brightening the dim light of the office. Chuck lurched slightly, though the round skittered to his right, zipping in the air past his right ear and zinging off the plaster of the far wall. Even as Chuck shifted his weight and moved forward, the Russian was swiveling and bringing his pistol around. Another shot roared, again just to Chuck's right, but he moved forward and brought his arm around, knocking the Russian's hand aside, pushing the pistol down towards the floor.

Opening up the Russian's right side, he drove his left fist into his ribs, then stepped back as the man swung his gun hand back in a tight arc, whipping past his moving chin. Chuck stepped forward, brought his knee up and kicked the man in the chest, sending him stumbling slightly, but his back struck the corner counter, and he easily recovered. He swung his hand with the gun back around, but Chuck intercepted the motion with the edge of his hand, striking his wrist, then punched his elbow with the other hand, striking a nerve cluster and forcing the gunman's fingers to spring open, dropping the weapon.

The man charged forward, barreling into Chuck and throwing him back, and he struck the corner of the fridge, pain shooting up his spine. Rolling to the side from the impact, he saw the man continuing forward, rage splitting his stone face into two carved statues of insanity. Reaching out, Chuck hooked his fingers in the fridge door and yanked towards himself, ripping to the left and swinging the door open, sending it crashing into the Russian as he advanced. Stumbling to his left, he grunted in surprise, then Chuck planted his feet and threw himself forward, bringing his knee up and around, crashing it into the man's stomach. He fought back with a glancing punch to the temple, but Chuck rolled with the blow, then torqued back around, crashing his own fist into the man's face, then followed up with a second punch, and finally lunged forward, thrusting his shoulder into the man's chest, wrapping his hands around his arm, spinning and flipping him high over his shoulder.

The Russian struck the floor two feet away, his shoulders and neck taking the brunt of the blow, the cracking thud echoing loudly in the tightly confined office. He moved slightly, but Chuck stepped forward and kicked out, drilling him in the head with his booted foot and the man lay still.

Chuck stood there for a few precious seconds, fists clenched, lips snarling, then wiped a trickle of blood from his mouth and stood upright, turning towards the extended area of the office. Already in the distance he could hear police sirens screaming.

CHAPTER 46

"Chuck are you there?" Rosa barked into her cell phone, desperate to reach her partner. The black van sat idling at the side of the road, a few miles from the house which had become the scene of an action film gunfight. A tall and broken building rose from the sidewalk ashes just behind her, the van itself surrounded by a vacant dirt lot, bracketing it in, but casting deep shadow over the vehicle, keeping it at least somewhat obscured from view.

"If you get this, come meet us. The safe house has been blown," she said into the voicemail box, as calmly as she could. "We're making our way out of downtown, trying to get some space between us and the Russians. Both them and the Blades are coming at us hot and heavy, I'm not sure what else we can do. Need your help, okay?"

She disconnected the call and glared out the windshield, trying to focus. Trying to think of her next step. It wasn't an obvious one, she had no actual place to go, she just needed to get some distance so she had some time to think. Hopping from side road to side road, she'd already begun her trek out of downtown, a somewhat slow and meandering wander, avoiding the main roads and snaking around the perimeter of downtown, searching for quiet travel lanes. To this point she'd been lucky. But for how much longer?

Above the city, the sun had crested and already begun its slow decent, crawling its way down the darkening sky towards afternoon. Rosa sat in the driver's seat, her heart slowly slamming in her chest. She worked to keep it under control, trying to ease her nerves. They wouldn't be able to sit here forever, she knew that for sure, but it felt like the whole world was swarming around out there somewhere just waiting for them to make a mistake. Throughout her entire time in the Blades, in the United States Army, or as a Fugitive Recovery Agent, she'd never once felt quite so much like one woman against the entire world as she did right now.

"What's the plan?" Stepan asked, leaning forward. "Are we going to just wait here?"

Rosa shook her head. "I'm trying to give Chuck a chance to call back, but we'll have to move soon. There's too much risk just sitting here."

As if on cue a police car screamed past them, a black and white blur with their siren blaring, trailing blurs of red behind it.

Rosa glanced at her phone, looking at the time. "Okay, we need to move. I don't like sitting here. Hold tight, okay?"

Stepan nodded and withdrew back to the back seat with his son, making sure he was buckled in as well. Rosa shifted into drive and pulled out of the vacant lot, out onto the road, a two-lane street with traffic leading both ways, then sent the van surging forwards, crossing an intersection. Up ahead, she could see the familiar line of hotels and parking garages that bracketed the interstate, and she veered left, angling towards the main highway, trying to find a good way to get access to Interstate 91 which could take her pretty much anywhere she wanted to go up and down the Connecticut River.

Seeing clear roads up ahead, she pressed on the accelerator, carrying the van forward towards the speed limit, finally cresting at forty miles per hour. Up ahead there was an intersection which led into a gradual right turn towards an on ramp, the interstate progressing above, casting the street below in obscured shadow. The van picked up speed, moving towards a rapid cruise, coming up towards the intersection and Rosa put the blinker on, indicating a left hand turn to make their final approach towards a four-lane road that might finally lead them out of harm's way.

The Ford pickup truck came from nowhere. It was a huge truck, probably an F-250, colored dark blue, and as Rosa blasted through the stop sign, it was suddenly there, on her left, moving fast and making no attempt to stop. The Ford slammed into the van at full throttle, nose striking the large, flat left side with a crushing explosion of metal and plastic, bowing the side of the van in, crumpling the support structure, and sending them into an uncontrolled spin, tires pulling and squealing against the unforgiving pavement. Glass shattered and sprayed along the ground as the van twisted and spun, Rosa desperately clutching the wheel, her forearms tightening into vein bulging tensed muscles.

"God dammit!" she had time to shout as the van hurtled around into a 180, the noise and splintering feeling as if it was coming from all around her. Her side window shattered inward, safety glass shattering all around her, her head whipping to the side as the once normal world became a swirling tornado of crash impact chaos, the van spinning completely out of control, the echoing impact still resonating in her unprepared ears.

Even before the van stopped spinning, doors on the Ford flew open and men burst out, weapons strapped around their shoulders, pistols clutched tightly in angry fists. They moved quickly, throwing themselves down onto the pavement and immediately breaking into a run. Rosa's head was spinning, her vision clouded by the unexpected impact and as she scrambled for the door handle with one hand and her pistol with the other hand, three men in tactical vests approached the side of the van. They didn't look like Russians, but she couldn't quite be sure.

Even as she was unbuckling her seatbelt, they reached the van and popped the handle, sliding the side door wide open, revealing Stepan and Jorge's frightened faces, both withdrawing as the outfitted soldiers of fortune pressed onward. The small swarm of men moved into the van, hands clutching and grabbing and even as Rosa finally popped the seat belt buckle, the swarming arms wrapped around the two innocents and yanked them from their seats, dragging them across the pavement.

Rosa closed her fingers around the stolen P30L, then kicked her driver's side door open and lunged out, lifting the weapon and firing three quick shots at the large truck, which beyond the slightly crumpled hood was relatively undamaged in spite of the impact. Three holes dug into the windshield, one right after the other, sending spider web cracks across the glued glass, but the driver held firm, looking back as his teammates hurled Stepan and Jorge up over the back of the flatbed into the truck. As Jorge crested the edge of the flatbed and was clear, Rosa adjusted her aim to focus on one of the men and fired twice more, striking him in the torso. He shouted and stumbled backwards, but arms reached out of the bed in back and hooked around his armpits, yanking him up and into the truck.

"No, no, no, no, no," Rosa shouted as she stumbled from the front of the truck, her pistol lifted. She fired twice more randomly, but her ears were ringing and her eyes dazed and both shots went wide right. With a scream of rubber on pavement, the truck surged backwards, then spun into a tight reverse 180 and accelerated, more rubber peeling and smoke rolling from the rear tires as the pickup lurched forward, grabbed purchase and hurtled away.

She stood there in the middle of the road, stunned and uncertain of what had just transpired. The van lay askew behind her, thrown into a lazy diagonal position, the side twisted and broken, the hood spiraling smoke, windows shattered. It sat there broken and forgotten, just like Rosa felt as she stared helpless at the rear of the pickup truck growing steadily smaller in the horizon, taking Stepan and Jorge off to God knew where.

She'd failed. They'd grabbed them. She'd been completely helpless and defenseless against the coordinated attack. How would she ever get them back? The men who had moved in on her had been highly trained, coordinated and relentless with a frightening military precision. They weren't the typical crowd. It struck her as a work for hire situation, which just ratcheted this thing up a few notches.

As she stood there in the middle of the intersection, looking lost and uncertain, a dark sedan rounded the corner and drew closer, slowing its approach as it reached her. She still held her pistol, pointed down to the ground in her relaxed grasp, her eyes wide and vacant.

"Rosa?" Chuck stepped out of the sedan and ran up to her, his eyes quickly shifting towards the broken and smoking discarded van.

"Rosa!" he shouted when he drew up near.

She seemed to snap awake and turned her head towards him. "Chuck! They got them."

"Who did?"

Rosa looked back towards the road where the pickup truck had vanished. "I don't know. I think they might have been Capozza's guys. They weren't Russians. They weren't Blades."

"Dammit."

Rosa looked over at him. "I messed up, Chuck. I couldn't stop them."

"It's okay, Rosa." He glanced around, and in the distance, police sirens grew louder. They seemed to be coming from every direction. "We need to get out of here. Buy some time to figure out how to handle this. Get in the car, let's go."

Rosa looked out towards where the truck had driven, her eyes wide and empty. Lost. "I failed them," she said. "I couldn't help them. It happened so quick."

Chuck stepped forward and placed a hand on her back. "This isn't over. Come on, we need to go. We'll get this figured out."

Rosa looked towards him, her grimace an uncertain, blank curtain of confusion. Chuck wrapped a hand around her shoulder and guided her towards the car, then led her way into the passenger seat. She sat there motionless while he buckled her in and the sirens began scorching the night air. He ran around the other side of his car and slid swiftly into the driver's seat, shifted into drive and threw the car around in a tight, screeching semi-circle. His car throttled and surged forward down the street, hanging a tight left and vanishing under the encroaching shadow of the overpass just as the police arrived, blaring their lights and sirens, flanking the van and moving in, not realizing the driver was already gone.

CHAPTER 47

Mitchell Capozza stood in the lobby of his in-progress masterpiece, the three-story framework of the Capital Galleria. Designed as an ornate and decorative entryway to this upscale office complex, the first-floor lobby was already framed out with smooth faux-marble floors and an assortment of rectangular support columns stretching from the dark wood reception desk all the way out to the glass encased front entrance. Sheets of plastic clung to most of the windows, but the lobby itself looked surprisingly polished.

Near the rear of the lobby was an elevator which was not yet installed and operational, while to the right of the large, square greeting area was an entrance onto metallic scaffolding, which ran up the East side of the building at a steep angle, before ending in a platform on the second level. Capozza had walked down through the second level while coming down and unlike the lobby, it was wholly unfinished, currently just a long and wide rectangular area with no walled-off offices and only the wooden and metal support structure visible. All throughout the second level was construction equipment, tools, and stacks of wood, material all staged there in preparation for the next flood of work, scheduled to resume within the next few weeks.

The scaffolding continued on the opposite side of this second level, again climbing up at a steep upward trend, then curling back into the third level which was the penthouse office area. Capozza spent most of his time here up in the penthouse instead of down on the bottom floor where he current was, looking out over the river and surrounding buildings, enjoying the window which took up the bulk of the wall itself.

Today, however. Today, he was waiting for someone. He was waiting for a few someone's.

He heard the dull roar of the truck's engine before he saw it, the V8 powerhouse throttled as it carried the dark colored Ford around one last corner and angled it towards the construction site. Capozza looked out the front door and squinted slightly at the smashed in hood, though the damage looked relatively minor and the truck was certainly moving as if it had not suffered any negative side effects of the apparent crash. He watched as the truck meandered across the lane and veered right, pulling into the small makeshift parking lot where it stopped, crooked and slanted.

Flanking the vehicle, two more cars emerged, black four-doors, and they pulled up around the truck and stopped clumsily on either side. The doors opened and men emerged, pushing out from the vehicles, looking somewhat conspicuous in tactical vests and military kits.

Capozza strode forward, pushing through the makeshift front doors and crossing the gravel lot in front of the skeletal start to his lifelong dream.

"Gilkison!" he shouted as he neared them. "Get that truck hidden! Did you find them?"

The man in the passenger seat of the truck turned and scowled at Capozza, baring his teeth.

"Don't need to tell me how to do my job," he hissed. Placing his hand on the ridge of the flatbed, he vaulted up and over the edge, landing inside the truck, his knees coiling. As he motioned into the rear, so did two men on the other side, and all three of them bent down, looping hands around the arms of the concealed captives. One of the other men scooped up Jorge, holding him upright, while Gilkison levered Stepan Federov into a half crouching stance, then twisted and tossed the man over the side of the flatbed, down onto the ground in a hard, twisting crash. He grunted noisily as he hit the gravel a few feet below, then rolled over on his side.

"Phil, come on!" he shouted to the other guy in the truck and he nodded.

"Yeah, yeah, Dan, chill the eff out will ya?"

"Gilkison! Reed! Just do your damn jobs!"

Capozza sneered as Gilkison, then Reed vaulted back out of the truck, landing next to the prone form of Federov.

"Signed, sealed, delivered," he said with a crooked smile, coming up into standing position.

"Well done," Capozza said. "Well done, indeed."

"Where do you want them?" Gilkison asked. Behind him a small crew of military garbed contractors had spread out and flanked the two captives. Two of them grabbed Federov's arms and hoisted him up, holding him there.

"Take them upstairs," Capozza said. "Tie them down, there are some chairs up there already. Penthouse office."

Gilkison looked back at his crew and gestured with his head, and they went into motion, walking towards the building, Federov and his son pinned between them all, moving in one large crowd. Gilkison turned back towards Capozza.

"Deal's a deal, Mr. Capozza. You know where to drop the money."

"Indeed. But do you think your crew might be up for a little extra bonus?"

"What are you looking for?"

"Well...there's another group who is looking for Mr. Federov. I think we need to discourage them from their search."

Gilkison looked at him dubiously. "I'm not sure what you're asking."

"There's a night club in Hartford. This other crew uses it as their headquarters. I'm thinking we need to go down there and send a message."

"A message? Yeah, that's not really our bag. And really, Capozza, do you think I'm that stupid? I know what club you're talking about and starting a war with the Russian mob is not in either of our best interests."

"I could make it very much worth your while."

"Doesn't matter how much money's sitting in my account if I'm a corpse. No thanks."

Capozza grimaced, looking at the team leader through narrow eyes. "Let's go inside and discuss, shall we?"

"Nothing to discuss, but just lead the way, bub."

The two men turned and walked back towards the building. Reed separated and slid into the driver's seat of the truck, pulling it out of the gravel lot, onto the road and around the bend to get it as far away as possible from the construction site. As it drove away, and completely unknown to Capozza and Gilkison, a dark car came down the road on the opposite side, passing the smashed pickup truck, then rolling past the construction site at a casual, observant pace.

CHAPTER 48

"You sure that's it?" Chuck asked. "That's the truck?"

"That's the truck!"

"All right then," Chuck hauled on the wheel, cranking it hard right and whirling the vehicle around into a swift, tire-screeching turn. He could see the vague movement of the driver in the truck as he looked back to gauge what was going on. Not wasting any time, Chuck punched the accelerator and hurled the vehicle forward, slamming into the tailgate of the truck at a swift, sharp angle. The rear of the pickup lurched left, and Reed tried to compensate, but over steered, sending the blue vehicle careening into a brick building. Glass exploded and metal crumpled, taking the tough looking truck and twisting it into wreckage, the unforgiving surface of the wall smashing it down like an empty can.

"Quick and dirty," Rosa chuckled. "I dig it."

Chuck spun the wheel back around, bringing the car towards a three-story skeletal frame rising out of uneven ground, reaching towards the slowly darkening sky. It was three blocks away, yet stood tall and wide, standing out among the shorter buildings surrounding it.

Chuck nodded. "That's the site of Capozza's new office building," he said. "Not much of a stretch to put two and two together."

Rosa turned slightly, looking back out the passenger rear window at the building. "The guys who snatched them were well-trained and well equipped. Even if we know where they are, that's a far cry from being able to go in and get them."

"I don't see what our choice is. We can't trust the cops. The Russians and the Blades are crawling all over this city like cockroaches. If Federov and his kid are going to get out of this, I think it's up to us."

"You know," Rosa said quietly. "You don't have to do this. You've already put yourself in harm's way. You got grabbed, beaten and you could have been killed, all trying to help me."

"Rosa," Chuck replied. "I know what I signed up for."

"You didn't sign up for this. This isn't what the company is for. This is more…personal. I think you understand that."

Chuck nodded. "I know. I don't know why, but I know."

"I'm sorry," she replied. "I can't talk about it. Not yet."

"I get it, okay? I understand, and I'm here of my own free will. I don't feel like I owe you anything."

"If anything happened to you," Rosa said, letting her voice trail off.

"Well, Ms. Guzman," Chuck replied sarcastically. "I do declare. Are you…concerned for my safety?"

Rosa smiled a wan, flat smile. "Very funny, smart ass," she replied quietly. "Don't tell anyone."

Chuck laughed softly.

Looking out the windshield, Rosa drew in a breath, making some kind of sound as a way to change the subject. "We've got two or so hours until dark. What are the chances of them staying there that long?"

"They're not going to want to move them if they can help it. I'm sure Capozza is feeling the heat from the other crews just as much as we are. He'll want to set up shop and get his boys in a defensive position."

"Then I guess we know what's next."

CHAPTER 49

The fingers of night spread and covered the purple clouds, darkening the city. All around them, streetlights began to flicker on just as the stars in the sky blinked into existence, replacing the curtain of light with several smaller pinpricks.

Chuck leaned forward, his elbows on the hood of his car, a pair of binoculars pressed tightly to his eyes. Up ahead, the soon-to-be Capital Galleria stood tall, bracketing the darkened sky with automated floodlights, casting the surrounding area in pools of pale light. Surrounding the building was a large square patch of gravel yard, with scooped piles of material scattered about the mostly intact structure.

"All right," he started, slowly moving the binoculars left to right. "Bottom floor entrance looks like the main lobby. Smooth floors and we've got the framework for columns built out. Looks like four supports, spaced eight feet apart maybe? The structure of a reception desk is set up near the rear of the lobby, just in front of a nonfunctional elevator."

"Points of entry?" Rosa asked kneeling behind him.

"Front door is it. Side exit leading to scaffolding, which rises at what looks like a forty-five-degree angle to a platform on the second floor. I can't really make out what that floor looks like."

"Blind spots are *no bueno*," Rosa replied. As Chuck looked through the binoculars, she fastened a tactical vest around her narrow torso and clipped it together. "Thanks for stopping by the office and grabbing my gear."

"I couldn't leave you high and dry," Chuck replied, thinking back to the three Russians who had been waiting for him there and nearly cleaned his clock. "I grabbed all your ammo for the Ruger, too, though I don't know why you continue to use a revolver in an automatic world."

Rosa pulled out her favorite pistol and spun open the cartridge door, checking to make sure it was loaded. "Don't have to worry about a jam, and with speed loaders, this baby is locked and rocked nice and quick."

"Hopefully, we won't have to use it much."

"I'm not feeling real good about that."

Chuck sighed and moved the binoculars up just a bit. "Scaffolding continues on the opposite side of level two, then goes up to the penthouse suite. We've got two big windows on the top floor, though the sheets of plastic blowing around make it tough to see.

"How many men?" Rosa asked.

"They're moving around a bit, and I don't have thermal imaging, but I'm counting around ten."

"Jesus."

"Yeah."

"What the hell are we doing?" Rosa asked, turning and leaning back against the car, then dropping down into a seated position.

Chuck dropped down next to her, lowering his binoculars. "Time to call in reinforcements?" he asked. "Just say the word."

Rosa rested her head against the cool surface of the vehicle, closing her eyes. She trusted Officer Bondalewski, there was no fear there, but it's not like she would come alone. No. No cops. That wasn't a chance she was comfortable taking.

Lifting her head from the metal, she shook it slowly. "No. I think this one's up to us, Chuck." She looked over at him with an emotionless, stern stare. "Are you okay with that? Do you want to back out?"

Chuck wrinkled his brow. "Hell no," he replied. "I'm in this with you. All the way."

She nodded. "So, what do we have to get through to get inside?"

Chuck raised himself back on his elbows, the binoculars back to his eyes. "I see two men at the front door. One just has a pistol, one has a submachine gun. We'll have to take them out to get inside."

"Quiet, though."

Chuck nodded, then set the binoculars down and turned to look at her. "Ready when you are, boss."

Rosa checked the pouches in her vest to make sure she had plenty of extra ammunition for the Ruger while Chuck did the same, verifying his magazines were all accounted for as well. They packed light, but not too light, so they could still move around easily, but both Rosa and Chuck suspected that tonight they'd probably need their sidearms.

Chuck broke off near the front of the car and ran off, low to the ground, vanishing into the darkness as Rosa separated and ran around the rear of the car, melting into the lack of light surrounding the building.

A few hundred yards away, the two contractors stood on each side of the front door. They each wore black cargo pants, though the man on the left with the pistol wore a blue T-shirt and the man on the right sporting the M4 automatic slung across his ample chest was outfitted in a dark commando style sweater. The man in the sweater also wore a black baseball hat turned backwards while his partner had no hat, nor any hair to keep the hat on. Shaved clean bald with a thick, unruly beard, his eyes were stern, but alert, scanning the gravel grounds around them.

"Messed up," said the guy in the sweater. "Racked and stacked like this is Baghdad."

"The Russians are the ones turning the city into a shooting gallery. They'll steer clear of this place if they know what's good for them." The guard in the T-shirt turned slightly and, for a brief moment, thought he caught a flash of movement out of the corner of his eye.

"Wait a minute—" he started.

"What?" The other guard followed his lead and turned towards that area of the building as well. The pool of lights from the floodlights above didn't quite reach out to where the movement had been. He lifted his pistol and aimed it in the general direction of the movement, clasped between his tight fingers. Just behind him the guard in the sweater pressed his automatic to his shoulder, leaning his eye down towards the tactical sight, squinting down the barrel.

"Did you see what that was?"

"Nope."

Both men walked slowly, crossing step over step, carefully approaching where the lights met the dim blackness. It transitioned in various shades of gray, and they couldn't see anything even several yards ahead.

The contractor with the M4 let it drift downward slightly, squinting. "I don't see—"

From behind him, Chuck moved quickly. Slipping into the pool of light from the shadows on the other side of the building, he moved in and wrapped his arms around the man's face and throat. Muffling the shout of surprise, he squeezed and tugged towards himself, twisting to pull the unsuspecting guard off his feet. As he twisted, he moved his hip in and tossed the man, flipping him up and around, then driving him down hard into the gravel, his weapon skittering away across the hard surface of the tiny stones.

"What the hell?" asked the guard with the pistol, and he swiveled, bringing his weapon around as he heard the sound of the scuffle just behind him.

Rosa was pressed tightly against the building just barely in the shadows and as he pivoted, she moved forward. Going in low first, she side kicked him behind the knee with a piston-shot, collapsing his leg and driving him into a rough kneeling position on the gravel. As he dropped, she lunged forward, slipping past him and slammed the pistol out of his hands, then swiveled, driving her elbow into his forehead. Rolling from the strike, he threw himself up and towards her, swinging wildly, and she parried his first strike, then struck aside his next blow, she drove a follow up punch into his jaw, then a second to his left temple, whipping his head back with each strike. Lunging one last time towards her, he spread his arms wide, but she moved inside his range of motion and swung around him, clasping her arms around his neck, then pulling back and down, driving his skull into the ground.

She remained crouched there, knee pressed into the small of his back and looked over towards Chuck who remained huddled over his unconscious guard as well. They both listened for any noise, any indication that the conflict had been heard from inside, but all remained silent on the Western front. Chuck signaled to Rosa, and she stood, grabbing the pistol away and Chuck slung the M4 over his own shoulder as they came together and moved towards the front door, a rectangular plate of glass with cardboard covering most of the window surface.

Chuck pressed his back to the door, and leaned out a little bit, looking through the slivers of glass uncovered by cardboard. The lobby was clear inside, a wide, flat area with four thick support columns and the wooden frame of a reception desk against the far wall. He saw one man leaning up against the desk and two more wandering through the vacant entryway carrying weapons. From this distance and angle, he couldn't quite tell what model weapons they were sporting, but at least two of them were toting full sized submachine guns, and they certainly didn't seem to be equipped with silencers.

"Scaffolding is that way, right?" Rosa asked in a quiet whisper, gesturing over to the right side of the building.

Chuck nodded. "Yeah, but we'll want to take these guys out first. We don't want to end up sandwiched between levels."

Rosa acknowledged him, then hefted her Ruger, making one last check for balance.

"Be ready, Goose, once this starts happening, we can't stop. We have to keep moving all the way to the top. I only saw ten guys, doesn't mean there aren't more."

"I get it, Chuck," she replied. "All or nothing."

"You sure about this? Last chance."

"I can't abandon them."

Chuck looked at her. "What is it about them that means so much?"

How could he understand? How could Rosa even think about telling him? She stole their mother...their wife...their innocence. She wasn't going to let anything else happen to them if she could possibly help it.

"Maybe we can talk about it over a beer someday."

"I look forward to that."

Chuck turned back around, glancing through the glass and tested the front door. It was unlocked, and it started to pull open, so he relaxed slightly, glaring at the men inside, waiting for the right moment.

Glancing back at Rosa, he barked one last command. "I'll make a beeline for the column on the front right. You hit the front left. Use those for cover as much as we can, though we don't want to linger."

"Yessir," Rosa replied with a faux salute.

"I did outrank you when we were in the Army, Specialist Guzman."

He pulled slightly, easing the front door open. Rosa stayed low, crouch walking up next to him, then took over holding the door open and let him slink inside, his knees bent. As he crossed the threshold, he stood and darted towards the column, his feet tapping lightly against the smooth floor.

"Who's there?" one of the guards asked, spinning and lifting a Heckler & Koch UMP 45 in two hands, his left hand wrapped tight around a vertical fore grip. As their attention diverted to the quickly running form of Chuck, Rosa finished her entrance into the lobby and rose, charging towards the other column. As she ran, she lifted her Ruger, sighting on the lead man who already had the UMP stuffed tight into his shoulder and zeroed in.

As she ran, she squeezed off three quick shots, echoing blasts that sounded more like TNT than pistol shots in this confined, echoing space. All three shots missed, but the guard with the UMP lowered it briefly and turned towards her, attention successfully diverted. As he broke away, Chuck swung around his cover with the Beretta clamped between his hands. Taking a few precious seconds to aim, while cursing himself for having to use the weapon, he pumped two quick blasts at the guard, striking him twice in the torso. He was wearing a tactical vest, but apparently no body armor beneath it, as a pair of quick clouds of red spun off into the air as he stumbled backwards, his submachine gun whipping up and chattering wildly into the air.

"Son of a bitch!" shouted a second guard, back by the reception desk, and he vaulted backwards over it to grab cover just as Rosa tracked down on him and fired twice, knocking splintered wood from the makeshift greeting area moments after the man leapt to safety.

As one of the remaining guards jumped away, the other lifted his own UMP 45, bore down on Chuck and unleashed a volley of return fire, which the bounty hunter narrowly avoided by swinging back around the column. Just as he swung around the side, sparks knocked away at the support structure, chunking apart the hard surface and sending jagged sends skittering across the smooth floor. Rosa cradled the Ruger in two hands, then slung herself around her own column, coming back around on the other side, trained the weapon on the second guard and unloaded one last quick shot before her chamber went dry. Popping open the weapon and speed loading a fresh round of ammunition she ducked back behind the column as the rapid explosion of return fire pounded away where she had just been.

This was taking too long. Someone was going to call the police and this would be over before it began. Not good. Not good by far.

At the other column, Chuck came out from cover and fired with his Beretta, the pistol snapping back in his tight grip, smoke had started to fill the lobby. Glaring at the man with the submachine gun, Goose dropped low behind her own column and leaned out slightly, ducking as two pistol shots smacked into the column a few feet above her. She saw the man with the UMP swing up and around, aiming his weapon, but she was faster. From her low crouch, she swung up the pistol, took a second to sight it and fired twice.

The first shot struck the gunman in his right armpit, slamming his arm up and back and springing his fingers open, letting the weapon fly. As he started to turn from the momentum, the second round drilled into his upper right chest and took him off his feet. Even as he went spinning wildly from his position, Rosa sprung to her feet and dashed forward, slipping around her column and working to position the second further column between her and the reception desk guard. He saw her ploy and adjusted his aim, shooting swiftly, but she angled her run just right and his return fire went wide. As if they'd coordinated the whole thing, as he stood slightly to fire on her, Chuck pushed forward and swung up his appropriated M4 Carbine, rattling off a swift three shot burst. Two more large slabs of wood broke apart from the top of the desk, but the third shot hit home, punching into the third man's right clavicle. He shouted and toppled backwards.

"Go, Goose, now!" Chuck shouted as he twisted with the weapon, covering the rest of the lobby. Rosa charged forward, running diagonally from her position of cover and towards the right exit door, leading to the enclosed scaffolding. Chuck broke away from his own cover and followed her, coming up near as she drove her shoulder into the exit, slamming the door wide open.

The sudden cold gust of wind took her by surprise, and she winced slightly. Up on the second level, sheets of plastic whipped in the strong cross-winds, slapping flush with the building, then thrashing, and whipping back out across the stairway towards the next level. As Rosa hesitated, Chuck pushed past her, turning to run up the stairs, but pistol shots immediately rang out from the level above, the gunmen hidden by the slapping, wind-blown plastic curtains. Chuck shouted as a shot struck him high in the chest, throwing him, his back slamming hard against the metal cage supporting the external stairwell. Even as the clang of backbone on metal still rang in the air, Rosa lifted her .357 and fired twice at the blurred motion of the gunman above. He shouted and stumbled back, then struck the railing with his lower back and went over, his legs swinging up and around, carrying him in a lazy back flip over the edge and down a full story to the unforgiving gravel below.

A second man lunged out onto the platform above, pistol firing, and Rosa ducked to the left as bullets rang and sparked off the metal behind her. She fired again, then speed loaded another six rounds, but as the man slowly descended the stairs, he pressed up against the slightly curved wall of the modern building, and she couldn't quite get a clear shot. She ducked down and to the left again as three more shots sparked off the scaffolding railing and cage around her. Up ahead she could see him slowly start to advance again, but still couldn't get a clear shot. He glared down at her as he lifted his pistol in a two-handed death grip, the barrel leveled directly at her as she huddled down in the corner at the base of the scaffolding. She had nowhere to go.

A thrashing gust of wind tore through the scaffolding outside, and Rosa shifted slightly, aiming for the smooth glass surface of the building, then fired a round into the pane of glass just next to the gunman. It exploded outward in a jagged shower, opening up the inside to the raging wind, and the next gust snatched the plastic sheeting and pulled it outside in a wild, snapping furry, the semi-translucent sheet snarling the gunman, curling around him and whacking at him with squared corners. He cursed loudly enough for Rosa to hear amid the wind and back pedaled slightly, pulling away from the side of the building just enough. Goose lunged upward, raising her revolver and squeezed off a pair of shots directly into his center mass. They punched through the plastic and thumped into his shadowed form, and he lurched wildly, wrapping himself in the sheet, then toppled forward down the stairs, pulling the plastic from its mooring and tumbled with it end-over-end, until he came to a rest at Rosa's feet, the opaque covering already starting to stain red.

Beyond the gusting wind, it fell quiet with no shouts, no pistol shots, and no apparent follow up to the swift, but fierce gunfight. Satisfied that they were momentarily safe, Rosa stepped over the corpse of the gunman and dropped next to Chuck.

"Chuck! Are you with me? Are you hit?"

Chuck lay still, his eyes closed, a hand pressed tight to his chest just above the tactical pouches wrapped around his lower torso. Rosa put her own hand to his chest and lowered her ear to his mouth, her heart nearly stopping in her chest as she anticipated the worst.

She could feel a light puff of breath exhale on her cheek. It was low, but rhythmic. Just beneath her hand she could feel his heart beating.

"Chuck!" she shouted again. "We're running out of time here, buddy. You with me?"

Chuck's eyes fluttered, and he nodded briefly. "Here. I'm here. I'm good."

"You sure? Where does it hurt?"

"A little of everywhere."

Rosa shook her head but reached out a hand. Chuck wrapped his own fingers around her forearm and allowed her to heft him up into a semi-standing position.

"I need you on top of your game, Chuck, got me?"

He smiled weakly. "Just try to keep up. Me and my Kevlar, we're gonna get this done." Turning, he charged up the scaffolding stairs, heading towards the second level.

CHAPTER 50

"What the hell is going on out there?" Capozza screamed. Gilkison pressed his fingers to his ear where a communication device was tightly wedged.

"Lobby guards aren't responding!" he shouted.

Down below the sound of gunfire had faded, but that didn't ease their nerves any.

"Is it the Russians?" Capozza demanded. "Did they send an army after us already?"

Gilkison walked over to the nearest window and glanced out. The penthouse suite had plenty of them.

"There's no other cars out there, sir," he replied tersely. "I'm not sure who's heading up this attack."

"God dammit. What the hell am I paying you for?"

Gilkison whirled around. "You paid us to grab you this asshole," he gestured towards Federov who remained cable-tied to a metal chair. "Mission accomplished, *sir*."

Capozza took a step forward. "Now I'm paying you to keep us safe. How about you accomplish that mission?"

"That's not what we signed up for," Gilkison replied.

Capozza shrugged. "Seems to me it's too late to back out now."

Gilkison looked over to where Federov and his son were secured. Just behind them, Jerome and Pietro stood, decked out in their three-piece suits, with visible shoulder holsters underneath their dress jackets.

"We'll drop our weapons and walk out right now. We'll let your two experts here handle it."

"That would not be wise."

Gilkison took a long step towards him. "Care to elaborate on that statement?"

Capozza rolled his eyes. "This isn't a dick waving contest, Gilkison, for Christ's sake. I just mean I'm willing to pay. Very well. Protect yourselves, protect us, it will be worth your while, okay?"

"Jesus Christ," Gilkison shook his head. "I'd better be able to retire after this crap, Mitch."

"That's my boy."

Gilkison turned away from Capozza towards the small group of contractors still huddled in the penthouse suite. "Get down there! Take these dirtbags out! Got it?"

The group made various acknowledgment noises, then dispersed, heading out the side exist onto another scaffolding and down to the second level.

Gilkison turned towards Pietro and Jerome. "You dipshits are staying up here, I assume?"

Pietro nodded firmly.

"Fucking wonderful."

CHAPTER 51

Chuck pressed his back to the smooth surface of the building, glancing around the edge into the second level. Even from this vantage point, he could tell the second floor was still very early in the construction process with the bare framework of walls set up all throughout, stacks of plywood five feet tall, and tools spread out across the floor in various nonsensical patterns. The lighting was dim, but there, a lazy strand of construction light bulbs strung along the metal rafters and hanging down providing the only source of illumination.

"I don't like this," Chuck muttered.

"Don't have to like it," Rosa replied. She pushed past him, keeping her pistol low, but gripped firmly with two hands and ready for use. She took several steps into the darkened room, her eyes squinting to adjust to the variations in light.

She couldn't track any movements or see any evidence of opposition, and she glanced back for a moment to tell Chuck it was clear.

Rosa never saw the man who blindsided her, she just felt the sudden impact and crushing weight of a man launching himself at her, barreling into her back and sending her sprawling forward. She went over forward onto her right shoulder, slamming into a toolbox and sending it tumbling as pain scorched her arm and ran wild down her right side.

"Rosa!" shouted Chuck and moved in, lifting his M4 rifle towards the man who had launched the sudden attack. As he did, gunfire exploded from the far end of the large, vacant area, and Chuck had to duck and charge forward, lunging for a stack of plywood near the middle of the room to take cover. Chunks of wood spun up into the air as they fired upon him, but he skidded to a stop next to it, managing to keep his head low enough to avoid the attack.

"A chick?" the man who hit Rosa from behind got a good look at her on the floor as he stepped forward, his pistol raised. "All this craziness from a chick?"

"Go screw yourself," she sneered back at him.

His face twisted into a snarl and his finger caressed the trigger of his pistol, preparing to fire. Rosa had a fifty-fifty shot. He squeezed the trigger, and she rolled quickly right.

She guessed correctly.

The shot careened off the concrete floor, smashing a jagged divot as she rolled over and wrapped her grasping fingers around the rubber handle of a hammer. Not wasting any time, she whipped her arm back around, releasing the hammer and sending it flopping end-over-end clumsily towards him. He withdrew slightly, but the tool still slammed into his wrist with a dull thud. Shouting, his hand sprung open, releasing the pistol and sending it tumbling towards the ground. Rosa swept her arm along the floor as she jumped to her feet and charged him before he had a chance to recover. Hurling a swift haymaker punch, he lunged at her, but she stepped easily aside and rebounded with the huge pipe wrench she'd picked up from the floor. It slammed into the side of his face, splitting skin and knocking a tooth out onto the floor. Planting his foot, he pushed back, slamming a fist into her stomach and sending her stumbling, then he pushed forward, throwing another straight punch, striking her in the upper chest.

The gunfire eased up, and Chuck swung up and around the plywood stack, his M4 leveled at one of the remaining guards.

Squeezing off another quick three round burst, the guard shouted and stumbled backwards as the last man broke away and headed towards where Chuck was huddled. As more pistol fire echoed in the air, Chuck dropped behind the plywood stack and shards of busted wood and smoking chunks of debris rained down over him.

Rosa took a few clumsy steps backwards as her opponent advanced. He attempted another desperate punch, but she sidestepped and brought her wrench crashing down on his arm, shattering bone and driving it downward. As he lurched forward from the momentum, she swung the wrench back and crashed it into the bridge of his nose, the cartilage blowing apart in a splintering crunch of metal on flesh. He faltered as Rosa spun around and brought the side of her foot against the side of his face, whipping his head around and throwing him roughly to the ground where he lay still. She tossed aside the wrench and scanned the floor for her .357.

Chuck remained pressed tight against the plywood as his attacker advanced, pistol held out in a ready position.

"Come on out, boy!" the man shouted, swiveling, his gun scanning the immediate area. Chuck jumped and planted his hand on top of the plywood stack, vaulting over it. The man shouted and stepped back, but it was too late as Chuck's sneakered foot slammed into his gun hand and knocked the weapon away, sliding and tumbling across the concrete floor.

"Don't call me boy, you racist asshole!" he shouted as he landed in a crouch next to the surprised contractor. The man lashed out with a punch, but Chuck ducked away from it, then launched a straight-leg side kick into his ribs, sending him shuffling backwards. Recovering, the man swung an angry fist, which Chuck parried for a moment, but only delayed the attack briefly as a second punch slammed into his ribs. Chuck tried to recover, but the man advanced again, striking him in the face with a follow up punch and sending him slamming backwards into the stack of wood.

"I'll call you whatever I want." He growled and charged again. Chuck ducked down and to the left as the man punched, his fist striking the edge of plywood instead of skin and bone. He shouted and pulled his hand back and Chuck moved in, slamming a fist up and under his chin, then a follow up to his stomach. Stunned, the contractor took an unsteady step backwards and Chuck swung a straight leg in a tight arc, drilling his instep into the man's face, then following the momentum with a follow up back kick, pounding his heel into the chest of the gunman. The air exploded from his lungs as he left his feet and slammed backwards onto the concrete floor, his eyes rolling back in his head.

Chuck looked back as Rosa approached, Ruger in hand.

"You good?" he asked.

She nodded somewhat uncertainly, rubbing her head and shaking out the cobwebs. They'd both taken some punishment and still had work to do.

"One more level. Any sirens yet?"

"Not yet, but it's just a matter of time."

"Let's finish this, huh?"

Rosa lifted her weapon and checked the ammunition load. Chuck checked his M4 and saw that it was more or less spent, so he cast it aside and returned to his Beretta, loading a fresh magazine from one of the pouches on his tactical vest. Up ahead the side door led to another metal scaffolding encased in an elaborate metal cage, which climbed up to the penthouse suite where Capozza was no doubt waiting.

"Yeah," Rosa replied. "Let's finish this."

She strode determinedly ahead, her weapon clutched firmly, her eyes two narrow slits as she glared towards the metal cage beyond the simple rectangular opening. Chuck fell in behind her and as they approached, the first, distinct warble of police sirens echoed in the distance.

Rosa turned briefly. "Dammit."

"Time's a wasting."

Moving to the side door, Goose pressed her back up against the wall, listening for any distinct movement on the metal stairs on the other side. Bending her elbow, she tucked her arm close, pointing the pistol up to the sky. Chuck fell behind her, flush against the wall as well, his own pistol pointed down towards the ground.

"Two outside, three in the lobby, two on the stairwell, three more on the second floor. That's ten total. How many did you see?"

"I saw ten," Chuck verified. "Doesn't mean there aren't more."

She nodded, stepping slowly out onto the metal, grated floor up on the second level. The wind blew around, battering at her face, and she winced slightly but remained half in and half out of the doorway, glancing up the stairs towards the next platform. It was a flight up from where she stood, and at first glance appeared empty, so she took another careful step out, pistol slightly raised, her finger just touching the trigger guard.

Her steps were soft, but still clanked quietly on the metal beneath her feet as she took another step towards the first stair, wind still whipping at her hair and biting her face like a hundred tiny, invisible piranhas.

She lifted her foot, moving to take the first step, but the blur of motion at the top platform caught her eye, and she shifted immediately, lunging to her left. Three swift cracks of gunfire echoed from the metal ledge above and in front of her, a dark clad man clutching a pistol firing down at her. Sparks splashed on the metal railing behind her as she ducked down and away, metal rebounding off metal.

Swinging around and through the opening, Chuck lifted his pistol with his left hand and fired twice up towards the shooter and he pulled his weapon close to himself and withdrew to avoid the return fire. The moment the gap in gunfire occurred, the eye of a lead-laden storm, Rosa threw herself forward, taking the metal stairs two at a time, hurtling up towards where their opponent was stationed. Gilkison recovered quickly, readying himself again to take aim at the man firing at him, but Rosa was too fast and was suddenly on top of him, slapping aside his gun arm with a hard strike to his inner forearm. The pistol spun wildly out of his hand and over the railing, and she followed up with a swift punch, but he parried the attack and threw out a swift front kick, catching her in the chest.

Leaving her feet, she toppled backwards, her shoulder striking the metal stairs hard and taking her over backwards into a clumsy, painful, bone-jarring somersault down the stairs.

As Rosa slammed back down onto the platform, grunting in pain, Chuck corrected his aim with his pistol again and drew down on Gilkison, rattling off another trio of gunshots. The lead contractor faked right, Chuck adjusted his aim again to compensate, but his enemy shifted back left and launched himself from the platform, going airborne over the row of metal stairs as Chuck's gunshots went wide right.

Chuck back pedaled slightly as the full weight of Gilkison hurtled down towards him, but it was too late for him to dodge. The man slammed down onto him, pounding his back into the metal cage behind him, bursting spit and blood from his mouth, pain exploding in his spine and racing on white-hot rails throughout his limbs. Gilkison pulled back slightly, closed his fist, and lunged forward, swinging, but Chuck dipped right and slapped the punch away, countering with his own rocket shot to the ribs. Gilkison didn't hesitate and rebounded with another piston-armed blow, but Chuck pulled back, letting the fist glance off his collarbone.

Rosa looked over, picking herself up off the metal, clutching her left shoulder and moving slowly, tears stinging her eyes. She could feel everything. Her limbs seemed to be moving okay and nothing felt broken, and she wrapped her fingers around the contoured grip of her Ruger pistol, pulled it close and glanced over at Chuck. She flashed him a concerned look, seeing him pinned against the cage as Gilkison pulled back his fist for another blow, but he returned her glance with a shift of his eyes, telling her to go. She nodded to him and leaped up, once again taking the stairs two at a time, but this time there was no one at the top platform to stop her, this time she had a clear path to the platform above. This time, Capozza was within her grasp, so close she could almost taste him.

The sirens wailed, louder and closer, and Rosa feared she was already out of time.

CHAPTER 52

"Pietro! Jerome! Get ready!" Capozza shouted as he stormed around the penthouse. Just outside on the scaffolding they could hear the pistol fire ratcheting up and ringing out loud. Bullet sparks rebounded off the metal surface just outside the entrance to the third floor. His men had never seen Capozza quite so rattled, his normal composure shattered by the sudden and effective attack by Guzman and Heath as they systematically punched through his well-trained defenses. A gunfight. It was an actual, legitimate gunfight in the middle of his brand new corporate tower, and he felt decidedly on the ropes.

The penthouse office was smaller than the second level, but still had direct access to the outside construction stair system. Two of the three walls were covered with windows and an ornate, partially constructed desk was perched near the rear of the square room. Directly in the middle of the half-built room two metal folding chairs sat with Stepan and Jorge Federov tied down to them with fierce plastic cable ties. Tears had dried on Jorge's cheeks, but his father maintained a firm and stern grimace, his scowl sculpted like stone etched from pure rage.

Capozza's two men came around the metal chairs, pistols raised in anticipation of someone coming through the opening, waiting for the right opportunity to shoot. The gunshots ceased from outside, but the labored grunts and shouts told them that combat was not yet over. They stood there, weapons raised and ready, barrels leveled, eyes focused on that single entry point. In their minds, they could see any number of scenarios, one person, two people, a whole squad of Russian operatives. Most of the ideas that flashed in Pietro's mind were frightening, a group of large, hulking men with tight crew cuts and submachine guns barreling through and chewing apart everyone within eyesight. Over and over and over again he saw that vision in his mind, and his pistol jerked left, then right, hovering there waiting.

To his right Jerome wiggled his fingers around the handle of his pistol, trying to keep feeling in them, trying to calm his nerves and steady his aim. Neither of them had any idea what was coming yet they were being expected to lay down their lives to battle it back.

The faint sound of bone on metal could be heard, a wild struggle against the scaffolding outside, then followed by the hollow slap of shoe on stairs, a series of echoing footfalls pounding up those last few steps towards the entrance. In the whipping wind it sounded like one person...or ten all at once.

"They're coming!" shouted Jerome and his weapon flinched slightly, moving, not sure precisely where to aim.

Blurred motion appeared in the doorway, a swift and sudden dark smear of movement, and both men jerked, then fired wildly towards the center of the opening, desperate to stop the oncoming barrage they were both certain was impending. Seeing that shift of motion, that shadow traversing from one place to another they were both certain they'd aimed their weapons directly in center mass and unloaded, envisioning that their onslaught was plowing into a thick cluster of oncoming Russian operatives. They could see the blurred motion spasm when struck, twisting and flying back, material flying from the impact, a spray of something, the blur of motion suddenly torqued violently the other direction.

All six wild shots seared towards Rosa Guzman as she moved,

bullets cutting through the air like hot blades through water, steaming and scorching.

All six wild shots soared above her as she dove, underneath the tactical vest she had thrown into the doorway to serve as a brief distraction.

Bullets pounded mercilessly into the pouched cloth, tearing into the fabric, shredding the straps, tearing the massive pouches into shorn shreds, nearly eviscerating the entire thing, spraying scraps into the air. Rosa slipped underneath, clutching her Ruger in two hands, striking the hard, smooth floor with her left shoulder, yet managing to keep her aim true, looking down the barrel, her body nearly parallel to the floor in a desperate, lunging, sideways leap.

Things felt like they were moving in slow motion, as if she was falling through some sort of clear gelatin, diving, yet almost floating as the two men stepped towards her, their weapons barking pulsing fire and smoke. She pulled the trigger of her .357 the moment before her shoulder struck the ground, jarring her aim, and the first two shots slammed Pietro in the upper chest, striking him like a mule kick. His feet shot out from underneath him, and he toppled backwards, his arms flying up in the air, sending his Glock pirouetting into the air. She grunted, her already sore shoulder and back muscles barking more fiercely as she continued her roll to the left.

Jerome adjusted his aim slightly and fired three more times, chasing her rolling form with a series of clumped fountains, chunks of hard floor spitting up into the air. With one last uncontrolled tumble, Rosa came up on one knee and threw out her foot, stopping her momentum, rising with two arms firm and hands clasped around her weapon. It jerked twice, blasting yellow from the stubbed barrel, the Ruger kicking with each powerful shot. Jerome tried to compensate, but the first shot struck him in the stomach, and he stumbled backwards, dropping slightly, letting the second shot pound into his sternum. With one final grunt he slumped over sideways, his weapon clanking across the concrete floor.

"Don't take another step!" Capozza shouted. "I mean it!"

Rosa swiveled in her kneeling position, glancing over towards them. Mitchell Capozza stood just behind Federov, a pistol pressed tightly to the back of his head, a firm grip on his left shoulder.

"I will paint my brand-new floor with his brains, Guzman."

Rosa lifted her hands, the pistol dangling from one finger by the trigger guard. "Take it easy," she said.

Capozza sneered at her. "Unbelievable. I paid you to find him, not to steal him from me!"

Slowly, Rosa stood to her feet, her hands still raised, her pistol clattering to the ground. "Yeah, clearly you have his best interests at heart."

"All I want is the data. That's all I ever wanted. I never wanted any of this." He was breathing sharp and heavy between each barked word.

Stepan glanced up at him. "You kill me or my son and you'll never get it."

"There are only so many places you could have hidden it," Capozza replied. "I think I could find it even with the both of you rotting in the ground."

Federov's eyes darted over towards Jorge before closing as if he couldn't even fathom a world where his son might no longer be in it.

"Sounds like we're at a stalemate," Capozza said. "Because if I don't get the data, I'm going to kill you both." He took a step to the left, moving the pistol over towards Jorge. "And I'll start with him first."

"Dammit, don't do this!" Rosa shouted. "Don't you hear those sirens? The police are almost here. How do you think this ends for you? How do you possibly get out of this unscathed?"

Capozza laughed. "You think I'm afraid of the police, little girl? You have no idea who you're dealing with."

Federov's eyes blinked open. For the briefest moment, Rosa saw doubt skitter across his face like a roach running from unexpected light. She caught his eyes and shook her head firmly.

"Oh, come on," Capozza said, catching the exchange. "Do you really trust what she's telling you?" he asked Federov. "Don't you know who she is?"

Guzman's eyes darted towards Capozza, widening slightly.

"Oh, you didn't tell him, did you?" Capozza asked, looking over at Rosa. "You didn't tell him about how you used to run with the Blades back in the day?"

This time it was Federov's turn to snap his eyes towards Goose, a mixture of confusion and curiosity etched across his face.

"Oh yeah," Capozza continued, patting Federov on the shoulder. "I bet she didn't tell you she was there the day your wife was killed, did she? That she was one of the punks turning downtown Springfield into a shooting gallery? She didn't explain all of this to you?"

"Those records are fucking sealed." Rosa hissed.

"Not to me, little girl."

Rosa's shoulders slumped slightly under the scalding burn of Stepan's glare.

"I was going to tell you," she said weakly. But that was a lie and both of them knew it. Stepan didn't reply, he simply shook his head.

"Okay, enough of this," Capozza said. "We're ending this." He stiffened his arm, pressing the pistol even more tightly against Jorge's temple, hard enough that the boy's head tipped slightly, tears spilling from his eyes.

"Don't!" Stepan shouted, his voice cracking.

"Capozza!" Rosa shouted. "You don't have to do this. I'll help you find the data! Take your hatred out on me, not the boy!"

He pressed on the pistol even tighter, moving his finger from the trigger guard to the trigger.

"You have three seconds," he said to Stepan, his lips split into a sneer.

"Okay, okay, okay!" Stepan shouted. "I'll tell you! It's in a safety deposit box! I've got the key in my shoe!"

Capozza smiled and turned towards Federov, but kept the pistol pressed tight against Jorge's head.

"See? Was that so hard?"

"Please," Stepan pleaded, actively sobbing now. "Just please, take the gun away."

Capozza shook his head. "You betrayed me. Betrayal must be punished, Stepan. That's the way this relationship works."

"No!" Stepan shouted.

Capozza pressed the pistol, his finger touching the trigger.

The gunshot echoed in the small confines of the penthouse suite, rebounding off the glass paned windows and unfinished walls. It was the loudest, most final sound Rosa had ever heard, and the exclamation point at the end of this operation.

CHAPTER 53

*R*osa's eyes had been pinched closed, not wanting to see, not wanting to believe what had undoubtedly happened. She'd seen all manner of things during her time in the gangs and her time with the Army, but those things had all been framed differently. Enemies. People she didn't know. She couldn't face it, couldn't stomach the idea that Jorge lay before her, face down, his head bullet torn and broken.

She heard Stepan's desperate cry first. A hoarse shout.

But it wasn't a shout of anguish. It was… something else.

Rosa snapped her head up, daring to pry open her eyes and saw it, Jorge stumbling, scrambling forward, crawling over the concrete as Mitchell Capozza went flailing wildly backwards, shocked by the concussive noise of the abrupt gunshot. A gunshot that, apparently, was not his.

Rosa moved, ducking and charging as Capozza righted himself, rebalancing his stance, moving his arm, tracing the movements of Jorge Federov with the large pistol clasped in his hand. Everything wound to slow motion, as if time was passing through transparent syrup, all movements dragged and sluggish, every single action a focus of hyper attention. Rosa saw Capozza's hand arc to the right, she saw his finger move towards the trigger, and she felt herself throwing her body forward, between Capozza and the child, without hesitation, willing and able to take the bullet. Capozza's eyes snapped towards her as she moved between him and his target, swinging the weapon around, his finger tightening on the trigger as he did.

The weapon fired again, a deafening, echoed snap, but Rosa pressed forward, not paying any attention to the trajectory of the bullet as long as it wasn't heading towards the child. She heard the whiz of the round scream past her left ear as she moved within the arc of Capozza's motion, slapping aside his swinging arm and plowing into him headlong. The pistol arced from his splayed fingers and he tumbled backwards, his shoulders slamming into the wall-sized window he loved so much, the impact starring the glass, bowing it out, then finally sending it exploding outwards, a wild, bellowing spray of shards. His face twisted as he looked back at her, eyes narrowed, mouth contorted in a split lip growl of rage. Hovering there for a moment, at the precipice, he cursed her, his eyes burning into her.

Then, he was gone.

He went over backwards, feet skidding from the glass covered floor, and then he was out and down, plummeting through the air, hurling down from the penthouse level, screaming in silence towards the ground below.

Moving towards the edge of the room, she glanced through the broken glass at Mitchell Capozza, laying sprawled in the grass and dirt. For a moment, she thought she could see him moving slightly, his arm reaching for something that wasn't there.

Stepan glanced wildly around the room, trying to figure out just what was going on, and his eyes finally fixed on Chuck Heath, who stepped slowly into the penthouse, a wisp of smoke still spiraling from the barrel of his Beretta 9mm.

Federov whipped back around to look at his son, eyes wide and hopeful, and Jorge looked back at him, tears rolling down his cheeks, but just tears, no sign of injury.

Outside, police sirens wailed and red lights reflected across the glass windows. Rosa and Chuck glanced at each other, then looked towards the scaffolding, suddenly quite concerned with what might happen next.

CHAPTER 54

Rosa Guzman was not necessarily accustomed to interrogation rooms and was certainly not accustomed to being the one in the metal chair at the opposite end of the table from two well-dressed men in black suits and boring ties.

"Good morning, Ms. Guzman. Good to see you again. If you don't remember, my name is Agent Pisani, the man next to me is Agent Howlett. We're with the FBI."

Rosa smiled and nodded. "I remember. I thought we worked pretty well together during that assassination case a few months back. Don't suppose that earned me any brownie points with the feds?"

Pisani couldn't help but return the soft smirk, though Howlett scowled at him for it. Pisani's shirt was unbuttoned at the top button, his collar pulled slightly askew, a five o'clock shadow running over his jawline and down the gentle curve of his neck.

"This is quite the mess you're involved with Ms. Guzman," Agent Howlett said. He sat on Rosa's left, his black suit offset by a dark blue tie, brown hair cut short. Pisani looked remarkably similar, only his tie was just as black as his suit coat, and he had no hair whatsoever. Rosa had already met them both during a particularly harrowing mission with an international assassin a few months ago, though neither man was acting as if she was a former partner.

She looked from one man to the other, her face solid and calm.

"I make no apologies," she said. "There were two lives at stake. They're safe now."

Agent Pisani leaned forward on his elbows. "You don't think the police could have helped with that?"

Rosa looked him in the eye. "I assume you've read the report. I'm sure your guys have torn apart the data on that hard drive."

Agent Howlett interjected. "Of course. But you left a trail of corpses in your wake, Ms. Guzman. And judging by your juvenile records, not to mention your military ones, this seems to be a trend."

Lacing her fingers together, Rosa clenched her hands into an interlocked fist, the veins standing out on her forearms. She didn't reply.

Agents Pisani and Howlett looked at each other briefly, then looked back at her.

"Ms. Guzman, you are right, the data collected from Mr. Federov's hard drive was extensive," Agent Howlett said. "Extensive enough that it caught the attention of our assistant director and the district attorney."

"We're prepared to overlook the incident at the Capital Galleria building site," Agent Pisani said. "Mr. Federov has insisted that we do so in order to ensure his cooperation."

Rosa smirked and nodded softly. "For me and Chuck both?"

Agent Pisani nodded. "Indeed. Both you and Mr. Heath are in the clear on this one."

"But make no mistake, Ms. Guzman," Agent Pisani said. "Let's not make this a habit, shall we? Or more of a habit than it is already?"

"Deal," Rosa replied. "I don't exactly take pleasure in this sort of thing. It just seems to happen around me."

"That is a fact we are both well aware of," Pisani said, nodding.

Howlett graciously ignored his follow up. "I hope it stops happening around you,"

"You and me both," Goose replied, pushing herself up from her chair. "Am I free to go?"

"Just a minute," Pisani said, his eyes darting over towards his partner. "Give us the room for a minute, okay, Darren?"

Agent Howlett nodded and stepped away, moving towards, and then through the small door, letting it click shut behind him.

"What's this about?" Rosa asked.

Pisani crossed his arms over his chest and looked at her over triceps bulging underneath the not-so-loose fitting pale blue shirt.

"Look, kid," he said, though Rosa thought she wasn't more than five years younger than him. "I don't know why I got this detail. Usually I'm in charge of some more…eccentric operations, shall we say? I suspect someone wants this swept under the rug."

"What do you mean?"

Pisani pushed up from the table and turned away from her, talking to the wall. "I have some…unusual beliefs. Some might call me a conspiracy theorist, but I prefer the term 'enlightened individual'. Whatever you want to call me, usually if I'm getting stuck with a particular detail that seems on the up and up, it's because the higher ups don't take it all that seriously."

"Okay?"

"Few months ago, they called me over to New Hampshire to check out a freaking werewolf attack. You believe that?"

Guzman chuckled, shaking her head. "What's that got to do with me?"

"My question exactly," Pisani replied. "They assigned me to your case, which tells me, they're just going through the motions. You either have friends in high places, or friends that just want you to disappear. Either way, I don't think you have a whole lot to worry about here."

"I've got no friends in high places, believe me."

Pisani shrugged. "Okay, then. Well, whatever. I can't tell you why, I just go where they tell me to go, and they told me to come talk to you. That says to me that they need to look like the FBI is involved without really bein' all that involved."

"Fair enough."

"That being said," Pisani continued, "you stir up stuff like this again, and I'll be back, okay? Just because you don't have fangs or weren't abducted by aliens don't mean I don't give a shit. So, keep your stuff straight, got it?"

Rosa nodded. "Aye aye, cap'n."

Agent Pisani sighed deeply, then gestured for her to leave, and she stood from her chair, turned around and walked out of the interrogation room. Pushing through the door, she walked out into the main precinct building itself, and almost immediately Helen Bondalewski stood from her desk and approached her.

"Goose, everything okay?" she asked as she came close.

Rosa nodded. "I'm clear. Stepan told them he wouldn't help unless me and Chuck were let off." She let out a long, relieved exhale, the force of which surprised even her.

"Good."

Glancing off to her right, Rosa's eyes narrowed on the office of Captain Hunger. The chair was empty behind the desk, but two men in dark suits were going through files inside.

Bondalewski followed her gaze. "Can you believe that? Even Captain Hunger was in his pocket."

"Unbelievable." Rosa looked past Helen, and her eyes briefly met Stepan Federov's who was walking into the precinct from another concealed room, flanked by more FBI agents. She smiled at him, and he looked as if he might return the smile, but then pinched it back down into a grimace.

"I'll be right back, okay?" Rosa asked and strode past Helen towards were Federov was approaching.

"Stepan," she said. "Can I have a minute?"

The three FBI agents walking alongside him all exchanged looks, but Stepan turned towards them. "It's okay. Give me a few minutes please."

They quietly dispersed leaving the two of them as alone as two people in the middle of a busy police precinct could possibly be.

"Stepan, I'm sorry. I should have been more honest with you up front about my past." Rosa chewed the words from pursed lips, knowing in her heart that even as she apologized for not being more honest, she was still not being completely honest. The secret of her role in his wife's death was a thick block of ice wedged between the two of them, cold and unforgiving.

Stepan's hard look softened a little. "Yes, you should have."

"I was young. I can't use that as an excuse, and believe me, I've spent a decade beating myself up over what happened."

"You'll have to forgive me if I have a hard time sympathizing."

Rosa nodded. "Of course. I'm sorry. It's not fair of me to compare what I'm going through with what you went through. That's not what I'm here for."

"Listen," Stepan said. "I get it. Mistakes happen. You got mixed up in something bigger than you. But I'm not at a point where I can think about this unemotionally yet, okay?"

"I understand."

"Give me some time?"

Rosa nodded. She was having a hard time processing her emotions. There was a fierce, lead weight in her gut, a feeling that felt like much more than just concern for the safety of a fellow human being. It felt deeper. It was a feeling she hadn't felt in a very long time.

"You saved my life, Rosa. You saved my son's life. Don't think I don't appreciate that. I just need to process all of this."

"I get it," Rosa replied. She reached into her jean pocket and fished out a business card, then thrust it at him, clamped between two fingers. "When you're ready," she said. "Give me a call, okay?"

Federov looked at the card and Rosa thought she saw a hint of a smile. He extended his hand and plucked the card from her fingers, then slipped it into his own pocket. His fingers touched hers and a strange warmth ran down her arm and up into her chest, her heart fluttering.

This time he did fully smile, then turned and walked away. Rosa wasn't sure if he'd ever call. She almost hoped he wouldn't. As difficult as it had been just admitting she'd been there when his wife was killed, what would he say if he knew she had actually pulled the trigger? Is that something that she could ever admit to? And if she didn't, and he found out anyway?

Yes, she decided that it would probably be best if he didn't call. Best for everyone.

Watching Federov as he was once again consumed by FBI agents, she strode towards the front door and pushed it open, wading out into the bright mid-day sunshine.

"'Bout time, Goose."

Holding a hand to her forehead to block the sun she saw Chuck leaning up against his car parked by the curb.

"Whatcha get? Twenty years? Thirty?"

"Very funny," she replied. "We're clear. Stepan insisted on it. He bailed our asses out."

"Good man," Chuck said, nodding.

Out of the corner of her eye, Rosa saw the dark sedan coming slowly up the street to her left. Shadows of heads were visible behind the lightly tinted windows, and as her eyes focused on the Connecticut license plates, her heart slipped a notch, downshifting to a rapid rattling thud.

"Oh, damn," she whispered. She had no weapon, and neither did Chuck. You didn't typically walk around police headquarters packing iron. Chuck whipped his head around and made the same immediate identification.

"The Russians," he said with a hiss.

Sliding past Chuck's parked car, the sedan veered softly left and wedged itself against the sidewalk just behind the hatchback. The back door eased open and the large frame of Vasily Sokolov peeled itself out of the vehicle and emerged out onto the sidewalk.

"Ms. Guzman, so we meet again," he said, his voice thick with accent.

"I've got no beef with you, Sokolov," she replied quickly.

He smiled a wide, friendly smile. "No! Of course not! No beef with us," he replied.

"So, your little war? Your hunting for Stepan?"

"Capozza is done. There's nothing else we care about at this point. Stepan and Jorge are family. They always will be. Capozza was all we were after, my dear."

Rosa nodded. "Good."

Vasily cocked his head slightly. "That's not to say we still don't have a small issue with how this whole problem was handled."

Their small corner of the world was quiet as he finished speaking, letting the words hang in the air.

Vasily laughed and slapped Rosa's shoulder with a thick hand. "Lighten up, Guzman! You did good. We're square."

He turned away from them and returned to the car, sliding in and slamming the door closed behind him. The sedan slowly pulled away and drove down the road, vanishing from sight.

Rosa looked over at Chuck. "So, what's next? We didn't exactly get our big pay day here."

Chuck shrugged. "Nope. But our name was in the newspaper for like three days straight. We've been getting a lot of calls. This might just turn things around for us after all."

Rosa nodded and smiled. "Great. Hopefully, they're not quite as exciting as this one was."

Chuck laughed and walked to his car as Rosa curled around the opposite side. The doors slammed and the engine gunned to life, leading them back to People Finders and back to their normal life, or whatever passed for normal in the life of a bounty hunter.

AUTHOR NOTES

Thanks so much for checking out Duck, Duck Goose, the first book in a series of thrillers starring Rosa "Goose" Guzman. I truly hope you enjoyed it.

I occasionally send out emails to my readers and those emails contain lots of new and exclusive material that you can only find as a member of my mailing list.

Subscribing will get you the following:

1. Exclusive Prequel Novella – "Goose" by Jackson Riggs
2. First in line access to the latest information on upcoming releases
3. Access to join the exclusive Fans of Rosa Guzman Facebook Group – a group of like-minded fans (and me) who offer sneak peeks and great discussion.

Like what you read? Please subscribe to my mailing list (books.to/riggsnewsletter) to stay up to date on all my latest work!

AUTHOR NOTES

If you love reading thrillers, also consider subscribing to the Muonic Press Thriller mailing list (books.to/muonicthrillers) for more gripping new reads!

You can follow my writing exploits at my blog at JacksonRiggsAuthor.com, and keep up to as well as my Facebook Page (www.facebook.com/JacksonRiggsAuthor).

ABOUT THE AUTHOR

Jackson Riggs was born in San Diego, California, yet managed to find his way on the East Coast later in life. Reading and writing for much of his life, Jackson finally took the plunge in publishing a short while ago, and never looked back.

Spending most of his life working in the field of Information Technology and consuming the literary works of Tom Clancy, David Baldacci and Lee Child, Jackson knew being a thriller author was where he'd always wanted to be.

He continues to live in the northeast with his wife and daughters.

Made in the USA
Las Vegas, NV
29 October 2020